BLOOD STEW

THE WINDSHINE CHRONICLES 3

TODD SULLIVAN

Mocha Memoirs Press

Other Titles in The Windshine Chronicles

Hollow Men

There Will Be One

To my family, with love.

GLOSSARY

abba.: father (informal)
ah-boe-ji.: father (formal)
ak-ma.: demon
banchan.: side dish
eo-moe-ni.: mother (formal)
gama.: wooden litter for royalty and aristocrats
gi-sa.: singer and announcer
hak-gyo.: school
hal-moe-ni.: grandmother (formal)
hanbok.: traditional South Korean clothing
Hangugeo.: Korean
Hanguk: Korea
hwando.: Korean sword
jeong-shin.: spiritual energy
jju-ggu-mi bokum bap.: a spicy Korean seafood dish
Jung-guk.: China
kimchi. : a staple in Korean cuisine; a traditional side dish of salted and fermented vegetables, such as napa cabbage and Korean radish
makgeolli.: a Korean alcoholic beverage

Mudeungsan.: a mountain in Korea
nakji-bokkuem.: stir-fried octopus
namul.: garlic
san-nakji.: a variety of hoe (raw dish) made with long arm octopus
seiza-style.: a standard, formal traditional way of sitting in Asia
seon-saeng-nim.: teacher
si-ah-boe-ji.: one's husband's father or father-in-law
si-oe-moe-ni.: one's husband's mother or mother-in-law
soju.: a clear, colorless distilled alcoholic beverage of Korean origin
Ssi.: an honorifc
yangban.: scholarly men

PART I: KIM NAM-GI

1. REQUEST

Nam-Gi raised the scroll before him, his dreams inscribed in flowing black letters on the rolled parchment.

"*Ah-boe-ji*," he said, politely greeting his father, Kim Joo-Won. "I have toiled over this request for two days. I have brushed out the words with careful strokes, using our best ink so that the lines would be long and flowing, and the curves graceful with delicate flourishes. I have ensured the language used is exemplary, without mistake, and of the highest standards of grammar."

He paused, his free hand resting on top of his walking stick. Without this support, he would wobble to eventually fall, the severe deformation that curved his spine leaving him hunched over and unsteady on his legs.

"If you have the time today, Ah-boe-ji, could you please call a messenger so that the request can be sent to the governor?"

Kim Joo-Won didn't pause his hammering of a nail into a wooden plank. Two hired men worked beside him, attaching other planks of the thick wood that would become the extended walls of the seafood restaurant. They glanced at Nam-Gi as their labor continued. The screech of seagulls and the slapping of waves against the nearby docks were his only replies.

Nam-Gi gripped the handle of his walking stick tighter, the knobbed end biting into his palm. It was cheap, cut from a thick branch and whittled down with a kitchen knife. Nam-Gi hated it, and the way people stared as he hobbled past them. When he wanted to disappear from the stares of others, every eye fastened upon him. Yet now, standing before his father, he wanted to be seen, but was being ignored. Frustration built within his thin frame, and it set his tongue to action.

"The renovations look good," Nam-Gi said, forcing a look of appraisal. "When the customers sit down to enjoy our many family specialties, they will have the fresh smell of the forest and the memories of recent hikes through green space to comfort them. I think they will enjoy that and love the experience of our restaurant all the more."

His father nodded as he placed another nail against the plank. "Expanding our establishment was a good idea." He gave Nam-Gi a sidelong look.

Nam-Gi remained quiet. He had been the one who hinted at the benefits of renovations months ago, planting the seeds in his father's head before the summer started.

"It'll be impressive," his father continued, "but it's going to be expensive. If we don't get a lot more customers soon…" His voice trailed off as he gazed over Nam-Gi's head at the crowded port down the long winding lane. Their restaurant had been in the family for generations and stood right before the old docks. An ideal location once upon a time, it had brought their grandfather prosperity when first constructed. But South Hanguk had become more popular to foreigners, and an increased number of arriving ships had led the governor of Busan to build a new port.

Kim Joo-Won took over the restaurant not long after

marrying, and by the time Nam-Gi was a few years old, nearby establishments were relocating. His father had planned on doing the same before it was too late, for business had already begun to dry up as customers chose the more convenient restaurants closer to the bustle of docked ships and unloading cargo.

As Nam-Gi aged, however, his parents discovered that he had been born disabled. His spine grew crooked, and terrible bouts of pain wracked the child. His mother, Gu In-Hye, was forced to take him to the herbalist for treatment. Nothing could heal Nam-Gi's back, but soothing potions imported from the country of Jung-guk eased his pain. The cost of such imports was immense, and their family was forced to stay where they were while other businesses moved to the extended sections of the port.

When Kim Joo-Won looked at him now, accusation hardened his gaze. Nam-Gi avoided his father's eyes and said, "Today is the last day to apply for a quest. If this does not reach the governor's office by sunset, I will not be considered to join a company of four."

His father grunted. "We won't be able to afford to hire help in the restaurant, and those quests can take weeks. Plus, they're dangerous. Few young men who go ever return."

The workers beside his father continued to hammer the planks of wood, but Nam-Gi was distinctly aware they were listening. The quests made heroes of ordinary men, and those who survived often became wealthy and politically powerful in South Hanguk.

"I appreciate your concern, Ah-boe-ji." Nam-Gi bowed. "But I have studied diligently the arcane arts. The foreigner has never taken on a pupil as young as I."

The two workers spat onto the ground to ward off evil at the mention of the foreigner, giving away their eavesdropping.

Kim Joo-Won turned to them, and the men quickly lowered their heads and began moving away. The day the foreigner agreed to teach ten-year-old Nam-Gi the magical arts was the only time his father had ever showed pride in him. His father didn't care that some Busan people didn't like the foreigner or spat when he was spoken of. Men in the highest levels of politics in South Hanguk were associated with the Dark Elves, and that included the Emperor.

"Finish your work," his father barked at the laborers, then turned back to Nam-Gi.

"Stay here and continue to study alongside the foreigner, and one day, you could become a governor's aide. You will live with a pencil and pen in your hand instead of chasing monsters with that crippled back and useless legs of yours."

Nam-Gi flushed, the outstretched hand holding his dreams quivering. Yet he couldn't give up so quickly. "Ah-boe-ji, imagine the notoriety after I complete the quest. Who would not want to visit a restaurant where the son is a hero?"

His father took out a fresh nail, placed it against the wooden surface, and hammered it into the plank. "You cannot sit long on a horse. An hour at most and the pain makes you sob like a woman."

The workers guffawed. White-hot anger flashed through Nam-Gi as his earlier flush turned into humiliation. Still, he kept the emotions bottled up, his face placid even as his hand tightened further on his walking stick.

"The governor will never accept a cripple," his father added. "You'll only slow down the other young men and, in the heat of battle, you could be the very cause of their downfall. That shame would be so much worse for our family than any imagined benefit from you becoming a hero."

His hammering grew louder, the impact behind each strike stronger, so that—if Nam-Gi wished to speak again—he would have to yell over the racket. In front of the workers, he knew that would only appear rude, which would anger his father further. Nam-Gi's dreams darkened. His hand holding the scroll began to drop, but before it fell to his side, Nam-Gi stopped it. The governor would get this request one way or another.

"Thank you for listening, Ah-boe-ji." He bowed, the pain ripping up his back. His father didn't respond, and he wasn't sure if he even heard him. Nevertheless, he turned and took a hobbling step away.

"Where are you going?" his father asked. "You don't have a lesson today. Get some rest before the afternoon diners arrive. Your grandmother's out diving for today's menu."

With the two men working beside his father, Nam-Gi had no choice but to acknowledge the order, and he gave another dutiful bow. But as he walked back toward the restaurant, he focused on the sun rays touching the ground beneath his feet and shimmering in the air around him. He spoke a simple displacement spell. His father and the hired men had gone back to their hammering, so they wouldn't see the light around him momentarily shiver. Nam-Gi stepped to his left as a wavering image of himself continued forward toward the restaurant. The distorted light became more stable with each step it took. As long as no one touched it, they would not realize the image was immaterial.

Nam-Gi couldn't hesitate. Watching his father out of the corner of his eye, he kept hobbling leftward. He tried to move carefully, for he could not move quietly with his awkward gait, and his physical form had not actually become invisible. Spells like that would require more preparation and more concentration to cast, and he didn't have the time to construct an alternate reality in his mind first, then slip it into the real world around him.

Nam-Gi held his breath, sweat trickling down his forehead with each tortured step he took. He kept going left towards the South Hanguk Strait. The land curved down, and he had to slow his pace so he wouldn't stumble and roll down the hill. When he had put some distance between himself and the restaurant, he doubled back towards the winding path leading to the new docks.

The early morning sounds of sailors calling to each other, and of merchants issuing impatient orders, echoed around Nam-Gi. Horse-drawn wagons loaded with goods to be transported into the city rumbled along the wooden docks away from moored boats. The ever-present shriek of seagulls swooping through the sky above the clamor filled the air. White guard dogs tethered to leashes sniffed with damp snouts and watched passersby with wary black eyes. When strangers came too close, the dogs barked and pulled at the ropes that tied them down. They all knew Nam-Gi, however, and sniffed at him silently as they watched him struggle along.

Nam-Gi raised his hand for a passing wagon, and the driver stopped, letting him climb into the back where several wooden crates were stacked. Nam-Gi made this trip several times a week when he went to study with the foreigner, so he knew exactly how long the ride would take and what level of pain to expect. He gritted his teeth and willed his eyes to remain dry as the wagon bumped along the ground, the horse pulling it to the city at a steady clip. The path beneath its hooves was uneven and full of rocks, and as it trotted over bumps, jagged darts of pain stabbed through Nam-Gi's spine. It wasn't long before the cursed tears his father had mentioned in front of the hired men filled his eyes. Nam-Gi wiped away at them and the mucous that slid down his nose with the sleeve of his *hanbok*. He counted the seconds in his head, as he did each time he made this journey, and fought through the torment that wrapped around him, pulling him to its uncaring bosom.

When he finally reached his destination and needed to get off, he knocked on a wooden crate with his walking stick to get the driver's attention. Most men would have just hopped off without the driver having to stop, but when the driver turned and saw Nam-Gi's haggard face, he pulled back on the reins of the horse. They came to a gradual stop. Nam-Gi eased himself to the ground. For a moment, he could only stand there with the driver looking down at him, pity in his eyes.

"You all right, little brother?"

Nam-Gi nodded. "Thank you kindly for the ride."

He wished the driver would move off, but instead the man continued staring down at him until Nam-Gi bowed and forced himself forward before his legs were ready. He leaned heavily on his walking stick, the knobbed handle again digging into his palm. There were better-made canes that Nam-Gi had seen the elderly use, but his family couldn't afford one of those to be crafted. Instead, Kim Joo-Won fashioned a new cane from a fallen branch every year as Nam-Gi grew taller or as the old one wore out. They weren't meant to be used for walking long distances. The place Nam-Gi went now was as far as he ever traveled from the family restaurant.

Nam-Gi entered the shadows of a narrow alley and hobbled along through many twists and turns before the foreigner's school came into view. The building was nondescript, the walls made of thick black volcanic stone topped by a thatched roof. Tucked away in even deeper pools of shadow, it was much longer than the surrounding buildings. The foreigner's school was neighbored by drinking establishments where men consumed alcohol and met women to spend the night with. The stench of piss and vomit hung permanently in the air. Often, a man in a drunken stupor could be seen slumped in a corner against the wall, oblivious to the filth covering him as the sun rose high into the sky.

Over the years, Nam-Gi had glimpsed corpses splayed in the alley, deep gashes torn through their bodies from vengeful blades. Yet here in the school he stood before, the most powerful yangban in Busan had studied, learning the many mystical arts of the foreigner. These men were few, for most South Hanguk people did not desire to be in the presence of the foreigner, and rarely, if ever, had seen him.

Nam-Gi was not one of those repulsed by the foreigner's presence. If his father had his way, he would one day join the ranks of the scholars, who spent all their time poring over scrolls and advising the governor. He would teach lesser officials the foreigner's secrets they had elected not to learn from the source.

This was if his father had *his* way. Nam-Gi had different designs for his future, however, and standing in front of the foreigner's door, he knocked on the heavy wooden frame. "Daesh *Seon-saeng-nim*," he said, "it is I, Kim Nam-Gi."

Moments of silence were the only response. The sun had risen higher in the sky, burning away the morning chill of the coming fall. Nam-Gi began to worry the foreigner had stepped away on other business. Lessons hadn't been planned for today, and the foreigner might have additional duties when he wasn't teaching the gifted young scholars of Busan.

As more time passed, Nam-Gi's hope diminished, and he despaired the scroll would get to the governor in time. Still, he would not budge. He would remain there at the door until the last minute, even if it meant he would be late returning to the family restaurant for the evening diners. Just thinking of his father's fury made him shudder. Kim Joo-Won rarely laid a hand on him, for there was not much Nam-Gi could do in the way of disobedience. He had no friends, and when he wasn't studying from the scrolls he kept in his wooden chest in the corner of their home, he was serving customers.

Yet if his father discovered why he had come here today, Nam-Gi knew his wrath would turn physical, even as his mother would plead with him not to cause their son too much additional pain.

Nam-Gi was determined to speak to the foreigner, but perhaps standing in front of the door as the sun rode across the blue sky wasn't the best strategy. He could set off in search of his teacher and ask people he passed if they had seen him. The foreigner was not someone who could easily disappear into a crowd. Wherever he went, the gazes of South Hanguk's people followed after him.

Deciding to brave the busy city lanes, Nam-Gi turned around and started with surprise. The foreigner, Daesh, stood behind him, staring with his strange blue and brown eyes. His long hair was swept behind his sharp, pointed ears and draped down his shoulders like molten silver. Nam-Gi flushed at the intense gaze the foreigner leveled upon him. The same thought that always came to him made his skin burn even hotter.

The Dark Elf was the most beautiful creature Nam-Gi had ever seen.

"This is unexpected," Daesh said, his accent making music of *Hangugeo*. Most people of Busan found the way the foreigners spoke Hangugeo to be grotesque but, for Nam-Gi, Daesh's pronunciation enchanted him every time.

Nam-Gi finally remembered to bow low in apology. "I am sorry for this unexpected visit, Daesh Seon-saeng-nim. If you have pressing matters, just say the word, and I will depart from your presence immediately." He kept his tone low to emphasize sincerity, though he meant none of the words he'd just spoken. He would not be going anywhere without pleading for assistance.

"I'm always busy, Nam-Gi," Daesh said. "But I'm curious to discover what has brought you here for this unscheduled visit, when you have never done such a thing before. You must have something important to say, and it must be urgent."

Without lifting his head, Nam-Gi retrieved the scroll from the pocket of his hanbok. "Daesh Seon-saeng-nim, there is an issue I would like to discuss with you. If you care to learn what has brought my life some difficulty, please take this scroll and read, for the answer is written there."

As the Dark Elf took the scroll, his hand brushed against Nam-Gi's. The feel of the smooth velvet skin of Daesh's long fingers touching his sent a thrill through Nam-Gi. He waited in silence at the sound of the parchment being unrolled; soon pinpricks stabbed into his back from the taut position of the low bow. He gritted his teeth, determined to remain bent over until his teacher gave him permission to rise.

"So, you have written a letter for permission to journey on a quest. You're my best pupil. Whatever challenge you would face at the end of your journey, I'm confident you'll overcome."

Daesh spoke softly, his tone neither boastful nor flattering. Nam-Gi knew that his teacher simply spoke the truth as he believed it. Normally, the words would calm the doubts and fears in his mind, his pride at his teacher's praise a salve for the torment he constantly endured because of his misshapen body. Today, though, they only fostered frustration, and once more Nam-Gi's eyes filled with tears.

Though his teacher could not see his face, Daesh said, "I sense there is something wrong." He touched Nam-Gi's shoulder gently. "Look at me and tell me what is the matter."

Stiffly, Nam-Gi straightened, his back cracking in the quiet alley and making him wince. He didn't meet his teacher's blue and brown eyes, respectfully staring at a space in the middle of his forehead. Tears slid down Nam-Gi's cheeks, and his frustration became embarrassment that he would present himself in this pitiful manner to his teacher who had just spoken so highly of him. To salvage some of his dignity, he switched to Elvish, a language only a few dozen South Hanguk yangban could speak.

"A father submit request must to governor," Nam-Gi said bitterly, the foreigner's language full of mistakes as he struggled with the unfamiliar grammar. "If a father does not so do, the son considered cannot join a company, four, a quest."

"I am aware of the tradition," Daesh said. "I was present centuries ago when the conditions that determined who could undertake a quest were set."

Nam-Gi gasped, momentarily finding the blue and brown gaze of the foreigner before politely looking away again. The Dark Elves held so many secrets, and only those who worked directly with the Emperor of South Hanguk were able to fully study them. All the regular people of South Hanguk had to go on were whispered rumors, almost none of which Nam-Gi was foolish enough to believe. Yet if what the Dark Elf said was true—if he was around when the traditions of the quests were fashioned—that would make him…

Nam-Gi inhaled sharply again. More than six hundred years old. That couldn't be possible, yet his teacher had never lied to him before. Could he be playing a joke on him now?

"You have asked your father to deliver the request to the governor?"

Nam-Gi nodded.

"And his response hasn't been positive? He doesn't think you are yet ready to go?"

Nam-Gi tensed as he tried to calm the tumult of his thoughts. "He never believe I ready!" Fresh tears filled Nam-Gi's eyes. His teacher's gaze bore into him, and Nam-Gi knew he couldn't stand there in front of him any longer in this pitiful condition. It had been a mistake to come here, for he had disgraced himself with his weakness. He had been so desperate, he had so wanted the chance to be considered for a quest like the other young men whose fathers thought they could become heroes.

"Forgive me, Daesh Seon-saeng-nim," Nam-Gi mumbled, switching back to his own language, and began to hobble away. He managed several steps before the Dark Elf spoke again.

"Nam-Gi. Turn to me."

Nam-Gi checked a sigh, turned around, and looked at the space right beyond his teacher's forehead.

"Before you knew I was standing behind you, I was watching you. Studying your aura. As you spoke to me, I continued observing the emotions at play inside of you." Daesh stepped forward, causing Nam-Gi to become acutely aware of his presence.

"There is only one emotion that will make your dreams come true. It is not hope. It is not love. Look at the world around you and consider the unfortunate circumstances of your existence." The brown of Daesh's pupils kicked up like grains of sand and whirled like a sandstorm in the blue corneas of his eyes. "Become angry, Nam-Gi. Feed upon your hate for all those who look down upon you in pity. Use that as your fuel to achieve great things. Only then will you be able to acquire anything that you most desire. Nam-Gi, let the world feel your rage."

2. YANGBAN

The sun hovered over the horizon, signaling early evening, by the time Nam-Gi waved down a wagon to take him back to the ports. Once again, the jostling of the wheels on the jutted road made tears spring to his eyes and slide down his cheeks. He ignored the looks of those he passed as he wiped away at his face with the cuff of his hanbok.

One day, he vowed to himself, he would show them all. His body might be weak, but his soul blazed with fire. He would dazzle them all with his achievements.

Arriving at the winding road once more, Nam-Gi stepped gingerly from the back of the wagon. The sounds of the bustling port greeted him. As he hobbled back towards his family's restaurant, the voices of sailors, the calls of merchants, and the echo of crates being loaded onto ships gradually fell away. It was much quieter in this section of the ports. The buildings here were older, their condition much worse than those that had recently been built further away. Thatch roofs hung limply over the stone and wood walls of the restaurants and vendors that couldn't afford to relocate closer to the heart of the new port.

Nam-Gi, noticing the contrast every time he came back from his lessons with the Dark Elf, had been the one to suggest to his father that—while they might not be able to move—they could renovate the restaurant their family had owned for three generations. Among all of the poorer buildings surrounding them, theirs would be a beacon to passersby, attracting more business and more money.

As he approached, he saw that his father was no longer working on the extensions, the two hired workers having departed for the day. That would mean diners had already begun to arrive. Nam-Gi was late, and his father would know he hadn't gone to rest as he had been ordered.

Before the doorway of the restaurant, Nam-Gi paused and listened to those seated on the mats inside. Several patrons shouted orders for food and drink to his parents from where they sat at their tables. Finally gathering his courage, Nam-Gi stepped in to see Kim Joo-Won laying a first course before a table of guests, a round platter of dishes balanced in the palm of his hand. His father looked up as Nam-Gi entered, his eyes instantly hardening.

Without a word, Nam-Gi leaned his cane aside and adjusted his stance so that he would not wobble and fall. Taking the serving tray from his father, he deftly arranged the rest of the dishes on the table. Gu In-Hye, in the back kitchen, had started off the diners with *kimchi*, rice, dried anchovies, tofu soup, shrimp, and grilled mackerel. At better establishments, there would have been plenty of each portion. Nam-Gi's family could only serve their guests meager side dishes, and disappointment was expressed in the way they gazed down at the offerings.

This, of course, was why Kim Joo-Won insisted Nam-Gi serve the customers whenever possible. That's when they would leave satisfied with their meals despite the fact the restaurant was unable to serve more, like the seafood places further down the port. His father didn't know how Nam-Gi did it. If he ever discovered his son's methods, Nam-Gi would be in more trouble than he would know how to deal with.

In his mind's eye, Nam-Gi visualized the food sitting on the table before the diners. Then he added to it, making the shrimp thicker, more juicy, and enhancing their fresh-boiled aroma. He reddened the kimchi so that it promised a spicy, tangy taste. The rice filled out until it was almost overflowing the bowl. The grilled mackerel lengthened, the tail now spilling off the plate. When he had these images firm in his thoughts, he concentrated upon the diners. Letting the magic stored inside of him loosen so that its ethereal tongues stretched out beyond him, he brushed the illusion against the men's perceptions in careful strokes, implanting the altered state of the food into their minds.

Immediately, the looks on their faces changed as the supplanted reality distorted the actual dishes on the table. Their eyes brightened, and they began to eagerly share the dishes with each other. They even called for more, as well as for bowls of *makgeolli*, and Nam-Gi went into the small kitchen where his father had retreated to prepare more food.

"Your mother is still preparing the next dish," his father said as he poured the traditional rice wine into a tin kettle, then put four wide saucers on the serving platter. His voice held no emotion, since the guests were within hearing of the small room, but his expression was cold as he handed the order to Nam-Gi.

"We'll talk later," his father added before turning back to the raw tuna he was filleting.

Nam-Gi kept his face neutral as he served the men their drinks. Even as they poured the makgeolli into their saucers, Nam-Gi conjured a greater quantity, a fresher taste, and then wove his magic through their minds to lower their mental facilities while increasing their pleasure so that the men began to behave as if they were actually inebriated.

Soon, a new group entered, and then another. The final group was three men wearing tall bamboo hats and deep velvet hanboks. Nam-Gi recognized their garb as that of Jeju government officials. His father greeted them profusely, bowing repeatedly as he led the guests to their mats.

"We are honored that you chose to visit us this evening," his father said, unable to keep the surprise from his voice. "We will do everything we can to ensure you have a pleasant experience."

The men brushed the legs of their long pants back before they sat down so that their hanboks remained neat and prim. Now all three tables in the restaurant were full. Once the renovations were completed, Nam-Gi's family would be able to seat double the number currently occupying the dining area.

"We wished to avoid the noise and bustle farther down in the ports." The one who spoke had the longest pointed beard of the three. It was neatly twisted and barely touched the top of his stomach. "We heard of this little restaurant some time ago and decided to see for ourselves if it lived up to its reputation."

Kim Joo-Won beamed with pride. "My grandfather erected these walls when he was still a young man and not yet married to my grandmother. For three generations our family has served the people of Busan the freshest seafood plucked right from the Strait and served to your plate. Once you have had a taste of our menu, you will know everything that has been said of our restaurant is true."

Gu In-Hye prepared the first course meal. Kimchi and crab soup, dried squid and shrimp. His younger sisters, Chansol and Chan-Mi, even added a bowl of snails. Skinny girls of seven-

and nine-years-old, they prepared this side dish reserved for honored guests very carefully. They added only two cucumber slices, a bit of carrot, and then sparingly spiced the dish with garlic and ginger. They cut four snails into three pieces to make it seem like there were more in the side dish. Like everything else, they had little of this expensive shelled delicacy, and when his sisters had finished, the bowl still looked woefully empty.

This would never do.

Once again, Nam-Gi built within his mind a heartier meal than that before their esteemed guests, and he reached out to implant the images into the heads of the *yangban*. This time, however, Nam-Gi noticed something, almost like a resistance, as he embedded the images into the others' consciousnesses. He didn't look any of the men in the face to confirm his suspicions, but a slight tremor shook his hand nevertheless. Out of the corner of his eye, he observed the government officials begin their meal. To his relief, they ate with relish, the altered taste and appearance seemingly affecting their perception of reality.

When Nam-Gi brought the *soju* that they ordered, however, he got the distinct feeling the men were paying a little too much attention to him. Even as they enjoyed their meal, he sensed a heightened awareness surrounding the yangban. Now, instead of a tremor running through his body, a sheen of perspiration broke out upon his forehead. Something wasn't right; his heart rate increased with his worry. Pinpricks of fear invaded Nam-Gi's subconscious. Used to maintaining his mental focus more than his physical focus, he caught his rising panic and shoved it away into the recesses of his mind.

Nam-Gi didn't make any further attempts to deceive the yangban. As the men drank, the soju seemed to be the only part of the meal that disappointed them. When they ordered a second bottle, and then a third, the one with the long pointed beard touched his stomach and said to one of his friends, "Everything here is superb, *except* the drink, don't you think?"

His companion nodded, and stroked his shorter beard in agreement. "I suppose it's how they make up for the abundance of food."

Nam-Gi began to breathe a sigh of relief, but then caught a knowing gleam in the eye of one of the government officials. His heart ratcheted up again. The evening shift seemed to drag on. Fresh waves of pain assaulted his back as his exhaustion deepened and his anxiety grew. Nam-Gi fought back tears, wiping his eyes often when he hoped no one was looking. The other two groups eventually left, but the yangban didn't seem capable of becoming satisfied. They ordered more fish, more squid, more shrimp, so that soon Gu In-Hye was serving them the food the family had planned to eat. The yangban even inquired if they had *san-nakji* or *nakji-bokkuem*.

"I am so sorry," Kim Joo-Won said. "We only have what we catch each day and had no success in finding octopus this morning."

By then, the soju bottles stood like green soldiers around the government officials. Their faces were flushed a bright crimson, and they ate loudly, their lips smacking with satisfaction.

"No san-nakji!" one said, shaking his head. "No nakji-bokkuem! We will have to remember this when we tell our friends at the governor's hall. Isn't that right, Myung-bak Ssi?"

"Yes, Hyun-wook Ssi, they will be very disappointed!" the long-bearded one, Myung-bak Ssi, exclaimed to his companion. "And we had heard such great things about this establishment."

Kim Joo-Won paled. "We will have it next time you grace us with your presence," he assured the men. "Octopus is not so easy to acquire, but if you send us a message in advance, we promise to have san-nakji here for you. We will even make *yeonpo-tang*, especially for you."

"And *jju-ggu-mi bokum bap?*" Hyun-wook Ssi asked.

"Of course."

"And nakji-bokkuem!" Myung-bak Ssi demanded.

Nam-Gi tensed as his father promised that dish, too. Octopus was eagerly sought after, and all they had was their grandmother diving the waters near Busan. She was old and not able to compete with the younger divers on the coast. This meant their family would have to buy octopus from someone else, and the price would be high. Would his father be able to purchase enough to satisfy the endless appetite of these government officials—and their friends if they brought them along?

Finally, the yangban stopped ordering food, made their last toasts, and rose to leave. Their footsteps unsteady as they walked to the door, they argued loudly among themselves as each tried to pay the bill first. Finally, the one with the longest beard thrust out several coins, which Kim Joo-Won took with both hands, head bowed low as he continually thanked the men for their patronage and implored that they return again soon.

"We'll be back," Myung-bak Ssi said. When Nam-Gi looked up, he noticed the man staring intently at him, his gazed focused and clear, whereas a moment ago he had seemed completely drunk. Then the three officials were out the door into the night. Gu In-Hye, who had been dozing in the kitchen, woke up with a start at the sudden silence. She swept into the dining area to clean up the dishes littering the table, and the soju bottles standing sentry around its edges.

"We did well tonight," Kim Joo-Won said to him. "When I'm done expanding the restaurant, we will have much business."

"Yes, father." Nam-Gi could barely remain on his feet, and

he leaned heavily on his cane, wincing as the knob again bit into his palm.

"The customers like your service," his father continued. "You will be necessary to ensure we are successful with our new extension."

The shift in his voice dragged Nam-Gi's eyes to his father's. The anger he'd thought dispersed flared brightly in Kim Joo-Won's gaze again.

"You will not leave here again without my permission." His father approached him. "You will not go on a quest. You will work here, and you will study with the foreigner. One day, you will be a yangban, and money will fill your pockets as you toil in service to the governor. This is why I pay to put you through the foreigner's school, not to go off on some quest and be killed. Do you understand?"

His father towered over Nam-Gi, who was bent over his walking stick, back inflamed from being on his feet all evening. Yet the words of the Dark Elf returned, and—though he nodded to his father now—Nam-Gi secretly nursed his hatred and fostered his rage.

3. VEILS

Days passed into weeks, and Nam-Gi watched the winding road leading to the restaurant for the yangbans' return. His father finished the extended room, paid the hired men, and sent them off.

"We will need welcoming plants," Gu In-Hye said, "so that all may know our business is growing."

So his father ordered two tall plants with slender brown stems and vibrant green leaves tied by colorful ribbons. They came in pots decorated with symbols of good fortune, and he set them on either side of the doorway.

"We will need an announcer to stand outside and let everyone know about the extra tables," Gu In-Hye advised. His father objected, but Nam-Gi's grandmother sided with his wife, so Kim Joo-Won went into Busan and came back with a *gi-sa*.

The slim young man stood outside of the restaurant in his silver slippers, the long puffy sleeves of his fashionable hanbok billowing at his sides. Cupping his hands to his mouth, he called out with an enchanting musical voice that turned the heads of sailors and merchants far down by the docks. The melodious syllables of his announcements echoed against the hulls of boats as he sang of the fresh catch being served that day, the comfortable environment of the newly-renovated interior of the restaurant, and the friendly service of the family who served all customers as if they were royalty.

Such men did not come cheap, however, and Nam-Gi watched his father each evening count their dwindling supply of coins. The restaurant now had six tables instead of the three Nam-Gi had grown up with, and the smell of fresh trees drifted off the wood walls. Despite the refurbishments, the green leafy plants, and the beautiful singer, the additional mats still went unused.

Eventually, the potted plants wilted in the humidity of the late summer, the once vibrant leaves drying out and becoming shriveled and brown. His father refused to throw them out, complaining often about their cost. After several days passed in which he underpaid the gi-sa, the pretty young singer stopped coming as well.

His father's mood darkened, and he barked commands at Nam-Gi when he spoke to him. Nam-Gi hobbled around the restaurant, cleaning the floor, straightening the mats, and preparing vegetables in the kitchen with his mother and younger sisters. Chansol and Chan-Mi must have sensed the desperate situation of the family, for they stopped playing, and whispered into each other's ears so as not to draw attention. Nam-Gi, however, couldn't avoid the simmering wrath of his father as he served the handful of regular customers who still frequented the restaurant, filling only three of the six tables.

Nam-Gi's only relief came when he went into Busan to study with the Dark Elf. His father somehow managed to find money for the expensive lessons, for it increasingly seemed that the hopes for the family's future rested on Nam-Gi one day becoming a yangban. Throwing away all of the money they'd already spent on his education was unthinkable, so his father went deeper into debt, having to borrow more from a lender in the city.

After Nam-Gi's unexpected visit to his teacher with the request for help, he worried there would be an awkward atmosphere between him and the Dark Elf. During the entire carriage ride there the next time he went for a regular lesson, Nam-Gi sweated beneath his hanbok, his legs and arms so tense they caused even greater stress to his back. When he finally clambered from the carriage, he wanted to wait and stretch to loosen his limbs, but he refused to be late, so forced himself to hobble into the alley leading to the school, his body jerking and shaking like a broken doll on strings.

Two other young men, Dae-Hwan and Eun-Sang, took lessons at the same time as Nam-Gi. They, too, bore the foreigner's presence in order to directly glean his secrets. Dae-Hwan, tall and strong, was the son of a government official, and wore brightly colored hanboks made in expensive fabric shops. Eun-Sang, a wealthy merchant's son, wore similar hanboks, and had a wide girth with a round face. Both young men lived in the city, and always arrived before Nam-Gi.

He saw them turn down the dark alley leading to the foreigner and immediately followed after, his back protesting at his quickened gait. He stepped into the shadows that led through the buildings standing close together moments after his classmates had already entered the alley. He had no choice but to take deep breaths of the air soured by vomit as he struggled to move quickly. Yet even pushing himself, he could not catch up with his two healthy classmates, and lost sight of them around a narrow turn. He only saw them again when they were standing at the school entrance waiting for the doors to be opened. Nam-Gi finally reached his classmates, his breath wheezing in his lungs and his clothes clinging to his body with sweat. He gave a polite bow, which Dae-Hwan and Eun-Sang returned. The door to the school opened, and the three of them filed in one after the other.

The smell of buds and pollen greeted the students. Someone had brought the teacher fresh flowers, which stood on both sides of the entrance. On a tall stand was a wooden bowl of brown seeds. They took off their shoes in the alcove and placed them in the shoe closet. Then they stepped onto the wooden floorboards and went into the center room of the school. Long shelves ran along the walls, and upon them were laid scrolls. Dozens, hundreds, thousands of various sizes that contained the teachings of the foreigner written in Hanguego. Nam-Gi had tried counting them out of the corner of his eye in the past, but the task proved impossible. There were simply too many of them, and he only had the moments walking to the mats where they studied in order to do so.

The three young men went to their knees *seiza*-style before a raised dais, where Daesh waited, seated in a wooden chair covered with a crimson cloth, hands folded neatly on his lap. Two daggers with long, thin blades crisscrossed each other on the wall behind him. Candles normally kept the room in contorting shadows that danced across the floor and along the walls. Today, fewer had been lit, and a deeper darkness pervaded the teaching hall. The school's roof rose high above their heads, and small open apertures allowed in fresh air.

Daesh's silver hair draped down his shoulders and stood in stark contrast to his black skin. He regarded the students with blue and brown eyes for several moments, staring at each of them in turn. Yet Nam-Gi sensed that Daesh's mind was focused most upon him, and his skin burned under the perceived scrutiny.

"Dae-Hwan, Eun-Sang, Nam-Gi," Daesh said, beginning the lesson. "You three have learned much of mind control in the time you have studied with me. But, in truth, you're far from being skilled in the art of manipulating those around you so they will see what you wish them to see. In order to achieve this feat, you must tap even further into your *jeong-shin*. You must learn how to increase the potency of the images you bring to life and embed them in the very thoughts of those you wish to bend to your will."

Daesh raised his hand and slowly opened his slender fingers. Glowing seeds Nam-Gi had not noticed before lay in a pile in his palm. Nam-Gi calmed the confusion this oversight wrought and struggled to perceive if it was an illusion. The image of the seeds would shiver, then dematerialize as if they were nothing but phantoms Daesh was conjuring inside their heads.

Yet they continued to slip from his teacher's black fingers and patter against the floor. A few seeds Daesh could have secreted away, yet this never-ending torrent pouring from the palm of his hand? How can this be real, Nam-Gi wondered, for their number seemed endless, and he had been sure his teacher's hands were empty when he first saw him sitting in the wooden chair on the dais.

"Are you so sure you saw all there was to see before you knew what to take notice of?" Daesh asked no one in particular. "Did you memorize every aspect of my appearance from the moment you first walked in? Were you studying me from the time you sat down to the time I began to speak?"

Now that Nam-Gi thought about it, he hadn't been. Why would he? He and his classmates had done what they always did, following the usual routine of coming to the mat and sitting erect and ready to learn the day's lesson.

"As illusionists, you must learn the nature of your targets' minds. What they know, what they don't know. You must make use of their gaps in knowledge and manipulate those shortcomings to your advantage. And more importantly, to their disadvantage."

The seeds now floated up to form a rotating cloud in Daesh's hands. The smell of spring drifted into the room from the alcove above their heads, accompanied by the sound of buzzing insects which filled the room. Around them, candles flickered to life and shadows sprang up to dance along the walls. Nam-Gi's attention was drawn to the hardwood floor, and he now saw flowers growing from the lined spaces between the planks of wood. These he knew had not been there before, yet a soft breeze sweeping in from the apertures in the high ceiling above their heads brushed against the petals. Black wasps flew from one flower bud to another, and they appeared so real that, even as Nam-Gi struggled again to break what he knew must be a spell, he found he couldn't see through a reality he was sure couldn't possibly exist.

"When you create an illusion upon the gaps in your targets' knowledge, it becomes even more real to them. So real what actually exists starts to feel like a dream."

The wasps drew closer to Nam-Gi, the breeze strengthening while the flowers lengthened, growing up past his hips to his stomach, the petals eventually reaching up to brush against his face. The overwhelming aroma of pollen filled his lungs, leaving Nam-Gi gasping for breath.

"When the created reality you implant into the minds of your targets become so real that it's their new reality, anything becomes possible."

He heard screams next to him, and he knew they came from his classmates. Nam-Gi dared not look, struggling to pierce the visions he heard his teacher admit to him weren't real. Yet he had seen seeds in the bowl at the entrance, and perhaps his teacher had taken some in his hand before sitting in the wooden chair on the dais. He had smelled the flowers, though he had not seen, or paid attention, to the floor that he sat on seiza-style every lesson. Had the flowers always been there, hidden in the unusual darkness of the room, only to be revealed when the additional candles flickered to life?

And if there was a breeze, then there could be wasps that flew in from the apertures above his head. If all of these different realities were possible, then all of this could really be happening. That angry buzzing sound mixed with the pained cries of his classmates, Dae-Hwan and Eun-Sang. That, too, could be real.

With that thought, Nam-Gi only had time to flinch before the wasps flung themselves upon him as well, stinging him. Their stingers buried themselves deep into his flesh creating a terrible burning sensation that attacked every nerve in his body. He opened his mouth and screamed. The flowers, which had grown taller than he was, now folded their long stems over his head, smothering him in a blanket of blues and reds and yellows and greens. Nam-Gi struggled to rise, but a gale tore through the school from the apertures above and crushed him to the floor so he could not move.

Laughter, quiet and cool, sliced through the tumult of the room, and the nightmare gradually dissolved. Nam-Gi lay on the mat, sweat-soaked, his hanbok clinging to his twisted body. He heard the harsh breathing of his classmates beside him, their moans intermingled. None of them were able just yet to rise back to a sitting position.

It took some time for Nam-Gi to finally push himself up. He saw Dae-Hwan and Eun-Sang still prone on the ground, large red welts marking the flesh exposed under their disheveled hanboks. He felt the raised bumps along his body, too. When he touched them, he yelped in pain.

"Was it real?" he whimpered to himself.

"There is reality, and there is the reality the mind

perceives," Daesh told him from the dais. "Because humans often lie to themselves so as to see only what they wish to see, their perceived reality always exists on a faulty foundation. Its weakness is what illusionists attack and reshape with their will."

Nam-Gi noted the other boys' current physical state while his own pain pulsated through his body. "But why are we hurt, Daesh Seon-saeng-nim?"

At this question, Daesh smiled, hints of cruelty revealed in the curvature of his lips. "Higher-level spells make reality seem so flawless to the enchanted that—to them—it becomes real. This is how you can kill your opponents. But the ability can go further than that." His voice fell to a whisper, and Nam-Gi glanced at his classmates. He did not know if they were listening or not, but at this moment, it seemed like Daesh was speaking only to him.

"Humans, in their short lives, seldom come to realize there is more than one reality. They believe that this," he opened his arms to indicate the physical world around him, "is all there is. But they are wrong. Other realities exist. Here, now. They are only separated by veils that give order to existence, for without the separations, there would be chaos. Yet, if you learn how to open the door a crack, you will view wonders and horrors beyond the imagination of mortal men."

A gleam came to his teacher's eye. Still speaking in that low voice, his blue and brown eyes trained upon Nam-Gi, he said, "I believe you have the ability to learn to push aside the veils, just a little, and at great mental costs. But once you do, you will be more powerful than other humans who walk on two good legs and swing mighty weapons with strong arms. For you will not only control the reality inside their heads, but also the reality surrounding them. You will be able to move further distances despite your crippled body by hopping from one point in space to another."

Nam-Gi's heart stopped. If he could one day learn to move through the world easily, even with his broken body, he would be able to go where he wanted without the pain of walking and the humiliation of crying.

"I will teach you," the Dark Elf said. "But remember that everything has a price. The jeong-shin necessary to lift the veils is greater than an ocean's wave. It will wash over you, and always threaten to drag you down in its current and drown you. Even more dangerous, Nam-Gi, is what you may find waiting on the opposite side of the veils. For, as in this reality, there is much that is cruel behind the veil, and you may encounter an intelligence that does not appreciate trespassers."

4. THE CLOUD ELF

A disembodied Eye blinked into existence above the Cloud Elf, Tsierus.

"Why did you land?" she asked Tsierus. "You cannot remain here long."

Tsierus stood atop a short green mountain and gazed down at a city nestled in the valley. Above him, pale clouds drifted below a stark blue sky. He had been traveling home when he'd sensed the presence of evil.

"There're Dark Elves in this country," he told his guardian.

The Eye directed her gaze to the city. "You would kill them for their transgression?"

Tsierus placed his hand upon the curved hilt of one of the two scimitars strapped to his waist. "I'm duty bound to."

Tsierus had been a child when the Cloud Elf Lord banished the Dark Elves from Heaven. The Lord had ordered the eternally-warring Dark Elf clans to never cross the borders of the nations they'd been exiled to into other lands.

"They've disobeyed His decree," Tsierus said. "Death is the punishment, and—as there's no one else to carry out the order—I must be their executioner."

"This is your first foray below the clouds," the Eye reminded him. "I will aid you as I can, but know this. Only your physical form stands here now. Your soul remains suspended in the Heavens above. Tarry on this physical plane for too long, and the threads connecting your body and your spirit may thin and eventually snap."

Tsierus gazed up, but the chariot he'd been riding in was invisible to his soulless eyes. Somewhere, it orbited around him, and would do so until he finally boarded it again. For decades Tsierus had been in transit, returning home from arduous studies in a distant region of Heaven.

"Is there anyone nearby I can call for help?" he asked the Eye.

The Eye turned towards the horizon. A series of multicolored lights flickered in the wispy shadows of its cornea. "Several of your classmates are in the perimeter, but if summoned, they would not arrive for many months."

"How many Dark Elves have infested this plane?"

"Twenty-four. This land is small, and they have yet to spread very far."

Two dozen. Tsierus had never directly encountered a Dark Elf, but he had studied them in books. Much had been written about the fallen ones. Every library in Heaven contained thick tomes on their disgrace. The Dark Elves specialized in violence, using negative emotions like anger and hatred to fuel their magic.

"They live among the mortals on this plane?"

"Yes. This land is full of humans."

Tsierus sighed. The Dark Elves' poison was sure to already have infected them.

"How long do humans live?"

"Several decades at most," the Eye said. "They rarely see a century."

The idea startled Tsierus. How could something alive have such fleeting lifespans? What of worth could be accomplished in less than a hundred years?

"Guardian, send a message to my nearest classmates about the infestation of Dark Elves in this land. I'll try to eliminate their evil on my own, but just in case, others must know that they've spread beyond the confinement of their borders."

More lights—reds, yellows, blues, and greens—flickered in the shadows of her cornea. "It is done," the Eye informed him.

Tsierus nodded, adjusted the longbow and quiver on his back, and took a step forward. Immediately, he collapsed to his knees, the air forced from his lungs. "Guardian!"

An enormous weight pressed upon him. He braced himself so as not to be crushed into the grassy knoll, his slender hands sinking into the moist soil. He groaned as his elbows buckled, the cracking of tendons reaching his ears.

A multicolored light extended from the guardian and enveloped him with a pulsating glow. Gradually, Tsierus was able to draw breath again, the terrible strain lifting. With a relieved sigh, he pushed himself to a crouch, steadied himself on his heels, and waited for the world to stop spinning. Carefully, he stood, and swayed until the vertigo passed.

"Tsierus," the Eye said, "you will be severely weakened here. I will have to constantly infuse you with energy, for the realm below the clouds is dangerous and not meant for your kind."

Tsierus rotated his shoulders and stretched his arms. The flesh he inhabited became lighter, buoyed by the guardian. His muscles tightened, strength flowing through his body. Staring across the grassy plain, he felt that, if he wanted, he could leap far up into the air and forward a great distance with little effort. Pleasure at this sense of invincibility pulled the corners of his lips upwards into a wide smile.

"Do not overestimate the power I am giving you," the Eye warned him. "I, too, do not belong here. By assisting you, I tax myself, and will be steadily reducing my capacity to protect you."

Immediately, the smile fled. Tsierus looked up at the Eye. "Am I putting you in danger?"

"No," the Eye replied. "Nothing in this plane can harm me. It is *you* that worries me. This body you currently wear, it is only your physical manifestation here in this reality. Unlike your heavenly form, it bears many flaws."

The Eye looked back towards the city where Tsierus was heading before he collapsed with his first step. "When you attack the Dark Elves, you must use overwhelming force. You must kill quickly, eliminating them effectively and efficiently. The longer the conflict lasts, the greater this body will weaken. I will only be able to strengthen you so much, and as I diminish in power, you will gradually become vulnerable to the magic of the Dark Elves."

Tsierus knew his guardian was trying to convince him to abandon the mission. He thought of the Heavens and the eternal peace of the Cloud Elves. "What would the Lord do? Despite the great risk, would He pass up the opportunity to do good? Should I not live by His example? Should I let fear influence my decision?"

"Cloud Elves do not die so much as transform," the Eye said. "You leave your families behind to become something else. Something greater. For your kind, Tsierus, physical death is a rarity, but it does happen when Cloud Elves leave the Heavens —as you have done—to adventure in the lower planes—as you are doing. If the physical form you inhabit now is injured beyond repair, your soul will no longer have an avatar. It will become lost in the ether.

"Death is rare for Cloud Elves, but here in this plane,

Tsierus, it is a common phenomenon. I apologize for stating this simple truth, but I must reveal all of the dangers you are placing yourself in. You must understand the great risk of the undertaking you are about to engage in."

"If I leave, I allow evil to flourish on this plane." The very thought caused a great sorrow to well up inside of Tsierus. Tears formed in his eyes and touched the ends of his lashes. "These humans, these men, do not deserve to be twisted by the perverted natures of the Dark Elves. I will not simply abandon them to their fates."

The Eye gazed down at him, the flickering lights in the shadows of its cornea focused intently upon him. "You have a good soul, Tsierus," she finally said. "I hope your pure heart will not be your undoing."

The concern in her voice touched Tsierus. She worried deeply about him, but then, she was his guardian. It was her reason for existing in this plane, the link they had shared since he was hundreds of years younger.

"I thank you for your aid and your service," he told her. "I'll wrap up this extermination quickly and rejoin my spirit to my body. I'll do what I can not to allow the Dark Elves' influence to spread beyond these borders."

Tsierus looked around again at this strange world. "Guardian, how many of the Dark Elves are in the immediate proximity?"

"There are two. One is in the city below. The other is in a grove of trees nearby. That one is alone, though a group of mortals head towards him."

"Can I reach him first?"

"You can."

"Then lead the way, Guardian."

Tsierus followed the Eye down the side of the short mountain. A cool breeze rustled the loose orange pants and yellow shirt he wore, his green cloak flowing behind him. He came upon a narrow path snaking past wide fields of green stalks protruding from standing water.

"This is a main source of the mortals' diet," the Eye told him. "These are paddies that farmers harvest, cutting the grass and drying it to retrieve the seeds."

"Can this body I wear consume it?"

"It should be able to, though you will not need much sustenance to keep it running."

Near the paddies were squat brick abodes with thatched roofs. Sharp caws periodically shattered the silence. Tsierus spied black-feathered birds in the fields picking at the seeds.

"I don't like the look of them," Tsierus said. The black birds seemed to share a mutual opinion of him, as they lifted their heads and followed his passage with intelligent, unfriendly eyes. When he passed them, their cries echoed from behind, to be repeated by other birds ahead of him.

"They're letting their brethren know I am coming," Tsierus said.

"They are not to be trusted," his guardian informed him.

The path took them beyond the fields to a grove of trees. Tsierus entered it, and, in the shade of the boughs, the temperature cooled. The body he wore felt weaker without direct exposure to the sky, as if the branches and leaves created interference with his connection to his spirit. Like his guardian had said, he would have to kill quickly and move on if he was to survive.

In the undergrowth running along the narrow trail, the sound of creatures scurrying among leaves drifted to him. Occasionally Tsierus spotted them, furry brown and black animals with bushy tails. Clouds of insects hovered beneath the trees. The first time he stepped through one, they tickled his skin and left him disturbed by their vast numbers. Trying to fan them away seemed to only attract more.

"They are harmless," the guardian assured him. Tsierus ran his hands through his hair to dislodge any of the tiny bugs that tried to settle there, and discovered he had long tresses that flowed down to his hips. He lifted a lock to inspect.

"It's the color of the sun," he said, pleasantly surprised. He wondered how the rest of this form looked. "I need a reflective surface."

"We are near the Dark Elf."

Tsierus let his hair slip through his fingers, and comforted himself with the knowledge he could view his reflection later. He slowed his pace as they came upon a clearing in the woods. Several wooden buildings with dome-shaped roofs had been built close together. A spiked iron fence surrounded them, but it did not seem like it would be difficult to penetrate. In neat script above the entrance of the widest building were a string of letters that Tsierus did not understand.

"Is that the mortal language? What does it say?"

"*Hak-gyo*. School."

"So this is where he twists the minds of mortals." Tsierus unshouldered his bow and leaned the quiver against a tree. He held three arrows in the fingers of his right hand and nocked a fourth.

"Let's bring him out, shall we?"

The Eye closed, disappearing. Tsierus spoke a spell into reality, and flame ignited the arrowhead. He released the bowstring, the arrow raced forward, struck the side of the school, and exploded in a wave of fire that engulfed the wooden wall. He immediately nocked another arrow as a force blew the wall outwards into shards, sending burning cinders into the surrounding trees.

A shadowy figure stood beyond the tendrils of smoke

swirling into the air. Tsierus targeted its chest as the individual stepped over the fire sprouting up in patches of grass. For the first time—beyond an image in a book—the Cloud Elf beheld a Dark Elf.

The outcast was male, tall, and slender. Like the birds Tsierus had passed in the fields, he was dark, his skin black like endless space. A mane of white hair flowed down his shoulders. He gaped at Tsierus with eyes that had blue corneas and brown pupils that shifted like dunes caught in a sandstorm. He approached the Cloud Elf, an expression of puzzled surprise marking his face.

"Who are you?" he asked in crude Elvish, his pronunciation as perverse as his appearance.

"I am purity," Tsierus replied, and released the second arrow.

A bubble of light engulfed the Dark Elf's hand. With a flourish, he deflected the arrow, sending it into a tree and igniting the bark with a roaring flame.

"Why do you attack me?" The Dark Elf seemed more curious than concerned. "Are you some type of elf?"

Tsierus nocked a third arrow. "I come from the Heavens. The Lord forbade your kind from leaving the restrictions of your borders. You have disobeyed His word and brought your evil into the land of humans. For that, I have judged you guilty, and am left with no recourse but to execute you for your transgression."

The Dark Elf's confusion deepened. As with the second arrow, he easily deflected the third, sending it to yet another tree that went up in an orange pillar of crackling fire.

"My name is Versi, and my companions and I live among the humans in peace," he said. "We left our homeland to avoid the conflict."

"Your kind cannot know peace." Tsierus let loose a fourth

arrow, which met the same results as the previous three. He clutched only one more arrow between his fingers, which he nocked. "The Dark Elves are cursed. To hate. To seek revenge. To destroy. Your influence is contagious, infecting all you come in contact with."

Versi scoffed, "You've never met me, and before even introducing yourself, you attack. Yet I'm the one who hates? I'm the one who's cursed?"

"You're the one that must be eliminated." Tsierus released his fifth arrow. With a laugh of contempt, Versi sent it to join the others in the now burning woods.

"If this is the best you pure elves can do, I suggest you leave before you stoke that hatred you mentioned, and I decide to actually fight back." The bubble of magic around Versi's hand flared with violent light, creating a gale of wind that tore at the brown robes he wore.

He stepped towards Tsierus, tensed to attack, then choked in pain as a beam of myriad colors pierced him, burning a wide hole through his chest. Behind him, the Eye hovered, and steadily maintained the shaft of light as it incinerated the Dark Elf's chest.

Tsierus grabbed a final arrow from the quiver beside him, nocked it, engulfed the tip with flame, and released it. The arrow shot through space, buried itself in the Dark Elf's forehead, and exploded. The headless body dropped to the ground.

"One down," Tsierus said to his guardian. "Twenty-three left to go."

5. BLINK

The magical flame from the deflected arrows spread through the trees, jumping from bough to bough and cutting a fiery swath through the canopy. Tsierus slung his bow and quiver over his shoulder and focused on the dancing tongues. He summoned strength from the threads connecting his soul to his body and tried to displace the flames into a different reality. The flames whipped down towards him in disobedience to the master that had conjured them. Tsierus leapt before being struck and rolled across the clearing towards the walls of the wooden school that still stood.

"Guardian! I need you!"

The Eye swooped down to hover over his left shoulder. Her cornea widened, and where her gaze fell, the flames died with an angry hiss of smoke and steam. The weight of this plane pressed down upon Tsierus once more, his arms and legs becoming heavier. Breathing became more difficult, and he struggled to remain standing as the blackened trees broke apart and toppled to the charred earth. Tsierus stumbled away from the smoke, forcing his feet to go one step after another, so that he could breathe fresh air. When the Eye turned her attention upon him once more, the effects of the plane finally lessened, and he took a deep, grateful breath.

Reaching the opposite edge of the clearing, he gazed out at the destroyed landscape. "This place is so fragile."

"In this realm, your magic is potent," the Eye said. "You must be careful, Tsierus, or you may do more ill than good."

"I don't want to harm humans."

"That will be difficult. I sense some of the Dark Elves living in solitude like the one you just disposed of. Others, however, live among humans in their cities. They may enlist mankind to fight alongside them."

Tsierus grimaced. What low depths would the fallen go to in order to avoid their punishment for breaking the decree of the Lord? How many innocents would they sacrifice through their evil?

"Guardian, I'll do all I can to protect humans," Tsierus declared.

"You are of a noble race," the Eye said gently. "I expect no less from you. If you show no hesitation in eliminating the infestation, you may, indeed, be able to leave humans unharmed during your quest."

Once he was sure all the flames had been extinguished, Tsierus went back to the path, crouched next to a destroyed tree, and touched its ruined stump. "Forgive me," he said to the nature spirits he could not see. "I will have to harm you a little as I weed out the poison infecting your beautiful land."

Tsierus stood and walked through the woods once more to reach the fields. Above him, the black birds hovered and shrieked down at him angrily.

"I don't like them," he told his guardian, "but I understand their current annoyance with me."

"Perhaps you should eliminate those circling above before they spread word of your actions."

Tsierus gazed into the blinking lights of the shadowy Eye. "I won't harm them if they don't harm me first. There's something malignant in how they communicate, but that is for humans to deal with. My mission is only to eradicate the Dark Elves."

"As you wish," the Eye said. "Know, however, I cannot continually peer into this reality. When you need me, summon me. I will leave you a reservoir of power, but as it depletes, you will weaken. Do not waste your strength, or mine, on useless endeavors. If you do, you will lose both and be left defenseless in this physical plane."

Tsierus bowed, and the Eye blinked out of existence.

The birds were not the only creatures stirred by the conflict. As Tsierus walked down the path, he spied movement around the farmhouses. Humans. He had never glimpsed mortals before, and he studied them as he approached. At one particular home, a man with a tan cloth wrapped around his thin frame stood beside a shorter, squatter woman. Five children of various ages, some wearing heavily-stained clothing, the smallest ones naked, gathered around the adults. The family stared up at the birds and the clouds of dark smoke on the horizon. Their lips moved as they spoke to each other. From this distance, Tsierus couldn't hear their language. He had seen the words on the school and wondered how the strange symbols would sound spoken into reality.

Tsierus saw a thin trail leading off from the main path to the farmhouse, and started down it towards the family. They were so busy staring upward they didn't see him. One of the children, a naked little girl with long black hair, noticed him first. She stared at him with ever-widening eyes. Tsierus smiled at her and waved. The girl took several hesitant steps towards him, which drew the attention of a second child, then a third.

Now the mother looked down at her agitated children. She followed their gaze until hers fell upon Tsierus. As he did to the children, he began to wave at her, but her sudden shriek made him freeze.

The man, startled to attention, looked at the Cloud Elf. Shock swept his features, and he spoke harsh words to his wife, who herded the children together and urged them away from Tsierus. The man spun toward the house, dashed inside, and emerged a moment later with a wood-handled axe gripped tightly in his hands.

Tsierus held up his own hands, empty palms facing the man. He knew they would not understand his words, but he still said, "I come in peace."

His Elvish speech seemed only to upset the man more. He rushed at Tsierus. When he reached the elf, he raised the axe high, the curved blade flickering in the sunlight, and chopped down at the Cloud Elf's head.

Tsierus's hand dropped to the curved hilt of one of his scimitars. He unsheathed it and parried the axe blow. Quickly he darted in, grabbed the man's right arm, and twisted it in a simple wrist lock, forcing the human to his knees with an anguished cry. The axe fell from the man's fingers onto the grass. At the farmhouse, the children screamed at the sight of their distraught father.

"Please," Tsierus said, the pointlessness of the plea painfully evident, "I don't want to hurt you."

He let go of the man, who immediately lunged to take up the axe again. Tsierus tapped him on the shoulder with the flat edge of his scimitar and spoke a sleep spell into reality. The man fell head first into the dirt.

"He'll recover," Tsierus said to the now-weeping children

and woman. The terror he saw in their eyes, trained on him like spears, made Tsierus cover his face to hide his own tears of shame. He stumbled back down the trail, his strength draining from him at the negativity of their emotions stabbing into his psyche. When he reached the path, he ran from the harsh words of their language following after him.

6. SECOND TARGET

His tears of sorrow dried in the cool breeze sweeping across the land. Tsierus glanced over his shoulder at the farm as it grew smaller. How had things gone so badly? What had he done wrong?

Until he figured out the mind of man, Tsierus promised himself to avoid direct interaction with humans from this point forward. They did not pose a danger to him, but trying to restrain them might have another heartbreaking result.

The sun dropped towards the horizon, the shadows along the road lengthening. With his keen sight, Tsierus saw, far ahead, merchants on wagons drawn by horses, merchandise in wooden crates stacked in the beds. Farmers sweated as they pushed wheelbarrows with an assortment of vegetables. Some of the humans carried wrapped bundles on their backs, their thin shoulders hunched beneath their heavy burdens, their bare legs thin. The urge to help those struggling beneath their loads filled Tsierus. He clenched his hands in frustration that he couldn't aid the scrawny, malnourished humans, their brows sweat-soaked, their bodies caked with dirt kicked up from their trek down the path.

Seldom did Cloud Elves interfere in the dealings of man. It was forbidden to aid mankind in any way that humans could do for themselves. Only in cases like Tsierus's quest, when an evil arose that humans simply weren't equipped to resolve, did Cloud Elves descend from the heavens to balance what had become unbalanced.

Yet as Tsierus studied the humans from a safe distance, he wondered if it be would be so bad to teach a small number of them simple techniques to yield greater produce from the ground. Or to teach them a few harmless spells to allow inanimate objects to move on their own, making it unnecessary for humans to strain themselves like pack animals.

After he eradicated the twenty-three remaining Dark Elves cursing the land, Tsierus considered staying on Earth just a little while longer before continuing his journey home. He would take careful note of the progress he made and would report it to the Lord. Maybe, just maybe, he could convince Him that small tokens to ease the burden of Man would have enormous benefits to those less fortunate existing in this lower realm.

Tsierus left the road and cut across a field of rice paddies. He approached a stone house and listened carefully to see if there were voices nearby. He heard nothing and saw no movement. Perhaps the occupants traveled to the city alongside those on the road, and would not return for a long while. He went to the side of the house so he would not immediately be seen. Sitting with his back against the wall, he waited, watching the road for a moment for when the flow of people ebbed.

The sun disappeared below the horizon, to be replaced by twinkling stars and a bright crescent moon. The steady trail of humans continued to the gates surrounding the city, and Tsierus realized that night markets must be popular. It did not appear the number of humans would lessen. With a sigh, he pushed himself to his feet. Running lightly across the field, he steered away from the busy portcullis of the wall surrounding the city. Guards stationed at various locations along the battlements paced back and forth, torches in hand to illuminate a wide radius around them.

Tsierus needed to locate the Dark Elf quickly and dispose of him without attracting too much attention.

"Guardian."

The Eye blinked into existence high above his right shoulder. Immediately, the reserves of power Tsierus had depleted in its absence were restored, new vitality flowing through his body.

"Can you lead me to the target?"

"I can," she replied. "But he is in a part of the city with dozens of brick and stone structures clustered close together. There will be many humans between you and him," she warned him. "If a prolonged fight occurs, the number of casualties may be high."

Tsierus frowned. "I will have to dispatch the evil quickly before he does too much damage. Let us make haste."

He let a sentry pass on the battlement above him, then scaled the city wall and dropped over on the other side. The heavy aroma of humans living close together washed over him in continuous waves of mingling smells. The pungent odor of sweat and human waste mixed in the air with the various smells of roasting chicken and pork and frying vegetables. Even here in the city, the brick dwellings all stood only one level and had thatch roofs.

This was so different from the elvish style of buildings soaring to great heights, allowing a hundred families to live in the brilliant spirals piercing the sky. Humans didn't seem to possess the technology to build higher than one level, which meant their homes stood close together to accommodate the large population living inside the city.

Narrow alleys snaked through the dwellings. Tsierus hopped to the top of a roof and darted on light feet, leaping from one building to the next in the direction the Eye indicated. Human voices speaking in the tongue he didn't yet understand filled the air. High-pitched cries of children playing, and the piercing sounds of babies crying, punctuated the deeper voices of adults in conversation. Tsierus longed to learn the meaning of the words so he could one day communicate with mortals. In their absurdly brief lives, he wondered if they ever broached deeper subjects? Or did they only spend their time in laughter and frivolous behavior since they knew they had several absurdly short decades before they lost their physical coils?

A fresh wave of pity swept Tsierus. How he longed to transform humans, to make them better than they were.

Before long, the Eye said, "There."

Up ahead on a main lane stood a building that was long and narrow. Like the others, it was made of brick.

"He is inside," the Eye informed Tsierus.

"Then let us begin."

Before, Tsierus had thought it best to draw the Dark Elf out into the open. This time, he decided to keep the fighting inside as long as possible, which meant he needed to get close to the target without being detected.

Tsierus focused on his body: his arms, legs, head, torso. He penetrated the outer layers of his physical form, and concentrated upon his heart, brain, veins, stomach, blood. Still further he delved within himself, glimpsing the cells making up his body, the molecules making up the cells, the separate atoms forming the molecules. He focused on the illumination shining down from the stars and moon, and the flickering fires of the lamps hanging from the buildings. He bent the light from these sources away from all of the particles making up his corporeal being so he would no longer be seen. The effort exhausted him, and the Eye had to continually reinforce his power with her own. He would have to move quickly to maintain the effect before they both became fully depleted of energy.

Tsierus leapt to the rooftop of the building where the Dark Elf dwelt, and dropped to the ground by the wooden door leading inside. He took the knob in hand and gently pulled to see if it was unlocked. The door cracked open, and Tsierus slipped inside. He stood in a small room with a single long table. Beneath the table were neatly stacked sitting mats. No lamp adorned the wall here, but in the next room, which was much larger, lamplight pushed back the darkness.

Tsierus went to the archway and saw the Dark Elf. In this room, too, a long table stretched from one end to the other. The Dark Elf sat at a low desk at the head of the room. He wore his pale hair loose and flowing down his shoulders. Back straight, he studied a thick tome and took a continuous stream of notes on a scroll.

The ceiling over Tsierus weakened the connection between him and his soul suspended in the chariot in the sky. The invisibility spell he had cast was draining both him and the Eye fast, so Tsierus entered the room and placed his hand upon the curved hilt of a scimitar. Just as he was about to strike, a loud knock resounded on the door, and the Dark Elf looked up, surprised. He spoke to those outside in the language Tsierus did not understand. Hurried voices immediately followed, and Tsierus tensed, waiting to see what the reaction from his target would be.

The Dark Elf leapt to his feet, the brown of his blue eyes swirling like a desert storm. His purple robes fluttered around his wiry frame as he spoke a seeing spell into existence. His gaze immediately fell upon Tsierus standing in the archway of the room.

"Guardian!" Tsierus yelled, but the Dark Elf was faster.

Speaking a quick, harsh utterance, he conjured three glowing swords. With a flick of his finger, he sent them racing at Tsierus. The Cloud Elf whipped backwards to avoid the one trained at his head, but the other two found their marks. One blade plunged into his shoulder, the other into his thigh. The swords tossed him back with the momentum of their force. He slammed into the entry door, the blades impaling him onto the wood.

A red glow covered the Dark Elf's hand as he rushed forward. Before the blow could strike the dazed Cloud Elf, the Eye emitted a force that shattered the door. Tsierus was propelled outwards past the officials and guards, who tumbled back at the explosion, the jagged pieces of wood tearing into their flesh. Hoarse screams ripped from their throats as blood flowered on the folds of their clothes.

The Eye bathed Tsierus in a pale glow that extracted the blades from his damaged body, and she began to heal his wounds.

"What are you?"

Tsierus looked up at the Dark Elf, whose eyes followed the shaft of healing light to the hovering guardian. Tsierus's wounds closed, but the lost blood soaking his clothing left him weak. Humans crowded around the damaged building, their unintelligible voices a roar in the night. He knew they were terrified, but for them, he must keep fighting. For the greater good, he must finish his mission.

Grasping the hilts of both scimitars, he unsheathed the curved blades in one swift motion and hurled them up into the night sky.

The Dark Elf gazed at the scimitars as they swiftly spun above the brick buildings to disappear into the dark sky. Then he leapt towards the Cloud Elf, his hand wrapped in a crackling red glow. He cocked his fist back and punched forward with incredible force at Tsierus's forehead.

The Eye reshaped the healing glow surrounding Tsierus into a shield. The Dark Elf struck it, smashing the barrier back into the ether. He grabbed Tsierus around the throat, and the Cloud Elf howled with pain as the red energy sawed into his skin. As quickly as the spell severed his flesh, the guardian healed him, repairing the injuries and barely keeping him alive.

"You can't keep this up forever," the Dark Elf growled as skin was sawed away to be replaced by more skin. "Now tell me, who are you?"

Tsierus stared directly into the brown and blue eyes of evil and spat out, "I am your death!"

The Dark Elf, caught in Tsierus's gaze, gasped. Behind him, the scimitars hurtled back down to Earth covered with a piercing light and slammed into the Dark Elf's back. The blades penetrated his body to their hilts, their sharp points also stabbing into Tsierus. The glow from the Guardian kept Tsierus from death as the Dark Elf pulled back and stumbled away, blood pumping from his heart to stain his purple robes.

"Why?" he whispered as Tsierus fought off the shadows of unconsciousness and staggered towards him.

"Because you have broken the decree of the Lord." Tsierus kicked the Dark Elf in the legs so he spun and collapsed to his knees, then yanked out both scimitars impaled in his back. With a short sweeping motion at the Dark Elf's exposed neck, he decapitated him.

Shocked screams came from the humans, yet those closest to him did not surge upon Tsierus and attack.

"Forgive me," Tsierus told them in Elvish. Then he leapt over their heads to the nearest rooftop and ran away towards the city walls.

7. THE LENDER

Nam-Gi reclined against the wall, resting after the last of the morning diners left the restaurant. He had a lesson with the Dark Elf and would need to travel to the city soon, where he would be until late evening. His petition to go on a quest remained in his chest, buried beneath studying scrolls. Summer days were coming to an end, though the heat and humidity remained stubbornly persistent. All day, Nam-Gi sweated as he worked in the restaurant.

At night, while everyone else slept, Nam-Gi sat outside with his scrolls and studied the lectures loaned him by Daesh. They were not the same ones his teacher gave his classmates. These new spells required significantly higher levels of jeong-shin, and some were actually written in Elvish. Nam-Gi studied into the early morning trying to unlock their secrets, the words like complicated puzzles with hundreds of tiny parts he had to construct in his head.

Daesh had given him a specially-brewed potion of ginseng to aid him in this pursuit. When he drank it, it coursed through Nam-Gi, revitalizing him, making the dawn brighter and his thoughts clear despite the lack of sleep. One of the potion's side effects, however, was that his nose would bleed after drinking the grainy liquid, and he would be forced to lie on his back and stare up at the brightening sky so that his hanbok would not be stained red. He timed it so he got the nosebleed under control right before his parents stirred and awoke from their slumber.

Another side effect of the potion was that moments of confusion assaulted Nam-Gi during the day. Sometimes he had trouble distinguishing reality from dreams. The lack of sleep didn't help, but despite the hurdles he had to overcome, he continued to push himself. No new quests had yet been delivered to Busan, but when one was, Nam-Gi planned on being ready.

As he sat in the restaurant that late morning, after cleaning up after the last of the breakfast guests, his eyes closed to slits, his mind racing over the spells he had been memorizing, a dark shadow appeared in the doorway of the seafood restaurant. A man in a dark blue hanbok and bamboo hat peered at Nam-Gi through the round spectacles perched on the bridge of his nose. Nam-Gi remembered him from a previous visit, and knew he was his father's lender.

The man lowered his head as he stepped into the restaurant so his tall hat would not be knocked off by the door-frame. In a quiet, commanding voice, he said, "Kim Joo-Won. I must speak with him."

Behind the lender, two of his financial assistants waited at the door, making their presence known by clearing their throats. Dressed in plain brown hanboks with leather armor protecting their torsos, their gaze roved continuously over the interior of the restaurant. Arms folded over their broad chests, they wore a short sword on each hip, and stood with their legs apart as if ready to pounce forward at a moment's notice.

In the kitchen, his mother and little sisters were busy

preparing ingredients for lunch. Chansol chopped vegetables, and Chan-Mi washed leaves of lettuce their grandmother had brought in fresh from the market. The old woman had gone out again to haggle for fish, snails, and squid. Money being tight, she would be gone longer than usual as she ambled from stall to stall searching for the cheapest price.

Nam-Gi heard the movement of his mother and siblings in the kitchen abruptly fall silent, and he knew his family had become aware of the lender's arrival. Nam-Gi still sat against the wall, summoning the strength to get his exhausted body to rise. His father stepped out before he had a chance and gave him a piercing glare.

Now Nam-Gi clambered to his feet and fought back a gasp of pain so he could respectfully bow to the lender. He leaned heavily on his walking stick, his back alive with fire after standing all morning serving the breakfast diners. He stared with envy at the lender's erect posture, at the way his hands were primly tucked into the wide folds of his hanbok. The neatly-cut beard and the finery of his garments bespoke great wealth.

"Your presence is most welcomed this morning," Kim Joo-Won said politely. "Have you already broken your fast?"

"I have," the lender replied. "There is a place not far from here that serves a thick abalone porridge with a strong green tea. It is a very delicious meal. I dine there whenever I am brought to this part of Busan."

"You must come here and let us serve you one day," Kim Joo-Won said. "You will be very pleased by what we can offer you."

The lender's eyes sparkled with amusement behind the lenses of his glasses. "I prefer exotic meals. Expensive, the taste delicious and a thrill to my senses. Down by the new ports is where the most diverse range of seafood can be found."

Kim Joo-Won's face crumpled. "We have many unique dishes at our restaurant. Tomorrow, we will have octopus. Come back, and we will prepare it with a special dipping sauce. The ingredients are known only to our family."

The lender gave his father a thin-lipped smile. "Octopus is a rare dish, indeed. Not many smaller properties can afford it these days, not with the competition from the larger businesses who own fishing boats with fearless young crews." He looked around at the empty seats. "Your expansion has improved your business?"

"The trickle will become a stream," Kim Joo-Won replied. "But our family is well known and deft at finding the best bargains. We do not pay the same price as those with less knowledge of the ports. We are not ones to waste money," his father added, and Nam-Gi picked up the venom in his voice.

"Ah, yes. I have given many loans to those farther down the road so they could open their establishments. Business has been good for them."

"I am happy to hear of their good fortune," his father said stiffly.

"A month has passed since you took out your newest loan," the lender continued. "By the terms of our agreement, we have come to collect."

The two men in the doorway had remained quiet as Kim Joo-Won and the lender greeted each other. Now, though, they cleared their throats once more, and unfolded their arms to place their hands on their waists by the hilts of their weapons.

Kim Joo-Won took a small purse from the pocket of his hanbok. Nam-Gi knew from how slim the cloth purse was that it was too light to contain the full amount owed. A quick assessment by the lender, his eyes darting to the pouch, then back to Kim Joo-Won's face, seemed to bring him to the same conclusion. His brow wrinkled in disappointment even before he stretched out his hand to take the money.

His father bowed low. "I deeply apologize for this inconvenience," he said in reverential tones, his voice low and humble. "We are still drawing in new customers. Soon our restaurant will be busy from morning to night, and we will have the full funds to pay off our debts."

The lender took the pouch, which disappeared into the wide sleeves of his hanbok. "You should not worry, this is not a problem. Often it takes a little longer for some establishments to attract customers to their location. Your place of business will be bustling soon, and coins will fill your pockets." The lender paused a moment, his gaze through his expensive round spectacles steady upon Kim Joo-Won, who was still bent over at the waist in a low bow. "I will only charge you the smallest of late fees. It will be no matter once customers fill your seats. An additional fifteen percent to what you owe will be a trifle."

In the back room, Nam-Gi heard his mother gasp. Nam-Gi wanted to flee the restaurant before the lender left and his father could turn his wrath upon him. The late fee was exorbitant. Their business would have to double immediately if they were to be able to pay the next month's debt to the lender. It quickly become obvious that, out of desperation, his father had made a terrible deal for the current loans.

Kim Joo-Won's deep breaths filled the brief silence. "That was our agreement," his father conceded. "But we would be able to purchase the rarest seafood to bring in more guests if we had more money to spend. Perhaps if the late fee could be lessened, it would mean we could pay off our debt sooner."

The lender's face revealed no emotion as he said, "Do you wish to back out of our prior agreement?" He cast his eyes around the wooden walls of the extended restaurant. "You did such a fine job adding on to your establishment. Yet down here at the edge of the docks, many accidents are known to happen to the less fortunate. This area is not as prosperous as it once was, and not all who walk near here are to be trusted."

The two men standing at the doorway cleared their throats again. Frustration flooded Nam-Gi, his heart racing, his anger making him become rigid causing added pain to his back. So the lender thought that this was power? Brute strength, strong arms, thick waists adorned with swords? The words of the spells swirled into Nam-Gi's mind, and he clenched his teeth as he struggled against the urge to call them up into reality. He would show the lender one day what true power was, he thought as he brought his body under control. One day, he promised himself, he would reach into the mind of the lender and twist it to his whim. And then the lender would learn that true strength was not physical, but mental.

Kim Joo-Won remained bent over in his low bow, his humiliation plain to his watching family. He was a simple man, deep in debt, and could not pay his bill. What would happen to all of them if the lender came back and the money was not there? In the kitchen, Nam-Gi heard Chansol and Chan-Mi stir. What would happen to his little sisters if his father lost this restaurant?

"Your money will be here," his father said. He did not straighten until after the lender finally took his leave, the two armed men casting cold glances back at Nam-Gi before trailing after him. When his father stood up, he turned to Nam-Gi, his gaze ablaze with rage. Before his father could speak, his mother stepped out of the back room, his sisters in tow.

"Fifteen percent." Her eyes were wide, her mouth quivering with worry. "Why is the late fee so high?"

"He was the only one that would lend to us." His father never stopped staring at him. "We have borrowed from too many others to pay for *his* medicine, the price of which has robbed us of any profit from the few customers we've had over the years. It was either that lender, or we wouldn't have been able to complete the renovations to the restaurant." His gaze hardened further, and without having to hear it, Nam-Gi knew what his father was thinking. The expansion had been Nam-Gi's idea, after all.

"How will we manage?" his mother asked.

To that, Kim Joo-Won made no reply. Nam-Gi kept his eyes on the ground, his thoughts racing. They needed money somehow, for he had to continue his lessons with the foreigner. He didn't know if Daesh would teach him for free, but if he decided to do so, and Nam-Gi's classmates of higher status found out and complained to the governor that he was being favored by the teacher, that could cause him many problems. It was already risky enough Daesh was teaching him spells he wasn't teaching the other two students.

No, Nam-Gi had to figure out how to solve his family's money problems before they lost everything. And as usual, he had to figure it out on his own.

8. THE RETAINER

Nam-Gi's grandmother stayed out diving all night in search of octopus. Buying it would tax what little money they had left, and Kim Joo-Won would do so only if they had no other choice. Sitting outside, the moon bright in a velvet sky filled with stars, Nam-Gi heard his father rolling back and forth on his sleeping mat, the floorboards creaking under his weight.

Time passed slowly. Nam-Gi meditated on the core of energy inside of him, storing and enlarging it for the coming day. He could not be sure, but he suspected he would need to use his magic in order to rescue his family if his grandmother was not successful in her dive. It wouldn't be easy to manipulate the lender, but he might have to start first with his grandmother, who would be distraught if she came back empty-handed. Making her believe she had actually caught something would force him to push deep into her mind, and there would be resistance. After that, he would have to affect the minds of his father and mother, but everything hinged on catching his grandmother first.

The horizon paled, then became flushed with hues of orange and red as the sun woke from its sleep. Nam-Gi removed a small vial of ginseng from his hanbok, uncorked it, placed it to his lips, and drank the golden liquid. It burned down his throat, warmth spreading through him followed by heat as his heartbeat ratcheted up. His breath coming out as quick pants, Nam-Gi lay down on his back, the familiar pounding assaulting his head. His sinuses burned, and blood trickled from his nose down his cheek. He used a piece of ripped cloth to wipe it away and tasted the rest of the blood draining into the back of his throat. His parents would be up soon, and he didn't have much time to get over the wave of sickness the potent potion of ginseng always visited upon him.

Nam-Gi picked up the crunch of footsteps on seashells as someone walked down the road towards the restaurant. His already pounding heart sped up further, and Nam-Gi lifted his head, causing the blood to flow faster against the cloth covering his nose. To his great relief, he saw it wasn't his grandmother. The feeling didn't last long, however, as the rounded black hat with black tassel the visitor wore, and the way his hanbok flowed neatly over his lean frame as he walked, bespoke government retainer. The young man eyed Nam-Gi curiously as he approached and stopped several steps away.

"Are you a member of the Kim family?" he asked in a firm voice.

Nam-Gi could only nod, worry flowering in his mind at the realization that this could only mean one thing.

The young man bowed. "I come on behalf of the yangban of Busan. Today, six of our members will visit your restaurant. They were told some weeks ago that if they gave proper advance notice, you would be able to prepare octopus for them."

"For such a request," Nam-Gi said, "the morning of the evening it is to be served is not enough time. We need time to prepare the special ingredients necessary to make the dish so delicious the diners will be enchanted by its taste."

The retainer looked past Nam-Gi to the restaurant, then back at him. "The yangban were worried this might not be enough time," he admitted. "I apologize for the abrupt notice. However, if you are able to prepare the meal for them, they will greatly appreciate it and give you a token of that appreciation in payment. Also," the retainer went on, "they will spread the word to other government officials of your understanding in this matter, which will encourage a steady stream of wealthy officials to visit your establishment."

Before Nam-Gi could say more, the retainer added, "The financial gain will be considerable, and extended over an indefinite length of time."

Nam-Gi swallowed the blood pooled in the back of his throat. If the restaurant became profitable as a result of the extension, his father would be able to pay off the lender threatening them. And if Nam-Gi was able to convince the yangban the octopus they ate there far surpassed that of other establishments, their family restaurant might become known for serving the dish, which would only increase their revenue earned. With the extra coins, Nam-Gi would be able to convince his father they could hire a waiter to take his place. This in turn would free Nam-Gi to study more in preparation for a quest.

Everything hinged on the yangban's experience today. Yet the way they had looked at him out of the corner of their eyes, as if they studied him, increased the risk of using spells to deceive them. Should he take the chance? But then, didn't the greatest gambles yield the highest rewards?

"We would be deeply honored to have the yangban dine with us tonight," Nam-Gi said. When he bowed, blood leaked down his nose and dripped onto his hanbok. The expression on the retainer's face didn't change, and he simply returned the bow.

"They will arrive in the evening."

The retainer turned and walked back down the road, his shoes crunching on the seashells beneath his feet. Nam-Gi immediately hobbled into the restaurant and took up the piece of black chalk his mother used to change the daily menu written along the walls. Leaning heavily on his cane, the knobbed handle jabbing into his right palm, he began to draw outlines of octopus, his left hand steady even as his heart thudded. His father stepped into the room and paused.

"What are you doing?"

Nam-Gi didn't want to waste time using words to convince his father. This level of manipulation could only be accomplished by using his jeong-shin, which he dipped into as he turned to respond. "Grandmother was successful, father. She found several octopus hiding in the fissures of the coast."

He conjured an image of his grandmother, her face wrinkled from the sun and years of diving beginning from when she was a child. He filled the pot she had carried to the coast with two large octopus, and two smaller ones, more than enough for the yangban and the lender. His grandmother hadn't caught octopus in years, no longer able to keep pace with the younger divers, so Nam-Gi sharpened the image by adding smells of the Hanguk Strait, the sound of the water sloshing in the pot, the excitement in his grandmother's voice as she announced her haul. He watched his father's eyes brighten at the images Nam-Gi embedded in his mind. Now he had to wait and see if his grandmother actually caught something or not, for—if she hadn't—their guests tonight would still have to be served meals cloaked in illusion.

What the actual food in each meal would be remained a mystery.

9. OCTOPUS

Nam-Gi cast spells over his mother and little sisters, his lies of grandmother's successful octopus hunt filling their heads. Their gazes passed over the images he drew, lingering on the crude depictions for only a moment as delighted smiles of good fortune touched their lips.

"Let's prepare the side dishes," Gu In-Hye told Chansol and Chan-Mi. Her happy face set the girls to dancing as they got the small knives and cutting boards ready.

A dull throb started in the back of Nam-Gi's head, another side effect of the ginseng potion. He had stayed up all night. Though he didn't feel sleepy, fatigue solidified at the edges of his consciousness so it felt as if he viewed the world from the bottom of the ocean. The colors of the restaurant rippled in his vision suddenly, to become garish, the walls and floor bathed in harsh, glaring light.

The daily nosebleed had stopped, for which Nam-Gi was grateful. He stuck the red-stained cloth into his pocket to wash later and stepped outside, but Kim Joo-Won called after him.

"Don't go far! You'll have to make sure there's no dust or dirt on the tables or floor tonight. Everything must be perfect."

Nam-Gi checked a sigh. Pausing a few steps beyond the door, he tapped his cane on the shells of the narrow path that led to the restaurant and waited for his grandmother. The presence of his father hovering behind him increased his agitation. As he sensed his father's patience running dry, he started to turn back to the restaurant to begin cleaning as he'd been ordered. Out of the corner of his eye, he saw his grandmother walking up the winding path. She carried a fishing pot, and by the way she gripped the edges, Nam-Gi knew something heavy must be in it. Hope rising, he hobbled down the path to meet her, his back aching with each quick step.

"*Hal-moe-ni!*" His voice boomed in his ears, making him flinch. Moderating his tone, he asked, "Did you bring something good back with you?"

His grandmother's face, tanned and wrinkled from years in the sun, bore a light sheen of perspiration as she strode briskly down the path. The sinewy muscles of her arms stood out against her flesh under the strain of the pot.

"You can see once I get inside," she said in a gravelly voice hoarse with age.

Nam-Gi couldn't let that happen. "Isn't it too much for you, walking all the way from the coast?" He wrapped a spell around the suggestion. "You have been so good to us, Hal-moe-ni, but you seem very tired. Don't you think you have gone far enough and need to rest now?"

Nam-Gi created a bridge between his mind and his grandmother's and eased his will over her own. He built a reality of her exhaustion from her dive and implanted it deep inside of her.

Confusion swept over his grandmother's features as she slowed. Whereas before her stride had been strong and purposeful, now she stumbled, her weakness causing surprise to creep into her gaze.

"It's gotten so hot this morning." She set the pot down and wiped her brow. "These legs of mine must be tired."

"It is okay, Hal-moe-ni. I will bring it the rest of the way for you. But first let me see how big the octopus are." Nam-Gi reached for the lid and lifted it.

"We'll have to tell the lender he can come back another day," his grandmother said as Nam-Gi peered into the water. In the pot swam long gray eel, but no octopus.

"I dove all night, but I wasn't able to find anything. If only the girls were older, they would be able to help me."

Nam-Gi trembled as frustration, anger, and despair surged through him. He swallowed in a throat gone dry but pushed down this surge of emotions as he summoned yet more jeong-shin. Steadying his voice before he spoke again, he said, "Hal-moe-ni, what do you mean the lender has to come back another day? You caught two big octopus."

"No, I just told you. I wasn't able to—" his grandmother started to repeat, but Nam-Gi laid false images over the squirming eel. His grandmother, motioning to the pot, gasped.

"But I swear I didn't," she muttered, shocked.

"Do not think too much on it, Hal-moe-ni." Nam-Gi rested a hand on her shoulder. "We have all been so tired trying to attract customers to visit the restaurant. After tonight, everything is going to be better. I promise. Now, let me bring this pot to father for you."

Nam-Gi tried to take the eel from his grandmother to get her moving, but she wouldn't relinquish it. She continued to stare into the water, disbelief sketching itself across the wrinkles of her face.

Gently yet firmly, Nam-Gi tugged at the pot until his grandmother finally released the handles. He braced it against his hip with one hand, the edges biting into his side, and hobbled back to the restaurant. He had to continuously feed his grandmother images to ease her doubt, but her perplexed look remained. When they finally entered the restaurant, his father rushed over to them.

"*Eo-moe-ni?*" Kim Joo-Won paused, searching the lines of her face. "Is everything okay?"

The old woman stood at the entrance, swaying on her feet. "I don't know," she muttered. "My head hurts. I must be tired."

"You were out diving all night." His father took the pot from Nam-Gi and set it down. When he opened the lid, his eyes lit up. "You really got them!"

She started and looked at the catch again. "Yes," she said quietly. "I did."

Gu In-Hye came from the kitchen trailed by his excited sisters, and took the pot from Kim Joo-Won. Chansol and Chan-Mi reached for the handles to help her carry it, but she shooed them away and took the pot to the kitchen. There, she poured the eel into a wide bucket. Like with the others, Nam-Gi continually maintained for her the illusion of octopus, now undulating in the water.

Kim Joo-Won took his mother's hand. "Go and rest, Eo-moe-ni." He led her to the single room where they all slept and helped her lie down on one of the mats. "You have done well." Kissing her forehead, he left her to return to the main room.

Nam-Gi rode the waves of his jeong-shin as he crafted a reality so strong no one in his family would question it as the day went on. He fed it into their heads, reinforcing the details to ensure the spell would not unravel.

In the kitchen, Gu In-Hye picked up an eel. In her mind's eye, she held a reddish octopus by two of its squirming arms. The illusion extended to Nam-Gi's sisters, who looked on with great amusement as the projected octopus sprayed a fount of water at them, splashing their hanboks.

For Nam-Gi, it was strange to watch them playing with air,

their movements mimicking the actions they would normally take if an octopus were actually present. He winced at the laughter that filled the room as his mother laid the illusion on the floor and flipped over its hood. With a sharp knife, she cut out the octopus's stomach, the blade slicing through the eel's tough skin.

The girls poured real water on the projected organs to clean them. Nam-Gi scowled as the liquid splashed the empty spaces on the floor. His mother cut out the octopus's eyes, the knife carving away at the air, and washed out the rubbery strains of brownish entrails before putting the eel back in a tub of clear water. Chansol and Chan-Mi prepared the fire pit. Once a low blaze burned, they put the tub over the flames and watched the water come to a slow boil.

Nam-Gi observed all of this in grim silence. This was the only way to save his family from the lender, he told himself, the only way to get his father to agree to allow him to go on a quest. He quelled a gnawing guilt over whether it was right or wrong to deceive his family. He was using his jeong-shin to create a new, sustaining reality to protect them, and he knew Daesh Seon-saeng-nim would be proud of his mastery of illusions and mind control.

Wouldn't he?

10. EVENING MEAL

The day darkened to evening. Nam-Gi, fighting off sleep and exhaustion, drank more of the ginseng potion, not wanting to let his jeong-shin diminish and the spells unravel. He had to cast yet another illusion to hide the nosebleed. He wiped away the warm thin trails snaking down his upper lip each time he bent over to sweep the floor. The room spun, forcing him to lean against the wall, eyes shut tight to steady the pounding in his head.

"You cannot rest," Kim Joo-Won scolded him. "The restaurant must be perfect for tonight."

Nam-Gi nodded, pushed himself off the wall with a deep grunt, and finished the floor. He proceeded to wipe down the tables and clean the corners of the walls where dust and spiderwebs lingered.

When he finally finished, he prepared yet another ginseng potion, his hands trembling as he mixed in the special ingredients his teacher had given him. He would have to get more eventually, but he had enough to last him for a while yet. He stared at the golden liquid, struggling to steady his rapid breathing and trembling hand.

"I will not fail," Nam-Gi whispered to himself. Placing the vial to his lips, he swallowed the ginseng, the potion burning down his throat. His nose bled again, but the spells that flared brightly into his mind were his consolation.

His confidence rose like a wave to drown his doubts. The lender and yangban would see only what he willed them to see. The power of his mind would overcome the physical limitations of his twisted body, and he would prove his worth to his family. Nothing would stand in the way of his dream of going on a quest.

The tempo of his headache increased, becoming a steady pounding in his skull. This, too, was only another obstacle in his path. Just as he had dealt with so many other physical ailments in his life, he would tolerate this newest pain.

Night gradually blossomed, the moon opening its eye in a black sky filled with a whorl of bright stars. His mother brought white magnolia flowers and set them in decorative pots on the tables. His father finally removed the wilted potted plants from the entrance and threw them out.

"Today is our real opening day," he announced. "After tonight, everything will change for us."

Gu In-Hye prepared side dishes of squid, shrimp, dried seaweed, lettuce, kimchi, rice, onions, garlic, and baby eggs. His sisters helped in filling the tiny plates. His mother didn't even have to threaten them to behave, the importance of this event not lost upon them.

"Everything must be perfect," his father repeated often, and Chansol and Chan-Mi picked up the mantra as they went about their chores.

"Everything must be perfect," they said, their shoulders tense as they wiped smudges off cups, plates, and utensils. The tension was contagious, and Nam-Gi focused on his own emotions so he wouldn't be infected by the others. Unlike his family, he needed to remain calculating as he wove illusion upon illusion to ensure the night was a success. Now wasn't the time for nervous excitement. He had to be cool, like Daesh Seon-saeng-nim, as he worked ever more complicated illusions into reality.

His father sent his sisters outside the restaurant as lookouts. When the two girls ran back in moments later, they exclaimed, "Someone is coming!"

Kim Joo-Won rushed to the door to gaze down the winding road.

"It's the lender," he told Nam-Gi and his mother. "It would have been better if the yangban had arrived first. We have to save the best dishes for the government officials, but we can't afford to insult the lender." He shook his head, perspiration marking his brow. "It's time to begin."

The lender, as before, was accompanied by his two associates, both still wearing leather armor and carrying sheathed *hwandos*. His father met them several steps from the restaurant and guided them inside with much kowtowing.

"We are so happy to see you here tonight," he said, repeatedly bowing. "We hope you have a pleasant experience. All has been made ready for you."

"So you really do have octopus?" the lender asked. "You managed to procure it so quickly."

"My mother obtained it for us," Kim Joo-Won boasted. "She has been diving along the coast of Busan since she was a child, no bigger than these two." He motioned to Chansol and Chan-Mi, who bowed low, their long black hair draping their sweaty faces. "The Strait is in her blood. She knows where to look to find the trickiest seafood hiding beneath the waves."

The lender regarded Kim Joo-Won through the lenses of his spectacles. "I'm sure she'll be proud to hear her son talk about her so highly." With a flourish, he sat down seiza-style on the provided mat. His two associates removed their swords, leaned them within easy reach against the wall, then sat down opposite the lender. Gu In-Hye brought out green tea in a tin kettle and filled the white porcelain cups with the steaming liquid.

Nam-Gi reached into the lender's thoughts when the man picked up the cup with one hand. He took a loud, noisy slurp.

"It's delicious," the lender announced in pleased surprise. "I'm truly looking forward to the main course. My associates and I are very hungry. We've traveled far today collecting debts and have had little time to eat. We've been looking forward to this special meal all day."

Nam-Gi brought out the first course on a wide platter. He settled the side dishes on the table, arranging them in a circle before the guests. He placed the plate of baked mackerel before the lender so that he wouldn't have to reach far to sample the succulent meat. The mackerel was actually less than six centimeters, but Nam-Gi elongated it in the guests' minds, and their eyes widened comically at its apparent length.

"I'm starting to see why you could not pay me," the lender said as he separated a slice of the fish with his chopsticks and placed it in his mouth. "You spend too much on your guests!"

"Once word of our extended establishment spreads throughout the ports, business will pick up, and you will get everything that is owed you," his father said with a low bow.

Nam-Gi noted bitterly that a look of relief did not cross the lender's face. Perhaps he preferred them being forever in his debt, their loan growing with interest month after month.

Nam-Gi's sisters rushed in from outside again, their bare feet slapping against the wooden floor. "There is a big group coming!" They pointed down the darkened path.

Kim Joo-Won went to the door and stiffened. He turned to Nam-Gi, anxiety written in the tightness of his face.

"They're here," he said in a breathless tone. This caught the attention of the lender, who turned and peered out into the night. Nam-Gi went back into the kitchen and handed his mother the platter, which she loaded with an array of side dishes. When the yangban entered the restaurant in their varying dark-hued robes, the lender's eyes widened even further in surprise.

Kim Joo-Won, bowing repeatedly, greeted them. "Welcome! Please, sit down and make yourselves comfortable."

He led the men to their table in the newer section of the restaurant. Six of them had come, just as the retainer had said. Among them were two from the previous visit: Myung-bak Ssi with his long-pointed beard, and Hyun-wook Ssi, who complained first about the lack of octopus as a menu item.

The yangban were tall, their black bamboo hats almost brushing against the ceiling. They went to their mats, which had already been pulled out from under the table and lined up for them. They sat down with precise, practiced grace, their backs erect, their hands neatly folded on their laps.

Nam-Gi approached their table with a kettle of green tea, which he poured into six porcelain cups. He returned moments later balancing a full tray in one hand until he settled his cane against the wall. He placed the many dishes around the table so each guest had an opportunity to sample the various foods with ease.

Gathering the emotions raging inside of him, he buried them deep within his subconscious so he could focus on the magic. He wove fictions into the minds of the yangban, his jeong-shin a roaring fire inside him as he continually stoked its flames to keep the different spells going. When he looked up and caught Myung-bak Ssi staring at him, worry escaped the pit he'd forced it into. For a moment, the different compartments he had stuffed all of his tortures: the pounding headache, his throbbing back, his fear of discovery, threatened to break their separate doors and crash over him.

Quickly, Nam-Gi turned back to the kitchen, but before he could escape, Myung-bak Ssi called after him.

"You're a student of the foreigner, are you not?"

Steadying his breathing, focusing on his mind, reinforcing the cracks appearing in his consciousness, Nam-Gi said in a breathless whisper, "Yes, I am."

There was no point in lying when he had so many other deceptions going. If the yangban was asking, then he probably already knew the answer.

"I haven't seen the foreigner in several months. He tends to stay holed up in his school, only showing up at the governor's office when a quest has been assigned."

"I've never seen him," Hyun-wook Ssi said. "But then, they're kept away from humans. Most islanders only know of their existence through word of mouth. I've always felt the Emperors don't particularly like humans being exposed to the foreigners."

"I've heard they're quite monstrous," added another of their companions. "Dark skin like shadows on a starlit night. White hair with the luminescence of the moon." He took a sip of tea. "I imagine them to be truly heinous to behold."

"They are indeed, Jae-seop Ssi," Myung-bak Ssi agreed. "I've seen the foreigner several times when he's traveled in the company of young men on quests. There is a degree of fortunate timing involved to catch a glimpse of one."

"Fortunate indeed," Hyun-wook Ssi scoffed.

"Well, fortunate *in* timing," Myung-bak Ssi amended. "But in all the years of my service, this teacher is the only one I've seen. He joins the quests most often from our region. I believe his name is Daesh."

A grimace threatened to disrupt the emotionless expression

Nam-Gi was maintaining on his face. The harsh manner in which the yangban uttered the Dark Elf's name seemed purposeful, as if it was meant to anger him. The urge to defend his teacher surged inside of him, the strain of handling all of these emotions creating an overwhelming pressure upon his psyche.

Rage! Nam-Gi heard the grinding of his teeth in his ear. Daesh Seon-saeng-nim had told him to use his rage in times of distress. It would focus him, give him strength when weakness threatened to overwhelm him.

"The foreigners are difficult to gaze upon," Myung-bak Ssi continued. "There are some who would like to do away with them altogether, but the foreigners have been in South Hanguk for so long, and the Emperor believes they make our country stronger. Especially with the threat of the Child-God of North Hanguk forever on our border."

"Nevertheless," Jae-seop Ssi countered, "it is important we always keep the foreigners under careful surveillance. They have dwelt in South Hanguk for generations, but can any human truly say they know the mind of a Dark Elf? Or how they influence those who study under them?"

The other yangban nodded in agreement, then continued on with their meals. Nam-Gi bowed, his body trembling, and escaped back into the kitchen. His mother had finished preparing the eel into a dish she believed to be san-nakji. Since the lender had arrived first, he was to be served before the yangban, though their servings, too, were almost ready.

Once again balancing the platter in one hand, Nam-Gi forced himself back out, hobbling to the lender's table. He laid the plate of wriggling slices of gray eel before the man and his two assistants.

"It looks delicious!" The lender clasped his hands together, his lips spreading into a thin smile. Out of the corner of his eye, Nam-Gi noticed the yangban had become silent. They stared at the lender's table as he picked up a squirming tentacle, dipped it in their family's specially prepared sauce, then placed it in his mouth.

Myung-bak Ssi stood and stepped over to the table. The lender's assistants ate the wriggling tentacles only after the lender had had several bites of what his eyes told him was octopus. All three men chewed loudly, satisfied looks beaming from their faces. Turning to Kim Joo-Won, the lender said, "Your restaurant will be known all over the island if you continue to serve san-nakji as delicious as this. We look forward to the next course of yeonpo-tang and jju-ggu-mi bokum bap."

"That's no octopus," Myung-bak Ssi said.

The lender's eyes narrowed in confusion behind his thin glasses. "Of course it is!"

The other yangban gathered around Nam-Gi. He stumbled back and bumped into one of them standing directly behind him. He cast his gaze around the restaurant, caught the confused look of his father, saw his little sisters Chansol and Chan-Mi staring, standing still with fear. Gu In-Hye, no longer preparing the rest of the yangban's meal, came to stand beside her daughters.

"Kim Nam-Gi," Hyun-wook Ssi said, "you are charged with using your jeong-shin for deception and profit. You are to come with us immediately to the governor's office and be kept in Busan's prison until your trial."

Kim Joo-Won took a step forward, but Jae-seop Ssi raised his hand, bringing him to an abrupt stop. His father could only stare in disbelief. In a strained whisper, he said, "Nam-Gi, what have you done?"

Nam-Gi pressed down upon the knobbed handle of his walking stick, the rough surface digging into his palm. Looking from his father, to his sisters, to his mother, he brought his gaze back to his father once again. The pain of this moment struck his heart, which thrashed in his chest and made the left side of his body go numb.

"I did," Nam-Gi gasped, "what I had to. For all of us."

And in doing what he had to, he had failed all of them.

11. THROUGH THE CITY

The yangban seized Nam-Gi by the arms. Stabbing pain shot through his spine, making him cry out. When they yanked his wrists behind his back, the room spun. Nam-Gi screamed, mouth gaping open as if he could expel the torture the men were inflicting upon him, but his suffering was going nowhere as they tied his wrists with a tight cord.

Gu In-Hye rushed forward and fell to her knees before them. "I am sorry, sir," she said, her palms pressed together. "He is sick; he has always been sick. Please, be gentle with him —he cannot handle such treatment."

The yangban holding him by the arms scoffed, and yanked Nam-Gi to the door, so that he cried out again. Short fingers of darkness stretched in from the corners of his vision. He was sure he would pass out any moment, and welcomed the loss of consciousness to escape the pain, escape the eyes of the guests staring at him, his little sisters crying, their heads bowed. Worst of all was his father's hard gaze, the features of his face settled into a rigid mask.

"Your son has shamed you," Myung-bak Ssi declared to his mother. "He has ruined your business's reputation and brought dishonor upon your family's name." He spat. "A thorough investigation will be done. We will speak to all the guests who have been served by the Kim family over these many years. Restitution will be made for every ill-gotten coin that filled your coffers."

His mother pressed her forehead flat against the floor as she continued to plead that they show Nam-Gi mercy. Even through the torment hazing his vision with swirling darkness, he glimpsed the way his father flinched at the accusations the yangban delivered upon their family name. They would be ruined by what he had done, there was no doubt. His ancestors looking in from the afterlife would never welcome Nam-Gi. In this world and in all future incarnations, Nam-Gi would be an outcast, alone and hated by all.

He moaned in growing despair at the future that opened itself to him, the condemnation that awaited him from this moment onward.

The yangban dragged him out of the restaurant to a waiting buggy. Hauling him up under his arms, they threw him into the carriage. Fresh pain brought fresh screams, and Nam-Gi shivered, tears streaming down his face to mix with the mucous leaking from his nose.

"Quickly, to the governor's office." Jae-seop Ssi and Myung-bak Ssi climbed into the carriage with him. One of the others took position in the box, and with a flick of the reins, set the horses off at a fast trot. Nam-Gi was thrown from side to side, his screams ripping from his sore throat with each new bump in the uneven path the wheels bounced over. His stomach lurching, he became sick, losing control of his bowels and soiling his hanbok. The yangban scolded him for his weakness.

"He is nothing but an animal now," one said. They cleared their throats and spat thick clumps of phlegm upon him.

Nam-Gi curled into a miserable ball of bodily waste as the

carriage tore through the city lanes toward the governor's office. He felt his mind slipping, fracturing, as wild ideas sprang forward. He could leap up and attack the men, tearing away at them with his teeth since his wrists were tied. He would make them all suffer before fleeing, but where exactly would he go? His father would never welcome him back to their home, and how could he exist in the city on his own? Everyone would recognize him as word spread of a crippled hunchback accused of terrible deceptions against those who had trusted him.

Voices rose and fell around him, but the roaring in his ears drowned them out as an ocean of his inner suffering washed over him in consecutive waves. At some point, hands gripped him again, pulling him out of the carriage and wringing out strained whimpers from his parched throat. They dragged him through a tall, familiar gate, and flung Nam-Gi to the foot of hard stairs. He collapsed to his side, and lay there, gasping for breath, his lungs burning as if they'd made him run from the coast to the governor's office steps.

As much as Nam-Gi wished to pass out, his stubborn consciousness refused to give him the peace of oblivion. Slowly, the thunder in his ears lessened, allowing words to penetrate the darkness cocooning him.

"…foreigner's pupil."

"He is one of…"

They were speaking of Daesh Seon-saeng-nim! Nam-Gi hoped they wouldn't bring his teacher here to see him like this, in the dirt, clothes soiled, face streaked with tears. His teacher had had such high hopes for him, preparing him to actually go on a quest when no one believed him capable to do so. What would Daesh think if he saw Nam-Gi now?

"…let the people know?"

Nam-Gi opened his eyes to thin slits to see who was gathered around him. All he glimpsed were sandaled feet. When he tried to move his head to look up, the pain in his spine roared with savage life, and he gasped sharply.

"He is awake."

When next a voice spoke, it was closer to his ear. "Your treachery has placed your teacher in a dangerous position. The foreigners are already distrusted by the people. Knowing one of their students has been conning them with magic he taught can create an uprising against the Dark Elves of South Hanguk."

Farther above him, someone said, "We should let the people decide the foreigner's fate."

"And disobey the Emperor's decree? No, we must do as we have been ordered. We will have to prove Nam-Gi's deceit goes beyond just him in the Kim family. His father and mother, his grandmother and sisters; even his deceased grandfather must be found guilty so the people do not turn their attention to the foreigners."

The voice closest to Nam-Gi drifted away again. "We will gather the evidence, and the Kim family will all be found guilty of deceiving their guests over the years. It is the only way to maintain the peace towards the Dark Elves."

Nam-Gi, whimpering, said, "You cannot do—"

Rough hands grabbed him, cutting off his plea. He was yanked to his feet so that the torture of his body assaulted him again. All he could do was cry out yet again as they dragged him to Busan prison and locked him away in a cold, lonely cell.

As he shivered on the cold floor, Nam-Gi's only consolation was the drifting of his consciousness into the vortex of nothingness he had been craving. Even as he sank into the darkness, however, he saw twisting shapes of nightmares rising up from the gloom of his subconscious, and he knew there would be no respite from the physical and emotional punishment his life offered.

12. A FIRE BURNING DEEP

Tsierus shuddered awake to a terrible burning sensation wrapped around his throat. He opened his eyes to thin slits. Above him, the stars created a canopy of bright lights in a black sky. For several moments, he wondered why the cosmos outside of his chariot spread out above him rather than before him as he rode through space. Then he remembered he had disembarked onto the plane below because of the plague of Dark Elves that infested this land of humans.

His vow to kill them all returned anew. The Cloud Elf tried to sit up and moaned as the sensation of fire penetrated his neck further.

"Careful." The voice of his guardian came from some place above him. "You are not dead, but you have hovered near the veil between death and life for days now."

Tsierus swallowed, and immediately regretted it. The flexing of the muscles in his neck sent the scorching flames to radiate through his flesh once more. He gasped, which immediately intensified the torturous sensation. He wanted to speak but feared the consequences of talking.

"The Dark Elf's magic left a curse mark upon you," the

Eye said. "There is a poison seeping through your veins from the wound in your throat. It has been attempting to reach your organs and attack you from the inside."

Tsierus's hands clenched feebly, in muted fury. The cursed race! Even when dispatched, they could still cause harm. This is why he must not die, and he must not leave this world of mortals until he has finished his mission. He must kill the twenty-two remaining Dark Elves. He would not forgive himself if he failed in this sacred quest he had placed upon himself.

His guardian floated within his line of sight, the blinking lights in the cornea of the disembodied Eye focused upon him. "Tsierus." It paused. "I gaze into your face and I know your thoughts. But I urge you now: you must leave this place!"

"Never!" The word came out in a pained croak, the price of the utterance sparking anew the fire of his injury. Yet Tsierus would not be cowed by the weakness of this body. "Never!" he proclaimed, louder this time.

"You are one against twenty-two. You are powerful, but the Dark Elves, in their own right, are also powerful. You will fail in this quest."

"The Lord would never flee in the face of evil," Tsierus gasped. "Even if it meant sacrificing His own life to save the souls of others!"

The Eye regarded him silently. Tsierus noticed that a soft light extended from its cornea and surrounded him with a gentle glow. His guardian was healing him again. He knew he put her at great risk as she delved into her power at great costs to herself, but how could he just go back to his chariot suspended above him in the sky? If he did, he might indeed live, but his guilt would haunt him for the rest of his days. That would be a hell of its own, for the Cloud Elves existed thousands of years. What would that be like, a lifetime of regret? A lifetime of wondering what he could have done for these humans if he had remained steadfast?

The Eye left his field of vision again, hovering somewhere near him once more.

"You will be healed again," she said, "though it will take time. Until then, you must rest."

Tsierus began to speak, but his guardian continued. "When you are ready, you will have to decide which path you will take next. I have located the next nearest Dark Elf in a large city some distance from here. It is near the coast by a mighty body of water in a city the humans call Busan."

"Then we will go there," Tsierus croaked, trembling at the pain. "We will go from city to city, and we will kill them all. This plane will be cleansed! I will purify it of their existence!"

Tsierus clenched his hands into tight fists. If he set upon this task with single-minded determination, he would rise above the challenge. He would kill them all.

PART II: KWAN CAPTAIN

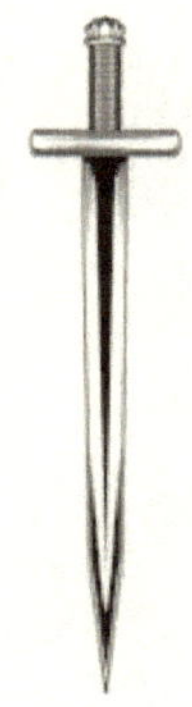

13. A BRIEF VOYAGE HOME

"Kwan Captain. Thank you for steering us safely across the oceans once more."

Kwan Han-Jae stood at the bow of the narrow sea guard ship, his gaze steady on the approaching docks of his hometown, Gwangju. He took a pull from his pipe, filling his lungs with sweet smoke, before releasing it in a funnel cloud from between his pursed lips.

They had arrived after five days of travel from their fort station in the village of Majeon, which was half-a-day's journey from the large city of Incheon in northern South Hanguk. The sun stood high in a clear blue sky. Though his mood should have been light, Han-Jae didn't relish returning to his wife, three sons and two daughters.

He turned to his first mate, Dora, who proffered a wooden bowl of makgeolli to him with both hands. Han-Jae took it, biting back a smile. His men had thanked him often: for a successful embarking, for clear hot days, for rain to cool off sunburned skin, for the sound of seagulls near the coasts, for the continued twinkling of stars in the sky. Each time, they passed around the wooden cup of rice wine. They spent most of the voyage drinking the cask of strong liquor secured against the stern of the ship, toasting their captain for even the ocean spray and wind against the sails.

Han-Jae placed the wooden bowl to his lips and drank in one long pull, the bitter liquid coursing down his throat. When finished, he handed it back to Dora, who bowed and went back to the men. They sat in a circle and snacked on seaweed and dried anchovies while gambling, tossing pebbles against the hull to see where and how they landed on the planks. Han-Jae turned back to the docks stretching out along the pier.

"Adjust the sails to face the coming wind," he said over his shoulder, and heard the dozen sea guards rising, their bare feet echoing against the bamboo boards of the deck as they went about their tasks. The creak of the sails being rotated reached his ears, and the boat's direction slowly adjusted into the familiar air current that blew off the coast. Han-Jae had taken this voyage home every four months for ten years. He would only be in Gwangju for two weeks, just long enough to take care of family business, visit his wife, and pay respects to his parents.

He dreaded each visit a little more every time.

The ship slowed as the sail caught the coming wind, the waves slapping against the hull with a steady rhythm. The day was already late, and Gwangju fishermen had all long since returned to port. Their boats bobbed in the water in a long row along the coast. Han-Jae directed the helmsman towards the fort of the sea guards of Gwangju where they would be allowed to tie their boat.

The sea guard forts, erected in every village, town, and city on the coast of South Hanguk, were uniform in appearance. Long structures of rough brick, they differed only in length. The fort of smaller populations like Majeon and Gwangju housed two dozen men. Larger forts housed three times as many, but seldom more. The sea guards were scouts for South Hanguk. They roamed the Hanguk Strait and ocean waves, looking out for North Hanguk pirates who raided fishermen and attacked coastal villagers to loot, plunder, and kidnap women. If they were forced to, the sea guards engaged in skirmishes, but their main role was to alert the Emperor's fleet to enemy intrusions.

And then, of course, the sea guards were always watching for foreigners who attempted to dock in South Hanguk beyond the port of entry. Han-Jae had yet to arrest any in his decade of service.

"Lower the sails," Han-Jae commanded. To his helmsman, he said, "Steer her into the western current."

They had been spotted by the sea guards of Gwangju. Several came out of the fort and watched their approach, tall halberds in their hands. Though Han-Jae's boat had the insignia of the turtle surrounded by rays of the rising sun, the sea guards would keep an eye on them to ensure they came in peace. The Child-God of North Hanguk was powerful in sorcery, and he played many devastating tricks upon unwary South Hanguk people.

With the sail lowered, they drifted on the current towards the dock. The men stopped moving for several moments so as not to disturb the flow and simply waited, the boat gently rolling beneath their feet. Han-Jae smoked his pipe and kept a steady eye on their progress. Always at his most alert during these last moments of their approach, he had seen many disasters in these last crucial moments from less-experienced crews.

When they were right alongside the wooden docks, two men standing starboard hopped off, rope in hand, and quickly tied the boat to the piling cleats. Others still onboard threw them another two ropes, and once all four were secured, Han-

Jae jumped onto the dock where he was met by several Gwangju sea guards, who bowed low.

"We welcome your return home, Kwan Captain." The one who spoke motioned toward the fort. "Please, follow us to Bak Captain. He is expecting you."

Han-Jae, Dora, and one other of his men walked behind the sea guard up the path, their feet crunching on shells thrown up on the beach. They ducked their heads to enter the low entrance of the fort. Inside, the stone roof was also low, so that the tallest of them had to stoop his shoulders so as not to hit his head. The walls were lined with different types of swords, daggers, a bow and arrows, and several spears. Several maps were also tacked to the bricks, representing the territories of South and North Hanguk, the borders in flux across different etched versions. One map even showed the countries of Il-Bon Nala with its string of islands to the east, as well as the massive Jung-Guk Nala to the north and its myriad kingdoms.

A wooden table stretched from one end of the fort to the other. One of the stationed sea guards was laying out an array of seafood and soups in wooden bowls.

"Kwan Han-Jae. It's good to see you again."

Bak Jong-Yeol sat on the floor at the center of the table, a pipe in hand, a trail of smoke drifting from his lips. Fifteen years Han-Jae's senior, he did not rise. Han-Jae and his men bowed low in greeting.

"I've been expecting you any day now," Jong-Yeol said. "It's been four months, after all, and your seasonal visit to your hometown was due."

"Thank you, Bak Captain." Han-Jae motioned to Dora, who brought forth a bag of dried ramen specially prepared in Majeon. "Please, accept this gift for your gracious welcome."

Han-Jae took the bag from Dora and handed it to Jong-

Yeol with both hands. His elder took it with a wide smile and adjusted it so that they could shake hands.

"Thank you so much for your gift," Jong-Yeol said, holding on to Han-Jae's hand for several seconds before releasing his grasp. He indicated for Han-Jae to sit down across from him. One of the men brought porcelain cups and filled them with green tea. Jong-Yeol lifted his to drink. Han-Jae did the same, and the other men in the fort joined them.

"Have you already eaten?" Jong-Yeol asked as platters of spicy kimchi, steaming rice, lentil soup, and an array of seafood were laid out. Han-Jae shook his head. When the dishes had all been neatly arranged between the men, Jong-Yeol started to eat first. The sea guards from Gwangju and Majeon soon followed suit, breaking apart the fish, spearing the shrimp, and slurping from the bowls of hot soup.

"I had hoped to hear you'd been assigned to Incheon," Jong-Yeol said when they had finished, and the platters were cleared away.

Han-Jae kept his face expressionless. In the last three years, this subject had always been brought up eventually. This was the first time it had been broached so soon after his arrival, however.

"My requests have been resubmitted to the officials in Incheon," Han-Jae said, his voice carefully polite. "I am currently awaiting a reply."

The wooden bowls of makgeolli had been served, and now they drank the cool, refreshing liquor to help them digest their meal.

"You must distinguish yourself," Jong-Yeol said. "It will be hard, in the rural village of Majeon where nothing ever happens. Nothing of significance, that is. The opportunity of a notable accomplishment will always be small, but you must find a way."

That, of course, was one of the many problems with coastal towns and villages. The fishermen were mostly hungry and poor. Their children ran naked, or in thin rags, along the coast while their mothers scavenged the rocks for seaweed and crabs. This led to laziness among the sea guards as the years passed, ambition cooling in the face of routine and boredom.

Dora, eating beside Han-Jae, said, "Maybe we should sail further out to find a worthy trial." He pointed to the maps on the walls. "Where the drawings of monsters lie."

"No!"

Han-Jae and Jong-Yeol said this together. The men at the table fell silent and stared at them in wonder. The two captains exchanged glances. They were the oldest of the sea guards in each of their stations. They had been promoted to captain because of their accomplishments while serving in the Emperor's fleet. Both men had traveled near the places where monsters were depicted, and now they drank deeply from their cups to steady their hands.

"Monsters are best left to heroes," Jong-Yeol finally said. The men continued eating and drinking without speaking for a time as the tension dissolved between them.

"I am getting closer to retirement." Jong-Yeol sighed and took a long drink from his cup, finishing it so Han-Jae could refill it. He looked off into the distance. "For years, I served in Busan, but as my instincts began to dull, and as the blades of swords came closer to striking and the twang of arrows made my hand tremble, I requested a village like Gwangju. Here, there is little excitement, and I spend most of my time in this fort while the younger men patrol the waters of South Hanguk. I am an old man now and soon I will join my wife in our small village and become a farmer."

Jong-Yeol drank deeply from the wooden bowl, and again Han-Jae immediately refilled it, while one of his men refilled his. "I am many years your senior. Do you wish to join me in retirement already, when you are still so young?"

The liquor was strong and burned as Han-Jae swallowed it down. He did not look at his elder, his gaze on the stone wall right beyond Jong-Yeol. "What advice do you offer me, Bak Captain? I will gratefully listen and do what I must to follow your wise words."

"Pray to your ancestral spirits." Jong-Yeol drank, his face red from the alcohol. "Ask them to send you a challenge so you may improve your status. When the obstacle comes and you stand tall over it in victory, go to Incheon with the news of your success. Send word back to me also, and I will ask those friends I still have in the city sea guards to put in a good word for you. Remember that whatever challenge comes to Majeon, you must stand firm. Do not back down! Never shrink from your duties as protector of that village!"

14. AN EAGER LOOK

Han-Jae stumbled out of Gwanju's sea fort several cups later. He refilled his pipe, struck a match, and took a deep inhale, letting the smoke fill his lungs. The sun sat lower in the hazy sky, but the world seemed bright in Han-Jae's eyes. He squinted against the glare, the makgeolli pulsing through his veins. Though his movements felt ungainly, he walked with purpose away from the coast towards the village.

Dora, unsteadily keeping pace beside him, said between gasps, "Bak Captain imparted great wisdom today! We can all be promoted to Incheon if we find a great trial to overcome!"

"Great trial," Han-Jae growled, the held-in smoke billowing forth from his lips in wispy clouds. "In Majeon? The worst thing there is hunger. Gaunt fishermen, their skinny wives, and their many scrawny children all crying out for more food."

"Incheon fishermen!" Dora spoke too loudly. His voice stabbed Han-Jae's ear, and he glanced behind him. Most of his men were still near the ship drinking makgeolli with the sea guards of Gwangju, their voices carrying up towards the village.

"Incheon fishermen," Dora repeated, as if Han-Jae could,

possibly, not have heard him the first time. "They are the cause of Majeon woes."

"And what would you have me do about that?" Han-Jae snapped. "Build bigger boats with wider nets for Majeon people so they can compete? They'd still be chased away from the most abundant fishing currents." He gave a bitter laugh. "The fishermen of Majeon are weak. Against the bigger fleet of Incheon boats, they don't stand much of a chance."

"Perhaps the monsters!" Dora waved his hands extravagantly. "We see where they are on the maps. We can go find one and challenge it!"

Han-Jae shook his head, the alcohol sloshing between his ears. "You've had too much to drink and know not of what you speak. We're not young men throwing away our lives to become heroes. We're sea guards trying to be promoted to Incheon. Stupid risks won't help us, it'll just get us killed."

Han-Jae had seen the destruction wrought by the beasts that inhabited the sea and attacked passing ships. Some monsters dwelled beneath the waves and had fearsome tentacles and maws filled with sharp teeth suitable for rending ships to pieces. Sea travelers with missing limbs and disfigured faces warned of narrow escapes, of crewmen pulled from boats. Or worse, of monsters that deceived, taking pleasant forms—like beautiful young girls. When men heard them singing, they stepped off their ships one by one and followed the songs of the seductresses into the dark cold depths to be feasted upon, their screams drifting across the waves to passing boats.

Over the generations, sailors had taken to marking dangerous areas on their maps with pictures of terrifying images like dragons, or skulls and bones.

Han-Jae and Dora reached the towering conifers Gwangju was famous for in South Hanguk. The trees stood tall, their long limbs stretched out wide, their branches full of green needles and bundles of brown cones. Han-Jae inhaled the sticky sweet aroma that permeated the air of his hometown. He'd grown up knowing it, had worked in the fields with his father and brothers, the smell a constant presence. Whenever he chanced upon a similar scent anywhere else in South Hanguk, he thought of his family here in Gwangju.

Unlike most homes of the country, which were constructed from stone dragged up from the quarries of South Hanguk, many of the houses of Gwangju were built of thick wood. Han-Jae followed the path leading to a busy market lane in the center of the village. People visited stalls where vendors called out the wares they were selling at the most affordable prices. When the villagers saw him, a native son returned, they bowed low in greeting to Han-Jae.

"They certainly miss you!" Dora looked back and forth, bleary-eyed. Once again, he spoke much too loudly, his voice braying from his lips. Han-Jae cursed beneath his breath and led him down a narrow path towards a small fenced-in home. He spied his three sons in the yard working a small patch of land and gave a shrill whistle. The boys turned.

When they saw him, they shouted *"Abba!"* dropped their tools, and dashed through the gate. Han-Jae dropped to his knees and the boys leapt into his arms.

"Dora Uncle!" The eldest son stepped away from Han-Jae and bowed low. "I hope you are well today."

"I am, Ki-Tae Ya," Dora replied with a wide smile.

"Have you eaten already? Mother was just preparing dinner. We heard father had arrived."

"We should be going inside, then," Han-Jae replied. Holding the hands of his two youngest sons, he walked through the gate, eyeing the wooden planks critically. He'd need to repair those before he left. Several had splintered and would shatter if struck with even a light blow.

The smell of flounder grilling drifted through the open door. Inside, Han-Jae saw his daughters preparing a long low table with bowls of boiled brown eggs, radish, lentils, kimchi, and buds of garlic, their long black hair braided and swaying as they moved. His wife, Myong-Sook, squatted over a pit in the center of the room, her shorter black hair done up in a neat bun. A low fire burned, and a grate was laid over the pit with four large fish spread evenly over the thin spikes.

"A feast!" Dora exclaimed, sitting down at the table. Han-Jae's daughters bowed politely to him, then filled his cup with tea as the boys sat down beside him.

"Where's the makgeolli?" Han-Jae asked, crouching next to his wife. She pointed to a tin pot on a shelf near the window. Han-Jae took it down, and—after Dora quickly finished his tea—he filled the mate's cup with the liquor, then a cup for himself.

"I see you two have already visited with Bak Captain," Myong-Sook said as she sprinkled a dash of salt on the flounder.

"How did you know?" Dora asked as he lifted his cup to toast Han-Jae.

"I smell it on your breath." She pointed towards the coast. "We see Bak Captain often around the village. Face always as red as the fire here." She indicated the flame beneath the grill.

Han-Jae shrugged, and took a long drink of the wine. "He's nearing retirement. Let him enjoy his prestige in his last years of service to the sea guards."

Myong-Sook called one of the girls over and placed the fish on a platter. "Serve your father first," she instructed, and retrieved lettuce leaves and long green hot peppers from a covered basket. She placed the leaves on the table between the two men and started to chop up the peppers.

"Will you be coming here to take his place?" she asked Han-Jae, who immediately frowned at the question.

"We'll be stationed at Incheon soon!" Dora exclaimed. Han-Jae threw a sharp glance his way, but his first mate didn't notice as he drank deep from his cup, then began to tear the fish into pieces with his chopsticks.

"I thought you had to prove yourself in deed to be taken up by the sea guards of Incheon." Myong-Sook placed the hot peppers on the table, and the children immediately grabbed slices and goaded each other into eating one.

"That's why we were with Bak Captain for so long!" Dora speared a slice of fish, popped it into his mouth, then followed it with a piece of kimchi. "He advised Kwan Captain to seek help from his ancestral spirits. Perhaps if he offers a tribute, they will gift him with a worthy task to improve his chances for promotion."

Myong-Sook paused in preparing the food and turned to Han-Jae, staring him directly in the eye. "Will you take it that far, to invoke the long dead spirits?"

Han-Jae met her gaze for several moments, the sounds of the children and Dora eating filling the house. "My father has mentioned how I would be better suited for Incheon than Majeon. Every time I visit Gwangju, he says it. It seems to be the only thing anyone cares about."

"You've been stationed at Majeon for ten years," his wife pointed out.

"I've been stationed at Majeon for ten years," Han-Jae admitted.

"We once thought it would only be a *year*," his wife added, her eyes still locked on his.

"So it was believed," Han-Jae said. He broke visual contact with her and polished off his cup of wine, then refilled Dora's.

Dora took the tin pot from him and refilled Han-Jae's, before raising his cup to toast.

"After Kwan Captain seeks help from the ancestral spirits, I'm sure they will listen," Dora proclaimed. "The dead seek honor for the family name just as much as the living. It increases their status in the next life."

Han-Jae drained his cup, the alcohol slamming into his mind to numb his doubts. He had been living lazily in Majeon since he'd been stationed there. All the sea guards had. Their greatest hardship was running out of good makgeolli and having to buy the local cheap variety the villagers drank. Did he and his men really want a challenge? Could they actually handle one? If he asked, would the dead give him a task greater than the sea guards of Majeon could overcome?

Han-Jae looked at his three sons and two daughters happily eating more food than many in the village of Gwangju. They were able to do this because the sea guards were paid decently, and when valuables drifted ashore from wrecked ships, they were able to split them among themselves. Han-Jae, being the captain, had first choice of whatever valuable flotsam washed ashore.

Prestige came with an Incheon position, but would it be as lucrative? There were a lot more sea guards in the city, and his position would be lowered, as there could only be one captain. If something happened to him, what would become of his family?

When he looked at his wife again and saw the eagerness in her eyes, Han-Jae knew that before he left Gwangju, he would entreat the ancestral spirits.

Perhaps, if he was lucky, they would not respond.

15. KYU HEH AH-BOE-JI

Han-Jae woke up the next morning next to Myong-Sook on their sleeping mat. Both were naked, her back against his chest, her buttocks pressed against his loins. He breathed in the musky fragrance of her black hair and listened to the soft breathing of her sleep. On the mats a little farther away, their children still dreamed. The rising sun paled the clear morning sky.

Han-Jae moved carefully so as not to wake anyone as he rose. He quietly reached for the hanbok on the clothing shelf, but not quietly enough, for his wife said, "Kyu-Heh Si-ah-boe-ji will be expecting you."

His wife's sleepy voice broke the silence. It seemed to have a magical effect on the children, who all began to stir. Myong-Sook pushed herself up and reached for her own simple hanbok on the shelf. Han-Jae observed her plump, healthy arms and legs with pride even as her morning greeting about his father waiting for him left him annoyed. His family ate well because of his work as a sea guard in Majeon, so why wasn't that enough for them?

"I can go see him after breakfast," Han-Jae said as he pulled on his shirt.

"Jang-Geum *Si-eo-moe-ni* wakes up at dawn," his wife countered. "She'll have food prepared."

Han-Jae scowled, but it was wasted. His wife wasn't looking at him as she set out the boiled eggs she had saved from last night. She sliced a cucumber, arranged the slices around a pile of dried anchovies, and poured water from a stoppered jug onto radishes for the morning soup.

Finished dressing, Han-Jae checked the tin kettle to see if any makgeolli remained. To his disappointment, it stood empty. He packed his pipe with tobacco instead, lit it, and stood in the doorway a moment, smoking. When he heard his wife clear her throat to speak again, he buried a growl and quickly stepped outside.

A breeze drifted through the village, carrying the smell of the sea from the coast. Two weeks he would be in Gwangju, but already Han-Jae was ready to put distance between himself and his family and return to Majeon. There, he gave the orders. Here, he found himself having to follow the commands of too many, all seeking to place a fresh duty upon him or remind him of a different obligation.

Han-Jae walked through the gate and took a narrow path leading behind his home to another within eyesight. His parents lived close to his wife. Myong-Sook helped them throughout the day while tending the children. A fence similar to his own surrounded his father's place. As Han-Jae passed through it, he saw planks were splintered here as well, and would also need to be replaced.

A farm ran along the right side of the house. Other villagers in Gwangju had small plots where they grew a few select vegetables. His father's was at least four times as wide as any of their neighbors' patches. Growing in neat rows this time of year were cucumbers, tomatoes, peppers, and potatoes. Much of it would be sold at the market, but the verdant garden also ensured his children were bigger and better fed than the average Gwangju child.

The beds would need rotating soon for the fall and winter crops. One of the reasons his father's farm could be the size it was, was because of Han-Jae and his visits, accompanied by the twelve men under his command. He would bring them here later in the day and, for the next two weeks, they would harvest the remaining summer crops, till the land, and plant the seeds for the next season's crops. This was yet another benefit of being captain of the sea guards of Majeon.

Han-Jae saw his father crouched down cutting away the growth points of a tall cucumber plant with a sharp knife. Long green gourds dangled over his head.

"Ah-boe-ji," Han-Jae said, causing his father to look at him through the green stalks.

"Han-Jae Ya." Kyu-Heh drove the knife into the ground and slowly pushed himself up, the creaking of his knees audible from a distance. He wore a light gray hanbok, and a hat with a wide rim that would protect his face from the sun rising steadily over the horizon. "I heard you arrived yesterday."

Han-Jae kept his face impassive. "I visited Bak Captain and had a long meeting with him."

"Good." Kyu-Heh wiped the sweat from his hands on the side of his pants as he approached. Han-Jae noted the wrinkles on his brown, weathered face, and the shuffle of his gait. His father wouldn't be able to keep up this type of work much longer.

"Ah-boe-ji, where are the men I hired? Why are you out here alone?"

"I don't like to wait. They'll be here soon enough after they've broken their fast." His father stopped in front of Han-

Jae. "Did Bak Captain advise you about how to be promoted into Incheon this year?"

Once, his father would have waited to broach the subject of his promotion, or lack thereof. Once, Bak Captain and his wife would have, too. Now it was the first thing they asked when they saw him return to the village.

"He did," Han-Jae said. "He told me I should implore the ancestral spirits for a task that will earn me a promotion."

Kyu-Heh raised an eyebrow. "It's something to try." He gazed off into the far distance. "The spirits must be asked for a favor carefully. Their perception of our living reality is not what it was, now they exist in the realm beyond."

He turned his attention back to Han-Jae. "You will do this today."

It wasn't a question. Han-Jae saw in his father's eyes that the older man believed he might back away from the idea if he took too long to carry through with it.

"I will do it today, Ah-boe-ji."

His father nodded, then led Han-Jae out of the yard into the house. His mother had laid out the first course of their breakfast. Potato soup with fresh egg layered throughout it, dark green spinach *namul,* kimchi, and rice were set on a small circular table.

"Han-Jae," she said with a slight bow of greeting.

"Eo-moe-ni." Han-Jae bowed deeply.

"You and your father should sit down to eat while I prepare the fish."

She poured them both warm tea as they settled down at the table on the floor cushions. Watching his mother work, Han-Jae thought back to his childhood. He used to watch her carefully when she prepared food to make sure he received more than his younger siblings since he was the oldest. His mother would give Han-Jae anything he asked for. His father often accused her of making him weak. When Han-Jae came in from working on the family's old farm outside of the fishing village, his body would be sore and his back stiff from bending over for hours. His mother would lay him down, wipe the dirt from his arms and legs, and massage his muscles to ease the pain away.

Han-Jae only worked half the day, and his father would accompany him back so that he could eat lunch before he set off to fish the waters of Gwanju all night. When he saw his wife rubbing the aches out of Han-Jae's body, a deep scowl would stretch his lips from ear to ear.

"You should leave him alone," his father would tell her. "The hurt is good for him. The world is full of it. He should get used to it now."

"He is still young," she would counter, and his father would shake his head.

"The monsters of the world eat the young just as quickly as they consume the old." His father towered over Han-Jae in those days, his face already deeply tanned from the sun, the wrinkles already setting in from years of working in the elements. When Han-Jae gazed up at his father all those years, he knew he was looking at his future. Exhausted from continuous work, short-tempered with his children.

"Stand up to pain," his father had often told him. "Never bow down to it. Never let it get you on your knees."

When Han-Jae joined the Emperor's fleet, he had done just enough to get his superior's attention, yet never went so far so as to put his life in unnecessary danger. He had done the same as a sea guard, rising up until he became captain in Majeon. There he had stopped for many years, but now his family was pushing him to prove himself so he could be promoted once more.

Was he strong enough? Or had he become too weak in the comfort of his current position?

When his mother finished preparing the breakfast fish, she laid it on the table between Han-Jae and his father, then sat down seiza-style at the round table and began to eat from a bowl of rice.

"We will go to the tombs today," Kyu-Heh said.

His mother nodded her approval. "You will cut the grass? Han-Jae never gets the chance to go since he lives so far away."

Kyu-Heh shook his head. "We will bring a monk with us. Today, we ask a favor from the ancestors."

His mother paused, the grip on her chopsticks tightening. Han-Jae watching her out of the corner of his eye, saw her face pale, noticing that—for a few moments—she did not breathe.

"Has something happened?" The tone of her voice had changed, a breathlessness making her words sound strained.

"Han-Jae Ya will be promoted to Incheon upon his return to Majeon. We will ask the spirits for their assistance to ensure this is so."

Han-Jae placed a piece of fish into his mouth. His attention never left his mother, who had continued eating. She stared forward at the table, but what she saw and the thoughts running through her head, he could not guess.

"I will be ready to go after we eat," she finally said, but his father immediately shook his head.

"We implore *our* ancestors. This is a matter for blood family. Only those directly connected will be necessary." His father motioned to Han-Jae. "You will start ahead of me. When you reach the spirits, prostate yourself before them. Commune with them until I arrive with the monk. Only then will we ask for a challenge to be delivered unto you that you will be able to overcome so you can be promoted to Incheon."

Han-Jae cast his gaze about the room for a tin kettle of makgeolli, and spied it on a shelf by the window. Rising, he poured the liquor into a drinking bowl and took a long swallow of the bitter rice wine. He would buy some more in the village on his way to the tombs.

Han-Jae didn't like communing with the dead.

To do so, you had to put one foot into the grave, and that was never a pleasant experience.

16. THE DEAD GIFTS

Han-Jae walked the path to the dead. It wound its way north from the coastal village through the tall conifers towards the nearest mountains. The sun rose high from the horizon as the morning grew old, the rays shining down from the cloudless sky to bathe the dirt path in bright light. Yet Han-Jae did not feel its warmth and shivered every time he stepped into fingers of shadows from the branches of trees stretched overhead.

High-pitched twittering filled the rustling leaves as birds streaked through the air from bough to bough. The drone of insects and the scurrying of wildlife through the undergrowth of the surrounding forest added to the song of nature Han-Jae would have normally savored as he smoked his pipe after a leisurely breakfast. None of this mattered to him today, though, as he walked this path that led him closer to the family burial grounds.

The mountains of Gwangju, covered with grass and trees, stood as silent sentries throughout the province. At the feet of one, *Mudeungsan*, were the mounds where the dead were buried. Every time he visited his hometown, he came to pay his respects to the ancestors, cutting the grass with the shears they used for such an occasion. Always, his sons, daughters, wife, and parents accompanied him. They wouldn't talk as they worked, their heavy breathing the only sound as they crouched down low to clean the squat mounds. Han-Jae had always found the difficult task peaceful. He especially enjoyed the fact that they did not speak during the labor. No one would ask him about Majeon, Incheon, or promotions. He would be left alone with his thoughts, the dead resting silently beneath his feet.

Today would be different. Today, there would be speech, there would be conversation. As the foot of the mountains came into view, Han-Jae's steps slowed, but he did not stop. His father wouldn't be far behind with the monk, and he couldn't allow them to catch up with him. Being sent ahead to be alone with the dead had been a test of his resolve his father had issued him.

Han-Jae stepped under the shadow of a towering tree at the end of the path, and a chill passed through him. Finally glimpsing the mounds, his heart beat faster. Not even the makgeolli he had quickly consumed before he started on the journey helped dull his growing anxiety.

The mounds bubbled up from the ground before him. There were three; a large one in the middle, two smaller on the sides. A short rocky barrier enclosed them, and an engraving with the family name marked each one. When Han-Jae reached the barrier, he could still hear the birds singing in the trees. The sun still shone down from the clear sky, washing the day with light. Despite this, his sense of unease did not dissipate, but continued to grow, a relentless buzzing feeling vibrating through his arms and legs and leaving him numb. How many times had he visited these tombs since he was a child? Never before had they affected him in this way, and this wasn't even the first time he'd seen the dead entreated for a boon.

It was the first time it was done for him, however. That seemed to make all the difference.

Han-Jae started when he heard footsteps behind him. Turning, he saw his father walking beside a portly man wearing gray robes. A wooden necklace of beads dangled from the monk's neck. He did not appear old or infirm, yet he supported himself with a tall wooden staff topped with a sharp point, leaning upon it heavily as he neared the feet of Mudeungsan.

"Thank you for joining us today," Han-Jae said when the monk stood before him. He bowed low. "With your assistance, we will commune successfully with our ancestors long gone from this world of the living."

Han-Jae kept his voice firm, though his heart still thudded in his chest. He'd been in enough battles during his days in the Emperor's fleet to know how to suppress his emotions, keeping them bottled up until after the battle was won. Never show fear in the face of a threat.

"The dead are never too far gone," the monk said. Reaching into the folds of his gray robes, he removed a wine skin. "They only exist on the other side of reality. With but a simple knock on the threshold, they will answer."

The monk unstopped the skin and handed it to his father, who took a long swallow. The monk drank from it next, then handed it to Han-Jae. "Drink deeply," he instructed him. "It will help you bare your true self to your ancestors."

Han-Jae didn't know how much he relished that idea, especially in front of his father. The smell of the fragrant wine made his mouth water. He eagerly took the skin and placed it to his lips. He immediately realized it wasn't makgeolli. The wine was sweet like summer grapes and went smoothly down his throat. The more he drank, the thirstier he became. Before he knew it, the skin was upturned over his lips, the last few drops plopping onto his tongue.

"Prostrate yourself before the tombs," the monk told him.

Han-Jae spun sharply on his heels, the world reeling around him. He had spent years drinking with his men, but even he was surprised at the strength the alcohol must have to make him feel so drunk so quickly. His mood finally lifted. He was able to appreciate the warmth of the sun rays now, and the clever songs of the birds flitting through the trees. The morning had grown into midday, the temperature hot and causing him to sweat beneath his hanbok. He dropped to his knees, and the mounds rumbled at his fall.

Moments of silence passed, and stretched forward. Han-Jae gazed ahead, unsure of what he should do next, when the sound of a child's laughter floated up to him. There was a familiar ring to it, and Han-Jae leaned forward.

Behind him, the monk spoke. "A favor from the dead requires an offering. What are you willing to sacrifice for this request to your ancestors?"

Another child's laugh joined the first one, and then another. They sounded sweet, carefree, but Han-Jae swallowed hard in his throat, his mouth suddenly dry. The monk stepped into his field of vision, and suddenly became transparent, as if he was no longer really there. The peals of children's laughter continued, rising up from the mounds and brushing against the monk's robes, rustling them with their passing.

Too much, Han-Jae thought to himself as the laughter continued. Somewhere around him, children were playing a game, the ferocity of their amusement sending chills to ripple across his flesh.

"The dead live by their own rules." The monk lowered the tall staff until the sharp point was level with Han-Jae's chest. "When the summer days have burned away, you must remember this moment, for if you do, *you* will *receive your promotion,* Kwan Han-Jae."

The monk leapt forward, thrusting the pointed end of the staff deep into Han-Jae's heart. Han-Jae reared back, screaming as the monk's transparent form splintered, breaking apart on the wind and rising up as a gray mist into the blue sky. Han-Jae grabbed his chest, but the staff had vanished. No blood soaked his hanbok. He looked wildly about him and saw only his father standing there, a wide smile on his face.

"You will be promoted," his father said triumphantly, helping Han-Jae to his feet. Han-Jae listened closely and could not help but wonder if it was truly laughter he heard from the children, or howls of torment and pain.

As the two weeks passed, Han-Jae woke up to drink, and passed the day drinking until the night came when he collapsed onto his sleeping pallet with only one hope: that he would not dream. Yet every night, as the darkness closed over him, he did so. The sounds he'd heard at the burial mounds plagued him so that he woke up exhausted. Every morning he crawled over to his children and hugged them tightly but said nothing of his fears when Myong-Sook asked him what worried him so much.

The dead had been entreated.

The sacrifice was yet to come.

17. NIGHT ON THE YELLOW SEA

A pale shroud of moonlight covered the shrunken corpse floating in the water. Seong-Hoon crouched over the gunwale of the small wooden fishing boat and raised the oil lantern to illuminate the dark waves. The body bobbed up and down to the rhythm of the Yellow Sea, its legs and arms splayed. The pool of yellow light traveled past the scrawny legs and sharply-defined ribs and splashed across the corpse's face.

Seong-Hoon inhaled sharply at the man's exotic features. He had been fishing in the Yellow Sea with his older brother, Yoon-Woo, for two days. They had caught nothing so far, and now this—a dead foreigner, adrift in South Hanguk's territory.

He turned to Yoon-Woo crouched at the starboard side, two lines in hand. Preparing bait for trout, Yoon-Woo tied a live squid to a black rock and held it above the sea. He watched the waves closely for the best moment to drop the weight into the dark depths.

"Older brother," Seong-Hoon called. "You have to see this. Quick, before it drifts away."

Yoon-Woo looked over his shoulder, the lantern lighting the frown on his weathered face. "Don't you see I'm busy?" He nodded upward. "Night is already half over. Wasting time will just cause us to lose another day out here without a catch."

Seong-Hoon turned from his older brother back to the body. The waves had put distance between it and the hull. In the darkness of the sea, it would be lost if they didn't act soon.

"Just come and look," Seong-Hoon urged, sparing a quick glance over his shoulder. "It's a foreign person here, dead in the water."

Yoon-Woo stared at Seong-Hoon, doubt etching itself across his gaunt face. "You lying?" he asked, a hint of worry infecting his voice.

Seong-Hoon shook his head. "Come see for yourself."

Yoon-Woo cursed. Quickly, he tied the lines to a notch in the side of the hull and dropped the bait into the water. The heavy rock entered with a splash, alerting fish to its presence in the inky depths. After a few moments, Yoon-Woo gave one line a sharp tug, yanking the stone free from the slippery squid and pulling it back up to the boat. He crossed to the port side, and Seong-Hoon pointed. Yoon-Woo peered out into the dark waves at the skeletal body drifting away in the current.

The brothers exchanged glances. By order of Incheon's governor, all foreigners encountered on the sea had to be reported immediately. If alive, they weren't to be engaged; if dead, the bodies were to be gathered and brought ashore for inspection. Even in their poor village of Majeon at the northern tip of Incheon, the brothers had to follow the official decree.

The floater wasn't bloated as other corpses they'd seen in the past had been. Usually, the fishermen of Incheon discovered debris from shipwrecks first. Still, enough wreckage managed to reach Majeon, that this was the third body Seong-Hoon had seen in his twenty-one years.

"Let the sea keep it," Yoon-Woo said, gaze focused upon the body drifting away from them.

"They'll want to know about him in Incheon," Seong-Hoon reminded his older brother. "And there might be a reward."

Yoon-Woo glanced at him, his narrow eyes widening slightly at that prospect. Still he waited a few more moments as the body bobbed further into the darkness of the sea. He swore, suddenly and harshly.

"Fine," Yoon-Woo growled. "Get it aboard!" He turned to the taut line he'd just left. "It's good that he's dead. We can wait till morning before we go back. Maybe we'll get lucky and catch something we can actually eat."

Seong-Hoon raised the lantern higher and searched the sea for other dead bodies. He saw no others, or the flotsam from a destroyed boat that had accompanied the previous corpses.

What else could have caused the foreigner to be here at sea if not a shipwreck?

The weather had been fair over the last month, so the man couldn't have been blown overboard by a typhoon. The body looked like it had been dead for a long time, its skin ashen and wrapped tight against its bones. He thought, once again, that it didn't have the bloated look of a corpse that had been in the sea for very long.

Yoon-Woo grabbed the gaff lying against the hull. Seong-Hoon settled the lantern on the port side and stood between the oars. With powerful strokes, he paddled the boat in an arc to overtake the drifting body. When they came close, Yoon-Woo carefully settled the gaff over the man's chest and with a thrust, pierced the ribs with a powerful jab into the flesh. Hooked thus, the body was easier to recover. He pulled it to him, the corpse rippling the water until it bumped against the hull. Suspecting the waterlogged body would be heavy, Seong-Hoon went to help his older brother lift it aboard. They grasped it under the arms, hauled it out of the water, and let it fall with a thud to the wooden boards.

The salty smell of seaweed clung to it. After touching it, Yoon-Woo scowled and dried his hands repeatedly on his baggy pants.

"Something strange about the way it felt, wasn't there?" Seong-Hoon said. He picked up the oil lantern and raised it over the corpse again. The light illuminated the body.

Both brothers stumbled back and fought to steady themselves as the boat rocked at the sudden movement. The corpse lay on something inky black that fanned out beneath it.

Yoon-Woo immediately looked across the Yellow Sea towards land, his breath coming in fast, harsh gasps.

"What do you think it is?" Seong-Hoon asked. He took the lantern from his brother and moved the light closer. Very slowly, he reached out, and with the tip of his finger, prodded the very edge of the protrusion. Behind him, Yoon-Woo hissed.

"Feels like shark skin," Seong-Hoon said, rubbing the protrusion between his fingers. He caught his brother's eyes and saw the deep fear there.

"We could flip it over," Seong-Hoon suggested, "to get a better look."

His older brother shook his head. "We did what we were supposed to do." He went to the baited line dangling in the water and began to reel it in. "We need to go back now," he added quickly, "and show this to the sea guards. Shouldn't wait till morning."

Seong-Hoon kept fingering the strange black mass at the bottom of the fishing boat. What from the sea could have attached itself to the foreigner? And could it still be alive?

"Maybe we should look at it now," he suggested to his older brother, "just to make sure of what it is."

Yoon-Woo pulled the live bait from the water, unhooked the squiggling squid, and let it slide back into the thin net. He then attached the net to the side of the hull and took up the oars. "You can look," he said over his shoulder, "and I'll start us back home."

Seong-Hoon thought of their wives and children waiting for them. Going home empty-handed was going to make the next week difficult. What would they take to the market to sell? What would they eat? His stomach grumbled at the thought. He could only imagine the state his young sons would be in, already thin at two and four years of age.

He crouched closer to the body, trailing his finger along the tough skin, across the sharp ribs, past the bloodless wound from the gaff, and to the shoulders. He felt along the shoulder blades and saw that there, too, the slippery mass had attached itself. What in the world could it be?

He turned to his older brother again—paddling hard, the splash of the oars resounding across the silent waves. Yoon-Woo's eyes were trained towards land, taking no note of what his younger brother was doing. For a moment, Seong-Hoon thought of reminding his older brother of the reward they were sure to gain for bringing in the strange body. Even if they received only a few coins for the discovery, that would make this the best catch they'd had in months of barely surviving.

Making a decision, he placed the oil lantern in the bottom of the boat and put his hands under the foreigner's torso. When he hoisted him over, he noticed the corpse was surprisingly light, almost as if nothing existed inside of him. Seong-Hoon hadn't realized that when they'd pulled the waterlogged body from the Yellow Sea. He grabbed the lantern and brought it closer to the corpse.

"Wings," he breathed out in awe. "They're wings!"

His brother didn't respond, but paddled harder, the tips of

the oars entering the water with loud splashes. Seong-Hoon touched the man's back and tugged lightly at the slick flesh. The wings seemed to extend from his collar bone down from where his shoulder blades should be to his hips. The wings were shriveled now, but Seong-Hoon wondered what the span of them would be if the foreigner were alive.

Again, he looked back out at the dark waters as a new idea took shape. Perhaps the man hadn't fallen from some boat into the sea.

Seong-Hoon looked up at the cloudless night, the moon bright and surrounded by her court of stars.

Perhaps the foreigner had fallen from the sky.

18. WINGED BANCHAN

When Seong-Hoon spotted the coast, the sun was already showing signs of stirring from slumber, bright shards of light stretching out from below the horizon. Yoon-Woo paddled the boat toward the narrow strip of pier. He had been rowing steadily, shaking his head whenever Seong-Hoon offered to paddle for a while. A sheen of perspiration covered his brow, his shirt clinging to his thin frame with sweat. He was breathing deeply in an effort to catch his breath. Now that they had reached home, a look of relief spread over his face.

Other fishermen had already come to port, their boats bobbing at the docks beneath shrieking seagulls swirling overhead. Men unloaded their cargo as waiting restaurant owners, who had shown up early to get the freshest catch of the day, searched the rippling nets and buckets of water. Wagons pulled by laborers and led by merchants rolled down the rocky path leading to the docks. Beyond the coast, the brothers' small village of Majeon could be seen, the shadows dissolving from the thatched roofs as dawn spread its fingers into the sky.

Somewhere, their children would be out collecting seaweed from the rocks slapped by the waves, and their wives would be preparing a breakfast of rice, kimchi, and soup. Since the brothers had not caught any fish, they would have no meat for at least another week. Once again, Seong-Hoon hoped the corpse of the foreign person would bring in some type of reward. His older brother had been made so uneasy by its presence.

He glanced into Yoon-Woo's face, and—for the first time since they found the body—saw that his older brother appeared to be smiling as they neared Majeon.

"We should come to port north so we can get this body off without a lot of people staring," Yoon-Woo said. He maneuvered to the edge of the wharf away from the waiting merchants. Seong-Hoon grabbed the thick mooring rope and jumped onto the pier's wooden boards. He wound it around the thick piling, pulling the boat closer with each tug of the rope before tying the knot. Yoon-Woo settled the oars against the hull, and Seong-Hoon climbed back onto the boat to retrieve the corpse.

"It feels even lighter now," he said as he hoisted the body over his shoulder. His older brother's faint smile retreated back into a scowl. Two children, a naked boy only a few years old and his older sister clad in a dirty white shirt falling to her knees, ran up to them.

"What's that?" the girl asked, pointing at the body.

Yoon-Woo, approaching them, raised his hand and cuffed the girl on the head. "Go back to your ma, Bong-Cha," he told her, for the brothers' family and her family had been in Majeon for generations. The girl glared at Yoon-Woo, but when he raised his hand again, she darted away, her little brother in tow.

"Let's get this to the sea guards," he told Seong-Hoon. He started along the wet beach towards the low stone building, and Seong-Hoon obediently followed.

The stone fortification of the sea guards stood on an

outcropping of rock jutting out into the Yellow Sea. Two swift boats with sails were docked there, and a lantern shone from a window looking out onto the coastline. A guard in a dark blue hanbok sat on a large rock outside of the oval entrance to the fortification. His tall halberd rested against the wall. At his feet lay his pointed helm, and beside that was a pot of makgeolli. He cupped a small wooden bowl of the rice wine in his hand.

As the brothers approached, their feet crunching on the shelled path leading to the fortification, the guard started in surprise and called out in a voice that carried above the lapping waves, "Stop, whoever you are, and announce yourselves."

The brothers paused. "Kang Yoon-Woo and Kang Seong-Hoon," Yoon-Woo called out. "We need to speak with Kwan Captain."

The guard sipped from his cup, the chalky wine staining his lips white. "Come back later! Kwan Captain has only just returned from a long voyage south. He's having his breakfast now and isn't to be disturbed."

Seong-Hoon saw Yoon-Woo tense, the veins along his neck standing out as his older brother gritted his teeth. He knew how much Yoon-Woo disliked the sea guards, who ate more than any of the villagers and did nothing helpful for the fishermen.

"We found something at sea we need him to see," Yoon-Woo replied, his voice tight.

The guard guffawed. "Fish caught fresh, is it? The captain loves his tuna, if that's what you've got. He might even buy it from you, if the price is right."

"It's not tuna." Yoon-Woo pointed to Seong-Hoon, and the guard's gaze followed the motion until it settled upon what was thrown over Seong-Hoon's shoulder.

"You're right, that's no tuna." Now the guard finally stood. "But what is it?"

"It's a body," Yoon-Woo replied. "A foreign person we found out on the sea."

The guard's eyes widened at the news. He drained his cup with a loud slurp, set it on the rock, and cautiously approached the brothers. His gaze fell on the corpse's back and a sharp gasp emitted from his lips. "There's something black growing out of him!"

"Wings," Seong-Hoon said, which drew an annoyed look from his older brother.

"We don't know that for sure," Yoon-Woo said quickly. "That's why we want to bring it to the captain. Let him see for himself what we caught."

"Are you sure it's dead?"

"My older brother gaffed it when we brought it out the sea," Seong-Hoon replied. "He stuck the hook in deep to pull it into the boat. The foreign person is dead."

The guard stared at the body for several moments as the waves slapped against the shore, the sky brightening above them. "I don't like the look of him," he finally said. "Tie weights around him and throw him back in the water. Let him sink to the bottom of the sea. Let the darkness have him."

Seong-Hoon's mouth dropped open in surprise as he struggled to think of a response. He knew they couldn't send the body to the bottom of the sea. If there was a reward for the find, it would be lost, and they would have to go home empty-handed. He started to explain this to the sea guard, but Yoon-Woo answered faster.

Nodding in agreement with the sea guard, his older brother pointed to rocks near the fortification. "We can use those there. That should get the job done."

"How are we going to take those rocks out on our boat?" Seong-Hoon shook his head. "We're not going to get far with them in the bottom."

Yoon-Woo hesitated for a moment, looking back at the two bigger boats by the fortification. "Those would be able to carry the weight."

The sea guard followed his gaze and immediately shook his head. "I can't take one without the captain's permission. If I ask him, he's going to want to see the body for himself." He glanced at the corpse again.

A deep frown had carved itself into Yoon-Woo's face as if he could read the shifting winds. Seong-Hoon couldn't understand what frightened the two men. The man on his back was dead, a corpse growing lighter by the moment. Plus, he was the one carrying it. He wanted to explain to Yoon-Woo what this find could mean for their barely-surviving families in Majeon.

"This will come to no good." The guard sighed long and deep. "Come on, then, to see Kwan Captain."

His spirits rising, Seong-Hoon followed his older brother and the guard into the fortification. The guard had to duck low to enter the low oval entrance. When Seong-Hoon entered, he saw the roof wasn't much higher than his head. The fortification was wide but sparse, with a single wooden table where three men sat eating a breakfast of raw fish and squid, rice, seaweed, soup, and makgeolli. Several swords, daggers, and two spears hung on the walls.

The men stared at the brothers as they entered. One, with a thin pointed beard, who smoked a long wooden pipe, gazed at the body over Seong-Hoon's shoulder.

"What's this terrible side dish you're attempting to serve me this morning, Kyung-Wan?" he asked the guard leading in the brothers. "Why do you bring this winged *banchan* to ruin our breakfast?"

"I am sorry, captain." Kyung-Wan bowed. "I did not want to disturb you as you ate, but the matter is urgent." He pointed to the brothers. "These fishermen caught a body floating in the sea. It is a foreigner. I thought it best to bring it straight to you so that you could inspect it."

Seong-Hoon noticed the guard didn't mention his idea of sinking the corpse into the sea. Under the sharp stare of the captain, though, Seong-Hoon became nervous, sweat pooling under his arms. Suddenly, he wished to leave this place and return to his family, yet he couldn't just abandon his find now, not before he discovered if there was any value in it.

"We saw this foreign person floating in the water," Yoon-Woo said, and Kwan Captain turned his gaze from Seong-Hoon to his older brother. "My younger brother and I pulled it from the sea."

"Did you?" the captain said. "Well, stand there and wait until we're done."

The sea guard who had led them in motioned for the brothers to stand against the wall. The captain and his men continued to eat their breakfast, frequently refilling each other's cups with the rice wine, which they drank in loud, thirsty slurps. The brothers' stomachs growled, as they had not eaten in some time, and even then it had been a spare meal of rice, seaweed, and a bit of eel meat.

The captain finished his meal and puffed on his pipe, the tendrils of sweet-smelling smoke drifting up to the stone ceiling of the fortification. Only after several moments had passed did he say to the other sea guards seated with him, "Clear the table."

When that was done, he addressed the two brothers. "Lay your burden down there," he instructed them

Though the man was dead, Seong-Hoon still laid the corpse down carefully on the low wooden table. He couldn't be sure, but the body looked even smaller now, almost the size of a large child; but its black wings hadn't shrunk any, the tips of them drooping over the edge of the table.

The captain's face twisted in disgust. "So you brought this to us, did you?" He turned to Seong-Hoon. "You didn't think to just let the sea keep it?"

Another asking the same question? Seong-Hoon looked from the captain to the guards, to his older brother, then down at the corpse. "But it is duty, sir." His voice trembled in the silence. "It is a foreign person."

The captain inhaled deeply from his pipe and released the sweet smoke with a deep sigh. "That's no person, you fool. That's a monster."

19. BLOOD STEW

Hunger sparked a flame of thought that wavered in the empty landscape of its mind. An ember flicked from the thought and landed on another, setting it alight. That one tumbled onto another, and then another, until a chain reaction of contemplation began to push back the darkness.

The thinker gradually became aware of its physical shape. Legs and arms tingled. Muscles connected to its wings tightened. Ribs throbbed from a fresh wound, yet no blood snaked down its skin. Its body had dried out and was now no more than a desiccated husk.

The fog in its mind continued to evaporate. Broken images fell together like pieces of a puzzle and built a memory of its past. It tried to recall its name, and soon remembered it had none except what the meat called it: Orsieg.

Its sense of smell returned. The familiar aroma of salt and fish and seaweed was heavy in the air. Searching for greater details of its identity, the Orsieg dug through its thoughts, tunneling into the depths of its mind until it reached the surface of its earliest memory: its rocky home, the crag.

In the beginning, the Orsieg had slept in the liquid fire of the inner earth. Then the ground had rumbled, waking it while the lava bubbled up out of its deep core, pushing the Orsieg into the open air above ground. Birthed from its rocky womb and gripped by a tormenting hunger, the Orsieg knew that it must feed or waste away.

Weak, it had gone after whatever was close at first, sucking the juice from large spindly bugs washed onto the rocks by the sea. As it grew stronger, the Orsieg discovered wings had grown from its shoulders. It began to fly over the churning waves of the ocean. With quick hands, it snatched fish from the water, its black wings riding the air currents buffeting the crag.

One day, it flew farther from its rocky home than it had ever been and saw a wooden shell of meat drifting by. The hunger directing it, the Orsieg swooped down and grabbed the squealing meal. The meat had struggled more than the fish ever did, lashing out at it with sharp pincers clutched in tiny hands until the Orsieg was forced to drop it from a great height onto the crag.

The meat was barely alive when the Orsieg began to feast upon it. It found the blood especially delicious, and noticed that soon after this feast, it had grown taller. Bigger. Stronger. The meat's blood, which did not exist in bugs and fish, seemed key to unlocking its true potential.

So, the Orsieg spent its days on the rocky crag, watching for the meat to drift by in their wooden shells. It realized that hunting during violent storms was easiest, as the meats weren't as capable of defending themselves with their sharp projectiles and pincers that came in a variety of shapes and sizes. The Orsieg's body grew quickly, doubling in size with each meal. Its wings could not take it far out to sea any longer. It would wait patiently until the times when the sky darkened with clouds and thunder echoed above the crashing waves.

During these wild storms, the Orsieg would fly from its

rocky home, break open the shells with its long fingers, and scoop out the meat from where they cowered. It bundled them in nets of silk spun from spiders crawling in the fissures of the crag and carried them back to its home. There, the Orsieg would choose one a day, bringing it to the top of the rocky expanse's highest precipice. It would strip the meat's flailing limbs and tear them in half so it could make blood stew in the clay bowl it had fashioned.

The Orsieg eventually learned how to keep the meat alive on seafood and seaweed, throwing fresh fish down to them to make sure they did not lose their weight or starve. On the days of its best catches, it would sometimes have two dozen meat in the caves of its rocky home. With nothing else to do, the Orsieg often listened to them from above, the strange halting noises emitting from their mouths echoing on the rocky shore. As countless seasons passed, it eventually learned to understand some of their utterances. This was how it discovered the chain of sounds they used to refer to it: Orsieg.

And the sound they called themselves: men.

Time passed, the sea always bringing it more meat to feed upon. Its body quickly shrank in times of want, but just as quickly filled out again after a hearty meal of meat and blood.

One day, it dawned on the Orsieg that the wooden shells drifting past its crag had dwindled in number. The Orsieg wondered if some sickness had afflicted the meat at their source. It was forced to fly farther and farther from the jagged rock of its home. Its wings tired under its massive bulk, and it often feared it would plunge into the sea and be unable to take flight again. When the longest stretch of time had passed between sightings of the wooden shells—leaving the Orsieg to feed only on fish taken from the sea that did not satisfy its blood hunger—clouds again darkened the sky. In desperation, it flew out from the crag, and finally caught what would become its final meal.

A dozen squirming and screaming pieces of meat it brought back in its silk net and deposited on the rocky shores of its crag. It made sure to disarm the meat of their projectiles and sharp pointed tools, then crouched down to look at the tiny animals.

"I know a little of your sounds," it told them, which set all but one of the men to scramble to the far rocky caves away from it. "Has something happened to where you come from?"

"Monster!" the meat shouted at him. "We've learned to avoid these cursed rocks and your endless appetite for human flesh and blood!"

The Orsieg sat back on its haunches, surprised. "If you do not come, I will starve," it said simply. "So, I must go to you?"

It then swept up the meat that had answered, flew to the top of the crag's precipice, ripped him in half, and drained his blood into its clay bowl. Every day, it feasted upon its stew of blood and flesh as it gazed out in thought at the horizon. When the last of the meat was consumed and the Orsieg was left only the bones to grind between its teeth, it made a decision. It leapt from its crag for the last time and flew past the point of no return.

The Orsieg often feared it would die of the hunger that plagued it as it flew across the high waves, its fat and muscles melting away. It had known nothing but its crag for all of its existence, so went without direction, only heading towards the horizon. Occasionally, it spied a wooden shell of meat, but luck was not with it. Those days were clear skies, and the meat would shoot the thin projectiles that sank deep into its body at it, making it lose precious blood and driving it away from them with the stinging pain they wrought.

The Orsieg's body shrank to much less than its original size.

Darkness crept in at the edges of its vision, remaining even during the brightest days. The Orsieg knew it was dying, but it kept flying over the rolling waves, the lights of its thoughts blinking out one at a time. Finally, it dropped from the sky.

The last thing the Orsieg saw was the blue sea rushing up to catch it in its cold embrace.

20. THE FEAST

Han-Jae struggled to maintain his composure in front of his men and the villagers. When the brothers had first entered the dimly-lit fort, he had thought they had covered the body with a black cloth. The moment they set it down on the table and he'd gotten a good look, he immediately knew the corpse wasn't human.

The fools!

Now, a monster lay where his breakfast had moments ago stood. Han-Jae stared at it, his heart thumping hollowly in his chest. Exhausted after the long trip back from Gwangju, he had planned to rest in the fort all day while his men went about their duties. Dora had gone out for the night's patrol, and would be back soon with reports on conditions in the territorial waters near the village. Han-Jae had commanded Kyung-Wan he wasn't to be disturbed until Dora returned, yet here he found himself with these two villagers and this winged creature, shrunken and grotesque, with the salty smell of the sea clinging to it.

The brothers should have built a pyre and burned it on the beach. What possessed them to bring it to him here on land?

As Han-Jae stared at it, an unsettling thought occurred to him. He wondered if more of the winged creatures hovered over the waters near South Hanguk. Like roaches, perhaps they would become an infestation, and this was only the first, a scout looking ahead, fallen for some reason and drowned in the sea.

Perhaps it had been good fortune for South Hanguk people to discover this dead one before the others attacked in force.

Had the ancestral spirits already answered his prayer? Would they really be so callous, to disregard his fears and present him with this most difficult of challenges to overcome in order to gain his promotion?

Be careful entreating the dead for a boon!

The monster was no bigger than a child, the thin arms and scrawny legs appearing as if the creature would have trouble walking on land. What type of weapon could that tiny hand wield that would be dangerous to South Hanguk men? The thing looked easy enough to kill, yet its presence continued to disquiet Han-Jae. At the moment it lay there dead, but—if alive—what threat would winged creatures such as this pose in greater numbers?

He would have to bring the body to the yangban in Incheon so they could dissect it and study it. Because of him, the people of South Hanguk would be better prepared by knowing what secrets lay beneath the skin of the creature. They would be able to find a weakness before other winged monsters had the chance to drop down upon them from the sky and attack. This foreknowledge that would lead to an easy victory for the South Hanguk people would be because of him, Kwan Han-Jae.

Now he glimpsed the wisdom of the ancestors, and his spirits rose. They had given him a monster, but this one was already dead and posed no threat. He had worried about keeping his promise to his wife and parents about being promoted before he returned to Gwangju, but now he realized the problem would be easily solved, and his doubts about his ancestors' intentions had been unwarranted.

Out of the corner of his eye, Han-Jae saw several village children peering through the door of the fortification, their eyes round as they took in the monster. Soon everyone in the village would know what the brothers had brought in from the sea.

"Kyung-Wan," he barked to the guard who had led the brothers in. The man came to sudden attention under the captain's stare. "Take this out to our ship and store it there."

"We will depart immediately?"

Han-Jae shook his head. "The yangban are scholars. They respect words written down more than words spoken. I must write a report first." He sighed at the thought. "That will take time," he admitted. The more detailed, the better the yangban would respond to it. Han-Jae would have to seek assistance in crafting it from a nearby scholar.

"We'll leave within two days," he decided.

Kyung-Wan turned to the two brothers. "Pick that up and come with me."

Han-Jae turned to the other two sea guards in the fort. "I don't want to be disturbed. Drive those children away from here," he instructed one. "Patrol the village," he commanded the other. "I want to know exactly what the people are saying about that creature. We cannot allow their tales to become outlandish and cause a panic."

And he could not allow news of the monster to travel beyond the village before he had time to write the report and travel to Incheon.

Both of his men bowed to him and left the fortification. Han-Jae watched the children scatter, driven back towards the village. Only when their voices could no longer be heard did Han-Jae move to the wooden chest that protected the scroll parchments from the coastal humidity. He removed the ink stone and bamboo brush and set it all on the low table. He would have to wait for the brothers to return to record exactly how they had found the corpse and exactly where they had been when they found it. That would give the yangban an idea of how far out from land a potential threat could be.

Han-Jae re-lit his pipe, the feeling of good cheer spreading through him and driving off his earlier fatigue. When he saw the brothers leaving the ship and heading back towards the village, he leapt to his feet. "Come back here!" he barked at them. "Where do you think you're going?"

"Our families are waiting for us," said the older one. "We're going to see them."

Han-Jae shook his head. "I need to take down the events of exactly how you found the monster as they unfolded. Come here, now!"

Han-Jae turned and sat down at the table. The brothers stepped into the fortification a moment later. He ignored their despondent looks and motioned for them to sit down.

"Will this take long?" the taller one asked, a petulant look on his face.

"It will take as long as it takes," Han-Jae replied, and took a puff of his pipe. "Now, tell me your names again."

"Kang Yoon-Woo," the older fisherman replied. "And this my younger brother, Kang Seong-Hoon."

Han-Jae wrote down the year, the season, and the day. Then he wrote the brothers' names and asked, "How far out from Majeon were you when you found the body?"

"Between the islands of Mibeop-do and Boleum-do."

Han-Jae puffed on his pipe and stared at the brothers through a tendril of smoke snaking from the round bowl. "You were in North Hanguk territorial waters?

Yoon-Woo shook his head. "We know the rocks that mark

them. We've been fishing in the sea since we were young children."

"Yet you were as far as Boleum-do? The Northerners send raiders near those parts to harass the South Hanguk island people."

"We got no choice," Yoon-Woo said, his voice hard. "I got a wife, three boys and a girl. My younger brother got a wife and two girls. We go out fishing and stay out till we get enough to come back home."

The brothers looked typical for this strip of coast. Thin, with stained brown shirts and pants that had been patched many times over the years. Their gaunt faces, tanned and cracked from their life on their boats, made them look much older than they probably were. The people of Majeon eked out a desperate life.

He peered past them and saw the village children running along the shore outside, having circled around after his men had driven them off the first time. They were like mosquitoes, swatted at to constantly return, their overwhelming curiosity needing to be sated. Most were naked or barely clothed with strips of old cloth wrapped around their skinny bodies.

He saw Kyung-Wan sit down on the rock outside of the fortification entrance and pour a fresh cup of rice wine. Han-Jae called out for a cup. Kyung-Wan rose, gave him his, and poured a fresh one for himself. The children still hovered nearby. From his post, Kyung-Wan barked at them every now and then to run off. This made them dash back a few steps, only to return.

Han-Jae took a deep drink from the rice wine, happy he had brought several casks back with him from Gwangju. The liquor burned his throat and quickened his thoughts. He wrote down the location where Yoon-Woo said they had found the creature. After he informed the yangban of Incheon, he would have to send a message to the nearby South Hanguk islands to warn them of a potential new danger. This would provide another good mark in his favor, especially if the dead monster originated in the north. Perhaps it had been created by the Child-God of North Hanguk, a secret weapon their age-old enemy was preparing against them in their war spanning generations.

Han-Jae could only speculate, which made getting the body back to the yangban even more urgent. The most learned of South Hanguk people, they might have vital information in their libraries of scrolls in Incheon. More important to Han-Jae at the moment, however, was discerning whether the monster had come alone or in a flock, like birds.

"Did you see anything else out there? Besides this winged creature?"

When Yoon-Woo shook his head, Han-Jae narrowed his eyes.

"We're always cautious out there," the older brother said. "We got to be, if a Northern patrol caught up with us, they'd throw us in the sea and steal our boat. Then our wives and children would be lost."

"Yet you take the foolish risk to fish that far out anyway," Han-Jae said sternly. "Stay closer to Incheon waters and you'll have the protection of the sea guards patrolling southern territory."

"The fishermen of Incheon got bigger boats with bigger crews and wider nets that easily trap tuna, carp, and eels," Yoon-Woo complained. "The sea guards only worry about the North Hanguk people, but we're in competition with fishermen from our own country. So we got to go farther and farther out to sea to ensure a catch. Sometimes we out there three and four days before we get enough to come back."

The way Yoon-Woo's face twisted as he said this gave away

his inner frustration at the richer city neighboring Majeon. He stared at Han-Jae, disappointment with the sea guards seeded deep in his eyes. It was in the expressions of all the villagers.

Whenever Han-Jae and his men passed the villagers in the markets, or on the paths winding through their stone homes, or dined in the restaurants of Majeon, they saw the hostility in the dark glances as the villagers kept track of their every movement from the periphery of their vision.

The sea guards protected South Hanguk people from northern pirates, who were a frequent threat in the disputed waters. Tiny villages like Majeon had a fortified base such as this one, but Han-Jae retained only two dozen men under his control, half of whom would be out on a patrol shift in two of their four swift boats. Why did these villagers think they had the numbers, or the authority, to settle territorial disputes between the fishermen of Incheon and the fishermen of Majeon?

"So, I know where you were, and how long you had been out to sea," he said. "Now tell me about the monster. Was there anything unusual about it?"

The two brothers exchanged glances. Han-Jae easily guessed their thoughts. A winged creature floating dead in the water isn't something a fisherman often sees.

"Perhaps a smell to it," Han-Jae suggested. "The color of its blood. Its weight. Anything that made you take special note of it."

The younger brother sat straighter suddenly, and for the first time since the interrogation began, he cleared his throat to speak.

"I'm not sure about a smell," he said. "Just the sea on it because it'd been riding the waves. After a while, it seemed to shrink."

Han-Jae puffed on his pipe. "How do you mean?"

"The foreign body," Seong-Hoon replied. "When we

dragged it out of the water, it was heavy. But the longer it was in the boat, the lighter it got. Like it had been filled with the sea, but then all the water flowed out of it. It got smaller."

That was indeed unusual. Human bodies taken out of the sea were bloated and floating on their face, their hands and feet often consumed by sharks, their bruised flesh riddled with sea bugs. The monster had been small, but if it had only recently died, why had it been on the surface and not at the bottom of the sea until its body filled with gas? And if it had been dead for days and risen back up to the surface, why didn't it have the waxy pallor of the dead?

If it was, indeed, dead.

Just as the unnerving thought struck Han-Jae, the screams started; high-pitched cries that came from the beach. Han-Jae leapt to his feet, and the brothers quickly stood also. He rushed outside to Kyung-Wan, who stood at the entrance of the fortification, the cup of makgeolli still in his trembling hand.

"What happened?" Han-Jae asked him.

Kyung-Wan shook his head. "I do not know. Suddenly, there were screams coming from the beach. The children, I think. Something has happened to them."

The man hadn't even picked up his halberd, which was still leaning against the stone wall. Han-Jae ducked back in to grab a hwando from a hook in the wall. Immediately he saw that it hadn't been sharpened recently, streaks of rust marking the blade.

"Follow me," he told Kyung-Wan, who started off without the halberd until Han-Jae reminded him. "Your weapon!"

Kyung-Wan returned to grab it and followed Han-Jae. Soon they saw the waves lapping the rocks were stained red. The winged monster crouched at the edge of the beach. It held a child's dismembered arm in its hands and was methodically skinning the meat from the severed limb with its teeth. At its feet, the small victim shuddered in shock, blood pumping from the gaping wound while his sister looked on in horror, her mouth stretched wide as screams poured from her lips.

"Ye Bin!" Yoon-Woo called out.

Han-Jae hesitated, fear flooding him.

"Save her!"

Han-Jae grimaced at the brother's command, then stumbled forward, sword raised. The monster grabbed the pain-dazed boy around his tiny waist. With a great flap of its wings, it propelled itself out of the water and above their heads. Kyung-Wan feebly threw his halberd, but the weapon was made for stabbing and chopping. The halberd flipped once awkwardly and missed. The monster, hovering in the air and clutching the mewing child, adjusted its wings. Catching a current, it started towards the tree line beyond the village.

"We should keep track of it," Han-Jae gasped, but Kyung-Wan didn't seem to hear him. The guard stared up into the sky in terror. Han-Jae, aware of the brothers' venomous gaze, ran forward, his heart thudding in his chest, his muscles burning at the unexpected exertion. The sudden dips from the rocky terrain of the coast soon tired him. The creature, having only the clear sky to navigate, quickly gained an advantage. It was not long before it had flown over the treetops to suddenly drop down into the leaves, disappearing from sight.

21. KWAN CAPTAIN

The wails of the missing boy's mother sliced through the sobs of the boy's aunts. The villagers crowded around the group of women who had collapsed on the wet sand of the coast, their clothes muddied as the waves lapped against them. The men tried to get them onto drier ground, but no amount of encouraging could get them to rise again as they wallowed in despair.

Han-Jae stood at the edge of the crowd and watched the blood dissipate in the water. He had been taken by surprise, he told himself. He had made an effort to save the child, yet when he looked at the villagers, he saw reproachful eyes gazing back at him and the sea guards under his command. The anger buried deep in their gaunt faces made Han-Jae take a tentative step back, his fingers tightening on the hilt of the rusting hwando clutched in his hand.

Han-Jae turned to Kyung-Wan. "We will rescue the child," he announced loudly.

Fear swept Kyung-Wan's face and was mirrored in the eleven sea guards that had joined them from the fort. What was the last battle any of them had fought? And on land? His men patrolled the waters of South Hanguk and were used to navigating the rolling waves.

Han-Jae didn't want to go into the forest after the monster, but the villagers were glaring at them, and he knew he and his men couldn't just stand there. Not when they were the only ones in the village with actual weapons.

He turned to his men. "We must prepare. Follow me."

He led the dozen men back to the fortification, the sounds of the women's wails dogging their steps. The rest of his regiment would be returning soon from their patrols near Incheon. In the meantime, they needed to take stock of their weapons and make repairs to any that had broken down from disuse.

They removed the daggers and swords from the hooks in the stone walls. All needed sharpening on a whetstone, but that would take far too long to do properly, and they had no time for it.

Kyung-Wan bundled the two spears in their arsenal. Looking over their equipment, Han-Jae immediately knew they didn't have the right weapons. This monster flew. A spear could take it down, but they only had two chances at that before they'd have to recover them.

Daggers could be thrown as well, but they would have to hit a vital spot on the first attempt. The sea guards did have half-a-dozen bows, and just as many full quivers of arrows. These would be their most useful weapons, but the sea guards didn't practice archery regularly and had left them strung up for months, leaving a permanently malformed curvature to the bows.

Han-Jae went to the rock that jutted out into the water where the sea guards docked and waited for the two swift boats carrying the other twelve men to return from their duties on the waves. The sails soon became visible in the distance until they were lowered so the men could paddle towards the forti-fication.

Han-Jae waved at them to make his presence known. When they came close enough, they threw the spring lines to the waiting sea guards, who tied them to the cleats embedded in the stone.

"Kwan Captain?" Dora said in surprise. "Are we late for the morning game of dice?"

Han-Jae shook his head and indicated the weapons the others held. "We have urgent business. While you were out, dark events happened in the village of Majeon."

Dora glanced back at the men he'd arrived with. Rings of fatigue darkened their eyes, and the smell of makgeolli drifted from their lips. "Can it wait until the afternoon, Kwan Captain? We've been up all night and would love to get a bit of sleep."

Han-Jae quickly related the story to his men, and watched horror embed itself on their faces.

"If those fishermen brought this evil into Majeon," Seung-Tae, one of the returning sea guards, said with a scowl, "then let them run off in the forest after it. It took their child, not ours."

The sea guards standing around Seung-Tae murmured in agreement. Han-Jae would have been inclined to agree before his trip home to Gwangju. The foolish brothers, he thought once more. Why would they bring a monster back from the water with them?

Dora was staring at him, however, a look of eager anticipation having dawned on his lined face. He must have come to the same conclusion Han-Jae had earlier. The ancestral spirits had delivered a task unto him. But a monster? Han-Jae was no hero and had no wish to become one. The thought of facing the unknown creature left him feeling hollow inside.

Han-Jae glanced over his shoulder to where the women still huddled on the shore, their wails carrying on the ocean wind. He wanted nothing more than to abandon this foolish quest, but that would ruin any chance of him being promoted. And his men had to at least put on a show of attempting to rescue the boy.

To Seung-Tae, who was still complaining to the other men, Han-Jae barked, "Lower your voice! It will stain our reputation if the villagers send word to Incheon we did nothing to help them."

He turned to Kyung-Wan. "Did you see how it happened? Where did you put the creature after you left the fort?"

Kyung-Wan lowered his gaze. "I had the brothers place the monster in the hull," he said. "We all thought it dead, captain. We saw no need to tie it up."

It would have been easier to blame Kyung-Wan for this misfortune, but Han-Jae decided against it. "How did it attack?" he asked instead. "Perhaps we can learn something about its abilities if we know how it grabbed the child."

Kyung-Wan's lips quivered as if he, too, was on the verge of tears. "I did not see that either, Kwan Captain." He swallowed. "I did not see the children double back around to the boat after they were driven away the first time. I did not even know the creature had risen until the young girl started screaming."

"Do you think the boy is still alive?" Dora asked.

"He was when the monster took him," Han-Jae snapped. "We must assume so until we have evidence to the contrary." He shook his head in frustration. "We should go now and get an idea of where the creature is. If we wait too long the trail will become too difficult to see."

The blood bled by the boy should still be visible in the trees for a little while longer. The sea guards had to go soon, for dark clouds marred the horizon, warning of a coming storm.

An ecstatic look blossomed on Dora's face, but he alone seemed enthusiastic. Han-Jae checked a sigh. Perhaps they would get lucky and kill the monster before the afternoon. If they brought back the shriveled monster, dead or alive, the villagers' grief would be mollified; their anger tempered. Word of that would get to the governor of Incheon instead of their failure, and Han-Jae would be able to get his promotion as had been promised to him by the dead.

"Eat quickly to regain your strength," Han-Jae ordered the men who had just returned, "and prepare yourselves. We leave to slay the beast."

The sea guards sat down outside of the fortification to a quick meal of raw fish, seaweed soup, kimchi, and rice. Then they stuck hwandos and daggers into the belts of their hanboks. They took up the halberds and spears, and Han-Jae instructed two of them to carry wide fishing nets just in case they were able to bring the monster to the ground.

Six of them strung fresh strings to the bows, Han-Jae among them. Although the bows were still warped, the taut strings should allow them to be of some use. Strapping the quivers to their waists, they started from the fortification. The villagers still stood outside, but the women's wails had quieted, tears slipping down their faces to plop into the mud at their knees. All eyes turned upon the sea guards as they marched past into the trees. Han-Jae didn't want the unconfident looks of his men to be focused upon the villagers too much, so he ushered them along quickly until the thick leaves fanned over them.

"There." Han-Jae pointed to splatters of blood marking the ground. The boy had been bleeding profusely, and the red trail was easy to follow as they cut through the forest undergrowth. The humidity increased under the trees. Soon sweat soaked their bodies, their hanboks clinging to their limbs. Han-Jae flinched at the noise of his men panting. Anything in their path would be alerted to their passing, but the sea guards were used to riding boats on the sea's waves, not moving across land at a fast pace. Again, doubt swelled inside of him, the truth washing over him. They were unprepared, and their pursuit, though necessary, was most likely to end in folly.

The tress grew closer around them. Birds flitted in the branches and small animals darted across leaves, keeping the sea guards on edge. Something heavy moving through the bushes nearby made them come to an abrupt halt, the spear men in front with their weapons lowered and ready to strike. When nothing materialized after several moments, Han-Jae signaled for the sea guards to move on.

"Captain!" Dora pointed ahead, and Han-Jae's slim hopes to find the boy alive vanished. Along the side of a tree, deep smears of blood marred the rough brown bark.

At the foot of the tree was a small skull without an accompanying body.

22. PERCH

The meat had been too thin, and the Orsieg had had no clay to collect the blood which spilled while it stripped the bones bare. The meal did little to increase its strength, and almost nothing to sate its hunger. It would need to feed again.

Soon.

Those with the pointed pincers had tried to bring it down. Before, killing the meat would have been a simple matter, but the Orsieg had lost too much weight, its size a pebble in comparison to its potential height. It needed to avoid the meat, but it also needed to feed, or it would starve. The Orsieg had no choice. It would have to go back to the coast and find more substance.

It decided not to fly, but used its thin arms to swing through the forest on the branches high over the ground. It curved its bony hands and let the momentum take it, swinging from branch to branch in the thick canopy. Even though it exerted little energy this way, it soon became fatigued, a light sheen of perspiration covering its emaciated body. The urge to give up, to fall to the ground like a rock, to curl up and let the earth take it back into its deep core, surged inside of it. The only thing that kept it going was its hunger, which seemed to have a life, and will, of its own. That hunger would not let the Orsieg die, would not let it rest until it had satisfied its endless need.

So the Orsieg swung through the branches of more tress than it had known could exist in its long lifetime. Around it, birds fluttered, and small furry animals darted through the canopy. They disappeared into the leaves of this strange world the Orsieg found itself in. Like them, it would have to learn to do the same until it was strong. It would use the trees as cover as it hunted its meat, hiding among yawning branches and surprising its prey when the opportunity arose.

When the Orsieg heard the sound of heavy breathing and the clanking of pincers, it altered its course. For now, only the smaller ones would be its target. Those would be easier to catch and rip apart with its weakened fingers.

It swung back towards the smell of salt and seaweed, back towards the coast from whence it had come. The sun had risen high in the sky but now drifted towards the western horizon. Soon, the voices of meat reached its shriveled ears. It paused at the edge of the tree line to view the land-shells the meat lived in when they weren't floating on the waves near its crag. The Orsieg's hopes dropped at the sight of the bigger men gathered in a cluster near the wet sand. It had seen them there earlier in the day when it escaped with its scrawny bleating meat. Still they remained there, mewling among themselves. It must be some strange ritual that kept them in place for so long. Grouped together like that, the Orsieg knew it could not take down even one of them for its next meal, though the flow of blood in those bigger bodies promised to be great, and its hunger was like a gale driving it forward to attack.

The Orsieg dropped to the ground as the sun dipped below the horizon. Shadows grew between the land-shells to create pools of darkness along the ground. Keeping low, it crept through the tall grass towards the brick structures. Dividing its focus between the structures and the big men on the beach, it reached the first land-shell, grabbed an oval opening carved into the stone, and hoisted itself up to look inside. This one was empty, so it dropped back to the ground and crept along to the next land-shell. This one, too, had an oval opening looking out onto the world. With its long arms, the Orsieg caught the edge and pulled itself up again. It emitted a short growl of satisfaction. Inside, several of the little ones, smaller even than the Orsieg, ate fish and seaweed wrapped in flat green leaves.

One looked up at the noise the Orsieg made. Upon seeing it, the meat began to shriek in a high-pitched voice. Quickly the Orsieg reached its long arm to the nearest and tiniest one and snatched it up in its thin fingers. The meat's limbs flailed as the Orsieg dropped back to the ground and ambled away to the sound of the big men running from the coast towards the land-shells.

The little meat's kicking and punching slowed the Orsieg down, so it paused to break the meat's neck, then slipped back into the trees before the lumbering men could reach it. Its hunger twisted through its legs, and the Orsieg stumbled. Desperate, it leapt to the closest tree and scrambled up to the branches high overhead. Fear gripped the Orsieg, for it had not been able to get far with its meal. When the men came in search of it, they would easily find it cowering above them.

From its perch in the tree, the Orsieg saw that the men stood at the tree line darkened by shadows, but did not come in search of it. Surprised, the Orsieg peered into their faces and glimpsed wide eyes filled with fear as they gazed into the gathering gloom of the forest. Realization dawned on the Orsieg, and it quietly laughed. It almost could not believe that—in its current, weakened form—the men were actually afraid of it! When it used to hunt the waves near the crag, it had witnessed this same terror as it attacked floating shells during storms. Then, it had been massive. How could they be afraid of it now, small as it was?

The Orsieg ripped off an arm from the tiny meat and lifted the appendage to its lips, letting the blood trickle into its mouth. Then it tore away at the scrawny muscle.

A little while longer, it thought to the men standing at the edge of darkness. When it had fed enough and began to grow back to its original size, it would really give them something to be terrified of.

23. TO AVENGE

Two children consumed in only one day. Seong-Hoon stared into the darkness of the forests, the sounds of flesh being torn apart drifting from somewhere in the treetops. His stomach twisted, his sides cramping as his body convulsed. Breath coming fast, he staggered back and fell to his knees, bile rising to flood his mouth.

"We must do something!" one of the other men said, tears sliding down his face and shimmering in the moonlight. Yet the gathered men simply stood there. Not one of them made a move to enter into the deep shadows that laid claim over the outskirts of Majeon. Behind them, women wailed. The second child was mourned now along with the first. The misery of the villagers became a deepening gloom settling over them all.

Seong-Hoon couldn't bear to turn back and face the mothers, and none of the other men around him seemed able to do so either. They kept staring dumbly into the forest, those awful sounds of tearing and ripping a constant reminder of their loss.

"What did we do to bring this evil upon us?" another asked.

"Where did it come from?"

Murmurs spread among the men, yet the answer was not forthcoming.

Seong-Hoon sat down in the grass, unable to control his shivering limbs as the question passed from mouth to mouth. Would the other villagers find out this was all his fault? What would they do once they discovered it was he who had cursed Majeon with his catch out on the Yellow Sea?

He should have left the monster out on the waves last night, should have left it to eventually sink into the watery depths. In his foolishness, in his wish to find wealth and improve his family's impoverished condition, he had brought the unknown into their small fishing village.

How would he ever make amends to these people he had grown up with? For did he not know the names of the two children that had been taken today? Had he not seen them as squealing newborns in their mothers' arms? Had they not played with his own children on the coast? In the end, had he not been the instrument of their deaths?

Yoon-Woo turned to look at him. In his older brother's wet eyes, he saw anger flickering darkly. Seong-Hoon averted his gaze, unwilling to be faced with the truth of all he had done wrong, to their families—and to the other families of the village of Majeon.

Soon, the feeding in the dark quieted. The men lowered their heads, their tears raining to the dirt beneath their feet. The forest grew ever darker as the heavy sounds of footsteps and the clinking of steel against steel reached their ears. Out of the trees at the other edge of the village, the sea guards emerged. Seong-Hoon immediately saw they were unscathed. They had not found the monster and had simply returned back to Majeon in failure. Would all of the men continue to prove powerless in stopping the monster from feeding upon the children of Majeon?

The sea guards paused some distance from them and eyed the villagers cautiously. Kwan Captain, standing in front of his subordinates, took a step forward, his eyes haunted. He started to speak but paused as he searched their grieving faces. In a hollow voice, he finally managed to ask, "Why do you gather there like that?" He swallowed. "Has a new evil befallen Majeon?"

"The monster took a second of our children," a man said, his voice flat and hard. "When you left us to kill it, it came back and snatched another boy from his own home."

The captain blanched. Behind him, the sea guards shifted uneasily. Seong-Hoon sensed the village men becoming tense, anger spreading through them, soon to become rage. All stared with dark eyes at the sea guards meant to protect the village from outside threats.

"What will you do?" Yoon-Woo asked, stepping forward.

"Tonight?" Kwan Captain's gaze flicked to the forest. "We cannot do much more. In the dark, we would be at a disadvantage, and my men are weary. In the morning we will plan how to kill the monster."

Yoon-Woo scoffed at these words and spat onto the ground. Anger at the disrespect to their leader flared in the tired eyes of the sea guards who were fanned out behind the captain.

"It wasn't us who brought this monster out of the sea," the sea guard, Kyung-Wan, who had first met the brothers at the entrance of the fortification, growled. "It wasn't *our* ignorance that couldn't tell a monster from a foreigner, *our* stupidity that brought it to land. We weren't the ones who set loose this plague upon Majeon!"

Seong-Hoon felt as if the attention of the village men shifted to him and his older brother. The world spun around him, his stomach convulsing, and he gazed down at the ground to steady himself.

"But it will be us who deliver the monster's corpse back into the deepest depths of the water," Kyung-Wan added, before the captain raised his hand for silence.

"Enough!" Kwan Captain barked, spinning to his man. "Since you enjoy the sound of your voice so much, Kyung-Wan, tomorrow morning you will go Hagun-ri on swift feet and speak to the captain of the fortification there. I have known him for many years. He will come quickly to our aid with the two dozen men under his command. When our numbers are doubled, we will track the monster once more, and this time we will catch it. This time, we will kill it."

The captain faced the villagers again. "Go back to your wives and children. We're going to set up a perimeter around Majeon during the night, but you, too, must remain watchful if you want to protect your families. The monster is small, but it has proven cunning. It may try and sneak in again. If you see it, call for help and fend it off as long as possible. I think it comes under the cover of darkness to attack because it is weak, so we must remain vigilant. We still don't know what the monster is truly capable of."

The men of the village and the sea guards exchanged exhausted glares with each other. Seong-Hoon tried to rise to his feet but found he could not conjure the strength in his legs to stand. All of his energy seemed to have flowed out of him into the ground beneath him. He wished to remain where he sat, away from everyone else. Alone.

Yoon-Woo came to stand over him. "We should go now," he said, his voice empty. He reached down, gripped Seong-Hoon under the arms, and hoisted him to his feet. The other villagers stared at the two brothers, their eyes distrustful and full of anger.

"We must somehow rectify this," Yoon-Woo whispered to Seong-Hoon as he helped him to the weeping village women huddled together with the children. They called out to their own wives and children to come along with them. Together, the two families returned to their small home of brick walls. They knew it proved no protection from the danger lurking outside, so their wives sat in the center of the room, their arms wrapped around their children. The brothers took the knives they used for skinning meat and stepped outside into the night.

"The captain said the monster is weak," Yoon-Woo said. "In the dawn light, we must go out and kill it."

Seong-Hoon gasped, drawing away from his brother. "The two of us, alone?"

Yoon-Woo tightened his grip around the hilt of the cutting knife. "How can we go on living in the village if we sit here and do nothing? Two children gone because of what we brought back from the sea. We have to do something if we're to find peace here again."

Seong-Hoon turned to the darkness of the forest and said nothing more. They took turns keeping watch, one brother sleeping while the other stared into the shifting shadows of the lanterns they kept burning. In the distance, footsteps could be heard as the sea guards patrolled the outskirts of the village. Always, they remained a safe distance from the trees. When dawn touched the horizon, Yoon-Woo shook Seong-Hoon by the shoulder.

"Come," he said. "The monster might be close by looking for another meal. We'll be bait. If it comes after us, we'll be ready for it."

Fatigue from a sleepless night settled heavily upon Seong-Hoon. In his brother's eyes, he saw the same exhaustion, coupled with an intense determination to make right what they had done wrong. In the distance, the weeping of mothers drifted from behind brick walls of homes as they woke up to their first morning with a lost child. The wails pierced Seong-

Hoon like swords, twisting inside his guts and making him grimace with pain. Alongside Yoon-Woo, he would avenge the children's deaths, for—as his older brother had said—how could they go on living in the village with their guilt if they did not?

The brothers took up their wide fishing net and the gaff. Skinning knives gripped tightly in their hands, they crept from their home to the edge of the forest as the sky became pale from the slowly awakening sun. The sea guards still patrolled the perimeter, their faces haggard with fatigue and haunted by fear. The brothers waited for a sentry to pass by before they scrambled forward, penetrating the forest.

Birds chirped in the boughs high overhead. Small furry animals rushed through the undergrowth. Clouds of gnats swirled around their hair and mosquitoes buzzed by their ears as the humidity closed in upon them.

It did not take long to find the tree where the monster had feasted. The rotting smell of death emanated from the area, and soon they saw the brown bark streaked with splashes of dull red. Seong-Hoon's stomach clenched. Yoon-Woo placed his hand over his nose, horror and revulsion sweeping over his face. Both brothers stood, transfixed by the nightmare that had become reality, unable to move forward, unwilling to go back.

"What do we do?" Seong-Hoon whispered, in a forest that had grown quiet.

"I don't think it got far," Yoon-Woo replied through gritted teeth. Seong-Hoon's eyes widened. Did his older brother really mean to follow the monster farther? Yoon-Woo stood rooted to the spot, breathing harshly in and out as the moments slipped by.

"I don't think I can go any farther," Seong-Hoon finally admitted, tears sliding down his cheeks. "I can't do this, Elder Brother."

Yoon-Woo's arms dropped to his sides, for the strength to continue the chase didn't seem to exist in him any longer either.

"Men," a deep voice said above them. "Do you look for this?"

The brothers, startled, looked up as a tiny skull dropped at their feet. Both brothers gazed in terror at the glistening bone stripped of meat, its small empty eye sockets gazing out at them. Seong-Hoon tried to move, tried to run, but fear cutting deep through his arms and legs paralyzed him as a dark shape dropped onto Yoon-Woo from high up in the tree. The figure, wielding a heavy branch, smashed it into Yoon-Woo's head. The momentum of the attack cratered his forehead, felling him with one blow. Blood splattered Seong-Hoon standing right beside him.

With an anguished cry, Seong-Hoon dropped to his knees, his heart racing. His brother twitched, the leaves rustling beneath him as life seeped out of his body. Tears blurred the image of his brother's death as memories rose up like a tide and washed over Seong-Hoon. He had never known a life without his brother, older than he, and so a constant presence at his side.

He lifted his eyes and stared, dazed, at the winged creature gazing back at him with monstrous, strange eyes.

"Such odd animals in this land," it said, raising the branch speckled with brain matter high above its head. Seong-Hoon had one last thought before the club fell with tremendous force.

The monster had grown a little taller since they had first dragged it up from the sea.

An explosion of light, then swift darkness, followed the branch smashing into his face. Yet Seong-Hoon did not die, and when he regained consciousness later, his screams were unending as the monster drained him of blood before consuming the flesh from his bones, one long strip at a time.

24. HANGU-RI

Anguished howls of wrenching torment woke Han-Jae from his troubled sleep and left him grasping for the hilt of his sword. The sound of hurried footsteps against the shells leading up to the fortification greeted him as he went to the opening and stepped outside into an early morning. Dora and several other sea guards stopped before him and bowed.

"What happened?" Han-Jae asked with sinking heart. He didn't want to hear more tragic news so soon, but the look on his subordinates' faces told him that whatever would be revealed would be as horrible as the previous day's events.

Han-Jae hesitated, then asked, "Was another child abducted?"

Dora shook his head. "We think it is adults this time. The screams are coming from the forest." Dora shuddered. His excitement that a monster had dropped from the sky into Majeon had faded, his face twisted with terror and revulsion. "I do not think the victim is dead, Kwan Captain," he whispered. "Not yet."

Han-Jae suppressed the stagger that almost overcame him at the horror of the news. He could not look weak in front of his men and bring their morale down even lower. "Quickly," he commanded them, and the sea guards ran back towards the village. The sounds of ongoing screams from the forest punctuated the air, the cries growing hoarser with each fresh volley. Already, the villagers huddled together near the edge of the trees. No one was foolish enough to enter.

"Did it attack people in their homes again?" Han-Jae asked.

"We're not sure," Dora replied.

They passed a brick abode where two mothers stood outside clutching their children. All of them were weeping. Where their men had gone, Han-Jae feared to guess. He recognized the women. The two brothers who had brought the monster from the sea were their husbands. Had they gone into the forest during the night? What madness would have possessed them to do so?

The villagers stared as the sea guards approached, the angry expressions from earlier replaced by terror. Once again, they would think the sea guards had failed them, yet hadn't Han-Jae set up a perimeter around the village?

"Who was on patrol here last?"

"I was, sir." A sea guard, Hyeon-Cheol, stepped forward and bowed.

"Did you see anything?"

Hyeon-Cheol shook his head. "I only recently passed this area. The forest was silent then, and I saw no one stirring in their homes. But I had not gone far when the screams started." He shuddered, his face paling further. "When I returned here," he continued, "the villagers had all come out of their homes to see what new evil had befallen them."

Han-Jae turned to the two women and their sobbing children. "Where are your husbands? Why are they not here with you?"

Moments passed in silence, and Han-Jae feared their grief

would not allow them to answer. Finally, the older of the two said through her tears, "I saw them! During the night, they hardly slept, making plans. To go after the monster. To find it and kill it to save the village."

Murmurs broke out among the fishermen. Han-Jae shook his head. So it was as he had feared. The two foolish brothers had entered the forest to fight the monster alone.

"They took their fishing net," the woman added, "their gaff, and their skinning knives. I saw them go into the trees, but it didn't take long before…before the screams." A fresh sob erupted from her, and she lowered her head as tears poured down her face.

"What do we do now, Kwan Captain?" Dora asked.

Han-Jae grimaced in frustration. The brothers had once again put the sea guards in a difficult position. It would have been wiser to wait for reinforcements from the village of Hangu-ri, where his friend, Lee Captain, maintained another fortification. Though Han-Jae had been reluctant at first to call for aid, as that would put his promotion at risk, he had decided last night to do so this morning. But better help than death, and as long as he took charge of the situation when Lee Captain arrived, he would be able to make a case to the officials in Incheon that the monster had been slain under his supervision.

With his friend's aid, their numbers would have been forty-eight strong. That would have been more than enough to hunt down the monster staying close to its source of nourishment—humans. No matter how clever the creature, with that many sea guards working together, their success would have been assured.

But now, though, how could they wait until reinforcements arrived? The villagers' terror was falling away again to the familiar glares of reproachful, angry eyes. They would want someone to be punished for their woes. If not the monster, then perhaps Han-Jae and his sea guards.

He could feel the tension drifting off the people of Majeon and radiating through the air. He sensed if he ordered the sea guards to wait a day for the reinforcements to come, and in that time, another person—especially another child—was taken, the reaction from the villagers could turn violent.

"Kyung-Wan," he said, stepping away from the villagers and lowering his voice, "Hyeon-Cheol, and Seung-Tae. You three, go to the village of Hangu-ri now and seek out Lee Captain. Tell him we are in dire need of his assistance, and he must bring all of the men under his control to Majeon as quickly as possible. They must make haste!"

He turned to the others standing behind him. "The rest of us will go into the forest in search of the brothers."

"Sir," Kyung-Wan said, "I can go alone since I am only carrying a message. You will need all the swords you have in order to fight the monster."

Han-Jae gazed into the forest again. "No," he said. "This monster is clever, and I have a feeling it's watching us. I should send half of you together to Hangu-ri, but perhaps that would be foolish. You three will go to Hangu-ri, and the rest of us will search for the brothers."

Kyung-Wan bowed. When he started towards the boats, Han-Jae stopped him. Quickly stepping even nearer to him, he lowered his voice and said into his ear, "I don't want the villagers to think we're not all going out to slay this monster. We will enter the forest together, and then separate. It shouldn't take you long to reach Hangu-ri on foot."

Once again, the sea guards collected their weapons. Han-Jae gave Kyung-Wan one of the bows, then they marched past the watching villagers and entered the forest. The humidity immediately closed its fingers around them in a tight fist, and soon the sea guards were breathing heavily as they trudged through the undergrowth. Han-Jae gave the order for Kyung-

Wan, Hyeon-Cheol, and Seong-Tae to start off under the cover of the trees toward Hangu-ri.

He led the other twenty-one men deeper into the forest. Once more, the area to where the monster had taken the humans wasn't far. Blood marked the leaves and trees, in much greater quantities this time because of the size of the victims. Many of his men averted their eyes and lingered far from the massacre. Han-Jae, stomach twisting, crept forward, with Dora at his side. The smell of death mixed with the odors of urine and feces permeated the area. Both men covered their noses as they approached the tree.

"There're only the remains of one body," Han-Jae said, voice tight. The bones had been crudely stripped of their meat, as if the creature had been in a hurry. This had to be the one who'd been only so recently screaming.

"Where do you think he took the other one?"

Dora shook his head. "I don't know, sir," he said. "But we must find out, for he may still be alive."

Han-Jae glanced back at the other twenty sea guards who would not come closer. Sweat poured down their brows, their hanboks clinging to their bodies. The folly of their task hit him mercilessly.

His men were not ready to fight this creature. If they moved forward, they would only survive if they were lucky. Han-Jae had been in enough battles during his service in the Emperor's fleet to know the fear etched across his men's faces would make their overwhelming odds against this single creature the reason for their defeat.

He peered up into the treetops around him. Perhaps the monster would return for these scraps of flesh it had left behind. They might be able to catch it that way if they laid a trap for it.

The patter of raindrops on the canopy above, announcing

a morning rain, made the air of the forest even thicker with humidity.

"We'll remain here until the sun begins to set," Han-Jae said. Dora arched his eyebrows, and Han-Jae added, "It won't be comfortable, but we don't have a choice. When the monster gets hungry, it'll come back to the village. We'll fan out and be ready for it."

"Should we not return to the village then?" Dora asked.

Han-Jae shook his head. "We can't go back with no sign of progress." Clapping Dora on the shoulder, he led him back to the other sea guards. He instructed them to move farther away from the corpse, which the men were thankful for, and set up sentries in a line through the forest. Two would watch together, and—though he knew they would prefer to stay in a group—his men followed his orders without comment.

The rain increased, thick raindrops splattering on Han-Jae and leaving him thoroughly soaked. All other sounds became muted in the downpour, and the feeling of being trapped in some large cage settled upon him. Han-Jae occasionally checked on his men to ensure they were prepared and watchful. As the day darkened to evening, terror settled upon them, and when he passed the sea guards, he saw their weapons ready; saw them flinch at sudden noises emanating from the forest.

Yet, to the relief of his men, and the disappointment of Han-Jae, the monster did not make an appearance. He looked back in the direction of the village of Majeon. Returning empty-handed was a discomforting prospect, but the feeling that the monster was no longer nearby crept over him.

Exactly where had it gone, and what mischief was it getting into now?

25. RICE WINE

The pants of Kyung-Wan's hanbok clung to his sweat-soaked flesh. Walking down the trail became more difficult as the fabric twisted around his legs. He sucked each breath into greedy lungs unused to this level of exertion. Hangu-ri, which he always traveled to by swift boat, seemed impossibly far away on foot through the entangling forest undergrowth.

Beside him, Hyeon-Cheol and Seung-Tae's labored breath mirrored his own desperate gasps. Gray clouds overhead released a steady rainfall, the drizzle becoming a downpour, yet it did not refresh them, the humidity growing denser still and making each step the three sea guards took more laborious.

"Do you think we'll reach the village before nightfall?" Hyeon-Cheol asked him.

Kyung-Wan shrugged, and wiped rain and sweat from his brow. He would never argue with Kwan Captain's orders, but reaching the neighboring village on foot seemed folly. They were sailors used to the open waves, not soldiers conditioned to march across hilly terrain.

"We should have sailed," Hyeon-Cheol said, speaking

Kyung-Wan's thoughts aloud. "Who cares what the villagers would have thought?"

Seung-Tae grunted in agreement. Kyung-Wan didn't reply. They had been given this order despite the fact the villagers had never shown proper appreciation for the sea guards' presence in Majeon. It had always been that way, though. This was one of the reasons why Kwan Captain kept a guard outside the fortification at all times.

The sea guards of Majeon remained alert for more than potential threats from the sea, which would have to get past Incheon first. Kwan Captain didn't trust the gaunt faces and skinny legs of the villagers, who outnumbered the sea guards more than ten to one.

He should never have allowed the monster to remain near the village, Kyung-Wan thought sourly. Kwan Captain had seemed as if he was going to blame him for following the orders given to leave the monster in the swift boat. They'd all believed it was dead! Why would anyone tie up the limbs of something dead?

Kyung-Wan shook his head. It was because Kwan Captain was always looking for a way to improve his status they hadn't thrown the monster back into the sea. He was desperate to be reassigned to Incheon, which made little sense to Kyung-Wan. Life in Majeon was easy. They did nothing during their time off-duty except sit in the village, drink makgeolli, eat the best foods, and gamble. What man would want to throw all of that away for a promotion, which certainly guaranteed more work and more responsibilities?

If Kyung-Wan had had his way, they wouldn't be in this situation now. He did not want glory, he did not need higher status. He only wanted a simple life, unburdened by tragedies and hardships.

"We don't have many provisions," Hyeon-Cheol said,

distracting Kyung-Wan from his thoughts. "We were in such a rush we only brought enough to last the night. By tomorrow morning, we'll have nothing left to eat."

The sea guards' stomachs grumbled as if in anticipation of the moment in which they'd be without.

"Let's rest," Kyung-Wan said, pointing to a spot beneath a tree with a wide trunk. The thick canopy overhead created a natural shelter from the rain. The sea guards settled among the roots of the tree, took out dried squid, rice and seaweed balls, and poured makgeolli into their wooden cups. In silence, they ate, as the downpour drowned out the sounds of the birds and scurrying animals in the underbrush.

When they finished, Seung-Tae stood to go off a little ways to relieve himself.

Hyeon-Cheol drained his cup and poured himself another. "Where do you think the monster comes from?"

Kyung-Wan shrugged. The constant drumming of raindrops on the canopy above him, coupled with the humidity, their meal, and the wine, was making him drowsy. He gazed into the rustling green leaves spanning out above him, his eyes narrowing to thin slits.

"In the Emperor's fleet, I've been to the border of South Hanguk's territorial waters," he said, voice thick as he wrestled to stay awake. "I've pursued pirates into the waters claimed by the Child-God of North Hanguk. But I've never gone farther than that, and so there is much I haven't seen."

Kyung-Wan placed the wooden cup to his lips, tilted back his head, and drank deeply. There was nothing better than makgeolli on a rainy day. He wished he was sitting on the rock outside of the fortification and dozing off to the sound of the waves slapping the rocky coast.

"The foreign world is full of dangers," he continued. "Most of our problems come from some other place. The evils walking South Hanguk are seldom born here. We do what we can to keep them out, but they're always finding a way in, no matter how narrow the opening."

"If the war between the North and South ever ended," Hyeon-Cheol said, "we would be able to combine our forces. Then we'd have enough men to plug up the holes that let evil creatures into our kingdom."

"*If* the war ever ended." Kyung-Wan guffawed at the thought. "We've been at a stalemate with the north for generations. Our fathers' fathers' fathers started this conflict, and each next son finds a new score that must be settled. How many soldiers are lost with each new flare up? How many comrades won't let the sacrifice of their brother be in vain?" Kyung-Wan shook his head. "We just watch each other, waiting for the enemy to cross a line before attacking. And when enough blood has been spilled, we pull back to our interiors, leaving our borders scarred and ravaged by this forever war."

Hyeon-Cheol poured Kyung-Wan more rice wine. "In my village, they say the Child-God of North Hanguk is eternal. He cannot die."

Kyung-Wan nodded. The same was said in his village, though quietly, as the Emperor did not like the people of South Hanguk spreading rumors of the north's might. It was bad for morale.

Hyeon-Cheol closed his eyes, and Kyung-Wan sipped from his cup. The rain maintained a constant rhythm on the leaves, but beneath the thick boughs of the tree, only light drops got through, and the two men remained relatively dry. Seung-Tae would probably be soaked by now, Kyung-Wan thought. The young sea guard had been gone for quite a while. When he returned, they'd rest a little while longer, maybe take a quick nap, and then press on towards Hangu-ri.

The need to relieve himself rose in Kyung-Wan's bladder as

well, and he stood. He had started in the general direction of Seung-Tae to see if he could find the third man of their group, when the leaves above him shook violently. Looking up, he saw a dark splotch fall from the highest branch straight down at him. Kyung-Wan issued a short cry of surprise, flung his arms over his head, and tried to leap, all at the same time. His confusion of movements made him stumble, and the object smashed into him, knocking him to the wet ground.

"What happened?" Hyeon-Cheol's slurred voice, thick with sleep and wine, drifted to him.

Kyung-Wan crawled from beneath the thing on top of him and saw that it was a body—bloodied and stripped of layers of skin and meat. It looked like something had been feeding upon it, pale bones peeking out from torn flesh. Kyung-Wan saw Hyeon-Cheol had risen to his feet, eyes wide in horror as he gazed at the corpse. He reached trembling fingers to pick up the bow he'd leaned against the tree, but a winged figure dropped right behind him, a spear in its hand.

"Look out!" Kyung-Wan shouted, but the terror in Hyeon-Cheol's eyes made Kyung-Wan's blood freeze. Hyeon-Cheol turned slowly, so slowly in fact that Kyung-Wan realized he didn't want to see what stood behind him. The winged shape drove the spear into Hyeong-Cheol's right side, and the sharp metal point erupted out of the left side of his rib cage.

Hyeon-Cheol screamed as the monster lifted him up and impaled the spear into the tree, leaving Hyeon-Cheol's writhing form suspended above the ground.

Kyung-Wan, catching the monster's gaze, unsheathed his sword with a trembling hand. Something had gone wrong, so terribly wrong, since he had carried the monster down to the boat. He saw the size and weight of the creature looming over him now, and realized it had gotten bigger. Muscle filled its bulky frame.

As the monster approached, Kyung-Wan saw it stood at least a head taller than him now. When it expanded its wings, their span blocked out the world behind it so all he could see was the creature, blood covering its face and dripping to the ground. Kyung-Wan raised his sword, but he did not swing. He could not defeat it. His arm shaking, his sword point lowered to the damp earth.

The monster reached out with its long arms. Kyung-Wan could only weep as rough hands closed around his throat.

PART III: HERO

26. A NEW QUEST

The faces of the dead stole Ha Jun's sleep for yet another night. He sat with his back against the wall, his eyes following the stars seen through the window as they sailed across the night sky. He hadn't slept an entire night in days now, a dull fatigue had settled inside of him like one of the black volcanic rocks of Jeju Island. He watched the darkness become pale as dawn approached. Soon fire from the rising sun torched the clouds. The sound of the farmers entering the orange grove drifted through the quiet morning, their shearing tools jingling as they walked down the path.

With a tired sigh, Ha Jun pushed himself up and went to the basin of water he had set out the previous evening. He peered at the shadowed image reflected back at him, then dipped his hands into the basin, making the shadowed water ripple in consecutive waves.

Before he left his room, he turned to the glyph sword lying on the floor beside his sleeping mat. He had been carrying the weapon wherever he went for years, the heavy sword strapped to his back as he worked in the grove. The constant burden had made him the strongest warrior on the island, capable of achieving feats regular men could not. With the help of the Dark Elf, Windshine, he had even managed to unlock the glyphs' secrets, mastering the power of the elements: earth, wind, fire, water, and lightning. The sword had helped him stay alive on the last two quests he had undertaken, even while he had watched many of his brothers fall.

Their deaths haunted his dreams. Ha Jun often thought perhaps it would have been better if he had never been given the glyph sword. Better if he had simply died alongside his companions on the dangerous roads they'd walked.

Another fatigued sigh surged up from a deep well of sadness inside of him, but he forced it down. Steeling himself, he stepped outside without the glyph sword, his exhaustion replacing the weapon's familiar weight on his back.

Ha Jun's mother had set already set out breakfast on a low table: rice and fish, kimchi and boiled eggs, and seaweed soup. The farmers sat in a close circle for warmth, a bowl of food, and a steaming cup of soup, held by each of them. Jeju's eternal breeze had grown chill teeth and nipped at their thick beige pants and blue shirts, the farmers pulling their hats low on their foreheads for protection. Ha Jun's father, Kang Jeong Seok, was already there in a simple gray hanbok. To start the morning, he always welcomed the men and made sure they had enough to eat for the long day ahead of them.

Ha Jun went to the table to get breakfast, but before he could fill his bowl, his father's sharp bark made him freeze.

"Where's your sword?"

Ha Jun's heart ratcheted up to a fast tattoo, yet he maintained a calm exterior as he turned and bowed to his father. "I hope you have slept well, Ah-boe-ji," he said politely.

"I have," his father replied. "Where is your sword?" he repeated.

"It is in my room, Ah-boe-ji," Ha-Jun replied without

straightening from his bow. He heard his father's sandaled foot-steps approach him across the earth still moist from dew.

"Why aren't you wearing it?" Kang Jeong Seok laid a heavy hand on Ha Jun's shoulder and roughly pulled him up. Ha Jun avoided his eyes, but his father's face loomed directly in front of him. "What's the meaning of this?"

Raw emotion surged through Ha Jun, and he caught it before it forced him to start shaking. All of the words Ha Jun wanted to bellow at his father struggled to be released in a mighty roar that would shatter the quiet dawn. He yearned to scream about the hardships of the two quests he'd undertaken. He wanted to wail about the close relationships he had formed, the brutal deaths of the gentle monk, Su Won; the noble mayor's son, Yeong-Su; the brave soldier, In-Su; the wise monk, Nam-Kyu.

Most of all, he wanted to sob over the loss of the master archer, Woo Jin, his friend who had shared his age and was crushed beneath a dragon after he slayed it with a single arrow. Ha Jun wanted to weep over the terrible secret he held about the Dark Elf, Blythe, and the harsh manner South Hanguk people had treated the foreigners over the generations the Dark Elves had lived among them. He wanted to curse the continued isolation of Windshine and the loneliness she was forced to endure on this island of men.

He wanted to proclaim that, when a man went on a quest, they never came back home. Not really. They walked those roads of peril and danger in their minds for the rest of their days, the memories as alive to them in the present as when they were formed in the past.

Ha Jun wanted to let all of these emotions, these words that fought to be freed, into the open world. The war raging deep within himself created an overwhelming urge to strike out; at his father, at the farmers. The tide of madness smashing against the dam inside of him begged for a release through physical action, through the destruction of everything around him. Visions of tearing down their family's stone house, burning down their grove, going on a rampage in Jeju, killing with his hands until blood misted the air and his terrible energy was finally spent, his mind finally at ease so that he could sleep, overwhelmed him.

Because Ha Jun knew none of this was possible, that he would never allow himself to hurt the people of Jeju, he kept the raging storm tethered inside of himself. In an emotionless voice, he said to his waiting father, "I will go get the sword now."

"*Your* sword." Kang Jeong Seok's amendment was sharper than any blade, and cut deep into Ha Jun, who kept the wound from showing as he suppressed a shudder from the blow.

"My sword," he said with a bow. He went back into his room, lifted the heavy glyph sword no one else on the island could carry, and strapped it to his back. When he stepped outside again, the farmers had finished their breakfast and had gone off to begin pruning the bases of the trees.

As Ha Jun crouched down for a quick breakfast, his father approached him.

"You'll be leaving soon. You have been assigned another quest."

In a carefully blank voice, Ha Jun asked, "When should I be ready to depart?"

Kang Jeong Seok did not immediately reply, but Ha Jun heard his quickened breath, and tensed. No matter how hard Ha Jun had tried to hide it over the years, his father always seemed to sense when Ha Jun disagreed with him. Every year Ha Jun had raised his defenses higher, making sure no emotion leaked out of the whirlwind of his thoughts, but it never seemed to matter.

"You should always be prepared to depart!" The words were tight, like the whip his father used to lash Ha Jun with as he rode on horseback behind him. "*When* should not matter. Even if it is now, you should be ready to begin."

"Is it now?" The quip forced its way out of his mouth, and instantly Ha Jun regretted it. His father took a step closer. It seemed a great heat rose off of him and engulfed Ha Jun. He prepared himself for blows he knew he would not defend himself against. The whip was nearby, in Kang Jeong Seok's room, and it would take only a moment for his father to retrieve it.

The snipping of the nearby shears of the farmers drifted through the silence between father and son. Time passed in which only that sound existed, then his father said, "I will discuss the details with you later. After the day's work is done. Now eat your breakfast and join the others. The morning grows late."

Kang Jeong Seok retreated. Later, after the farmers had left and the two of them were alone, there would be pain. Of that Ha Jun was sure, but that wasn't what concerned him.

Another quest. His father would have already sent in a request for Ha Jun to join, and since he had already survived two, where so many had died, Ha Jun knew the governor would accept the application.

Ha Jun braced himself on the table, the sword on his back growing heavier. What danger would he and his companions be sent into this time? What new relationships would be formed? And more importantly, how many bodies would he have to bring back to the island to hand over to grieving parents and siblings?

Ha Jun knew he would find out all too soon.

27. GWANG MIN UNCLE

A request for Ha Jun to meet the governor at his office in Jeju arrived by official courier two days later. The attendant rode up on horseback, excitement in his eyes as he handed Kang Jeong Seok the scroll. Even before his father unrolled it, Ha Jun knew what was written there. Once more, he kept his emotions bottled as his father turned to him.

"You have been summoned for another quest," Kang Jeong Seok said with a broad, satisfied smile.

Ha Jun only nodded but made no further response.

The following morning, he awoke before dawn. He packed a week's worth of provisions, retrieved the fire lance given to him by the soldier Seong Min, cleaned the long barrel with a thin cloth wrapped around a stick, then shouldered the weapon. He strapped his glyph sword to his back, and wondered, once again, whether he would ever sleep in this room again.

He sat down with his mother for a brief breakfast. She had risen early, too, and had prepared a meal of chicken and rice porridge, diced radishes, and kimchi jjigae. He ate quickly as the morning sun peeked over the horizon, then told her his goodbyes.

"Don't be away too long," she told him, deep pride tinged with motherly worry for her only living son warring in her eyes. Word would be spreading throughout Jeju Island today. With yet another quest, Ha Jun was slowly coming closer to being named a hero by the Emperor of South Hanguk.

Ha Jun bowed to her request, then went out to his father waiting for him at the stone fence surrounding their home.

"You will return victorious," Kang Jeong Seok said simply.

"I will return victorious," Ha Jun said. Bowing low in farewell, Ha Jun stepped onto the familiar path leading away from their orange grove. He walked through the trees, the birds waking for the day and filling the cool morning with song. When he reached the perimeter of their property, he stepped out of the grove and walked the road past his uncle's horse ranch. To his surprise, he saw Gwang Min Uncle already up and carrying a bale of hay to feed the mares for the start of the day. His uncle walked with a pronounced limp now, and Ha Jun rushed over to him.

"Let me help you," Ha Jun said, but he was immediately waved off.

Gwang Min Uncle eyed Ha Jun closely, and Ha Jun lowered his gaze, the familiar shame welling up inside of him. His uncle's limping gait was his fault.

It had happened before his first quest. His uncle had ridden up to Ha Jun on this same road running past the ranch, in this same spot Ha Jun stood now, and had tried to stop him. He had demanded Ha Jun come with him so they could talk, believing that, at sixteen years old, Ha Jun wasn't ready for a quest. Many young men throughout South Hanguk tried each year, and most died along the way.

When Ha Jun had declined, Gwang Min Uncle had

unsheathed his sword in an attempt to force him to obey. The threat had startled Ha Jun. The suppressed ball of emotion chained deep inside of him had come untethered, filling him with rage. Without thinking, he had attacked the horse his uncle rode on, killing it with a single blow to its head. When the animal collapsed, it had fallen on Gwang Min Uncle, pinning him beneath its heavy bulk and crushing his leg.

Instead of helping free his uncle from the dead animal, Ha Jun had continued on down the road. He had had to reach the other side of the island in time for the official quest ceremony at the governor's office.

The broken bones had never mended properly in his uncle's leg. This morning, as he stood there with a bale of hay on his shoulder, Gwang Min Uncle looked at Ha Jun, his eyes lingering on the fire lance and sword. He shifted the hay so that his good leg took more of the weight, and he said, "I can do this much on my own, at least."

Ha Jun flinched. More than a year had passed since the incident, and Ha Jun was now nearing his eighteenth birthday. Whenever he passed the ranch, he stepped in to see if his uncle needed any help. Memories of Gwang Min Uncle's kindness to him as a child remained in his mind. His father had been brutal in training Ha Jun, and the scars that criss-crossed his body were the price he had paid for the strength he developed that led him to be able to wield the Elven-made glyph sword. Of everyone Ha Jun had met on his journeys, only he could swing the magical weapon. All others struggled to even lift it.

Yet, while his father had made him strong, his uncle had given him fresh meat to eat, the choicest cuts of horse that Gwang Min sold for a high price at the market. During festivals and religious observances, his uncle would give him coins to buy treats. He taught him how to handle horses, and now Ha

Jun both tended the orange grove and worked for his uncle as a hostler.

When Ha Jun had initially come back from the first quest, he had worried he would never be allowed to speak to Gwang Min again. His father had dismissed this concern, however.

"Jeju is a small island," Kang Jeong Seok had said, "and our family can't afford the gossip that would come with a feud. It would be bad for business, both for our farm and your uncle's ranch. Never forget it's not only the living that watch us and judge our behavior.

"We won't speak of what happened to anyone," his father had said, "and will simply let everyone believe Gwang Min had an accident out riding one day. We will not dishonor our family name with public disagreements."

His uncle had seemed to agree, but the love that used to shine in his eyes toward Ha Jun had cooled. An emptiness existed there now, and it pierced Ha Jun to his core. Even when those he cherished did not die, he always seemed to be losing people in his life. Would this road to becoming a hero always be plagued by grief and loneliness?

"You're going to Busan?"

Ha Jun nodded. The sun was rising, and the road beckoned him, but still he lingered. Unlike his first quest, he wasn't late. He was, also, always reluctant to leave his uncle, though being around him made Ha Jun feel awkward. He wished he had the words in mind he could speak to erase that past incident between them; or at the very least, to apologize for the attack that had left his uncle crippled. But since the men did not talk about it, Ha Jun had never had the opportunity to say he was sorry for the injury he had caused that would now afflict his uncle for the rest of his life.

"Do you know what the quest will be?"

Ha Jun shook his head. "They do not tell us until we arrive for the official ceremony."

"No, I guess they wouldn't, would they?" Bitterness infected his uncle's voice. "I guess it might scare some of the young men from going."

Ha Jun lifted his eyes to his uncle, then averted them again. "You do not approve of the quests for anyone?"

His uncle didn't respond for several breaths, and Ha Jun began to wonder if he would answer. He hadn't wanted to appear rude in asking, but he was genuinely curious.

"The quests are necessary," his uncle finally admitted. "With so many men in the Emperor's army on guard against a potential attack from North Hanguk, we simply don't have the means to send arms whenever other dangers appear in South Hanguk. If we lower our defenses, even for a moment, the Child-God would attack. His spies in our lands are numerous, and no matter how often the Emperor has tried to root them out, they still persist, looking for weaknesses."

Like his father, Gwang Min had served in the Emperor's army. All men of South Hanguk had mandatory service requirements. One day, Ha Jun's own deployment would come, though his father had been delaying the inevitable through bribes to Jeju government officials. He wanted Ha Jun to become a hero first before he did his mandatory two years. As his father often said, if Ha Jun waited until after, his chances would be lost.

The opportunity to distinguish oneself is small, Kang Jeong Seok had told Ha Jun when he was still a young child, *and disappears when one isn't looking.*

"I understand the need some have to reach for greatness above their peers," his uncle continued. "All of the governors of South Hanguk are heroes, and they're the most powerful men in the country outside of the Emperor. Going through the quests is how the Emperor decides who's worthy of leading a province." His uncle took a deep breath. "But then, there are the great risks young men take who aren't ready for the hardships of quests. In their rush to beat the competition, they throw their lives away. With the constant threat from North Hanguk, we can't afford to have our best and strongest die before they're ready."

Ha Jun thought back to what Seong Min, the soldier, had said on their quest to slay the *ak-ma*: *if everyone could be successful on the quests, there would be no point in going.* It was the extreme challenge and the fact so many failed that gave value to the effort.

"Doesn't someone have to slay the monsters?" Ha Jun kept his voice small and soft. Questioning his uncle in this manner could be considered rude, but the way Gwang Min saw the world, and the way his father and the men he'd gone on the quests with saw the world, was so different he genuinely wanted to understand what set the two groups apart.

"The monsters have to be slain," Gwang Min conceded with a nod. "But do the quests have to be a competition between provinces? Do we have to go out against each other, instead of working together to eradicate the dangers? The governors risk young men's lives for the glory of each separate province. But we're one nation, all South Hanguk people. We should work together as one, not race to see who can be first."

Even as Ha Jun listened to his uncle's explanation, he knew what Gwang Min wanted would never happen. The quests were voluntary, and their purpose was to prove one's worth. If they all worked together, how would they know who was better than the others? How would they know who was superior?

Ha Jun glanced at his uncle again and saw a sad smile curving his lips.

"It does seem good, doesn't it?" his uncle asked, as if he'd read Ha Jun's disagreement in his mind. "To be remembered, to have songs composed about your deeds. To gain status in your province. To have your name repeated by each successive generation far down into days you will not see. But remember, Nephew, everything has its price. You must be sure you're ready to pay it, as the cost might be more than you can handle. And once you're far enough in the hole, there may be no way to climb back out again."

The faces of the dead young men he'd journeyed with on the previous two quests floated up to Ha Jun to cloud his vision. He blinked rapidly, the weight in his heart growing heavy once more. Looking away from his uncle, Ha Jun dared ask no further questions before his steadfastness wavered further.

28. JEJU GOVERNOR'S OFFICE

Ha Jun entered Busan's gates alongside farmers and merchants who were traveling to the city to set up their wares for the popular night markets near the ports. The bustle along the Hanguk Strait started early, when the fishermen sailed back into the docks. Restaurant owners would meet them at dawn and haggle over the fresh catch of the day.

As the morning burned away into afternoon, the clatter of wagon wheels on the wooden boards of the docks resounded across the port as merchant ships brought in their wares from the mainland of South Hanguk and beyond.

In the evening, the third wave of sellers entered Busan. These were mostly farmers bringing in vegetables, and animals for slaughter. Ha Jun threaded through the steady stream of people and went toward the center of Jeju where the governor's office was situated. The sun hung low over the western horizon, the sky darkening as evening crept across the city. He had made good time in reaching Busan, running over the volcano, Hallasan, in the center of the island. He took the trip often to retrieve his uncle's horses when a customer rented one to carry them to the island's northern ports, and had memorized every feature of the roads between his village and the city.

The official ceremony for the quest would be the last meeting of the day for the governor of Jeju. When Ha Jun reached the fence surrounding the office, he saw the governor seated in the wooden chair on the raised platform, his attendants lined up on both sides of him.

Standing at the foot of the stairs leading up to the office were three brothers in red hanboks. One carried a drum strapped to his back, another a case carrying a stringed harp, and the third a flute dangling from a cord around his neck. For the first time in many weeks, Ha Jun strode forward with light steps, a smile breaking out on his face.

"Elder brothers!"

The three musicians turned to him, broad grins curving their lips from ear to ear.

"Ha Jun!" Jae Jin exclaimed, stepping forward. "We wondered if you would be the fourth person on this quest."

Ha Jun bowed deeply, which Jang Jae Jin, Jang Kia Ha, and Jang Jae Ho, the three champions of the spirit, returned.

"We're glad to see you with the mighty glyph sword again," Jae Jin said. "Without it last time, we would have been lost."

"Thank you." Ha Jun bowed. "But in the end, I give all praise to Woo Jin, who finally slew the dragon with his bow and arrow. If not for him, the village of children would have perished."

The four companions fell silent for several moments. Woo Jin hadn't been the only person they'd lost on the last quest. The soldier, In-Su, and the monk, Nam-Kyu, had both given their lives in order to ensure the quest's success. Their faces floated up into Ha Jun's mind, and his chest tightened with grief.

"What of the old soldier, Kun Woo?" Ha Jun asked,

breaking the silence. "I have heard nothing of him since we parted ways."

The three brothers shook their heads. "After the return ceremony, Kun Woo took his leave with several of the government officials. I believe they were discussing the foreign religion that the people of Goseong converted to."

Ha Jun had learned little about that religion during the brief time he'd been in the company of the village of children. He had been mortally injured early on and had spent much of his time resting from his after-death experience. Supposedly, Woo Jin had been taught the religion's secrets by the village leader, Ji Su, but—when he died—he took the knowledge he'd gleaned with him.

And then there was Ji Su herself, whom Ha Jun had only interacted with briefly while they fought off the attacking northern soldiers of the Child-God. Beautiful, with a bright, fierce spirit, Ji Su was strong-willed and stubborn, endangering the success of the quest with her zeal.

Once the quest was competed, the companions had evacuated her and the other villagers to the nearest city, turning them over to that governor and thereby completing their mission. What Ji Su eventually revealed to the officials about the foreign religion, Ha Jun could only guess.

A Busan government aide came down the stairs and motioned for the companions to join them so they could begin the quest ceremony. The companions ascended the steps to the audience hall where the governor waited in his oaken chair. His office had no walls, symbolizing transparency. From the top of the platform, those in attendance could see the rooftops of Busan stretching to the walls. The height of the governor's office even allowed them to glimpse the ports of Hanguk Strait, and the water beyond.

The companions sat down seiza-style before the governor,

who favored them with a smile as bright as the gold and red hanbok he wore.

"Returning warriors," he began, "you three brothers who successfully completed the last quest and brought great honor to Jeju. I welcome you!"

The attendants and officials standing in straight lines leading up to the governor's chair clapped in unison at the pronouncement.

"And you, Kang Ha Jun, who have now completed *two* quests, and at such a young age! Only eighteen years old! Your exploits have already been woven into song. Tales of your prowess are repeated among families during meals. Your name is even known among the province governors of South Hanguk. You are on your way to becoming a hero. Soon even the Emperor will learn of your feats!"

Those in attendance gasped at Ha Jun's introduction, and he bowed low to show his humility. He would have liked to feel some joy at the governor's words, but the weight of those lost on both quests created an emptiness that perhaps would never be filled.

"Tonight, you four will journey on another quest and bring even greater prestige to the island of Jeju, and to yourselves." The governor extended his hand, and an official laid a scroll in his palm. With an elaborate flourish, the governor unfurled it and read the message within. When he looked at the companions again, he laughed.

"You four are perfectly suited for this quest. It has been reported that a strongman from across the ocean has landed on the shores of South Hanguk. This foreigner has taken up residence on the outskirts of Incheon near two small villages that run along its coast. The strongman is said to have great power in his arms and stands taller than many South Hanguk men."

The governor laughed. "We will show him how tall the

warriors of Jeju can stand! It is destiny that you, Kang Ha Jun, go against this giant and reveal to him the true might of South Hanguk people. And you three—the champions of the spirit—you will play songs to inspire Ha Jun to vanquish his foe and cut off his head to bring back to Jeju as a trophy. We will place the head on a stake at the gates of Busan so that all can see how our Jeju men overcame this threat from beyond the horizon."

The attendants and officials clapped again at this prediction, and the four companions lowered their heads in a deep bow of gratitude for the governor's confidence in them. When Ha Jun looked up again, a tremor of excitement passed through him. Standing at the edge of the officials was Windshine staring directly at him. He hadn't seen her since their parting after the last quest, but she had often been in his thoughts. Every chance to glimpse the Dark Elf was a rare treat to Ha Jun, who felt that Windshine, more than anyone else on the island, understood his true self.

Staring at her now, he admitted the truth to himself. He wished nothing more than for her to become a constant presence in his life.

29. INTRODUCTIONS

The older he became, the more women had begun to catch Ha Jun's attention. When he traveled to Busan, his gaze lingered on their black hair, neatly woven into a thick plait on their backs, or tied in a neat bun, bringing their feminine features into sharp relief. He appreciated the beauty of their faces, oval and pale; their black eyebrows neatly arched, rouge applied to their slender lips.

Busan was the height of fashion on the island, and the girls wore expensive hanboks of the latest styles, the colors perfectly matching each season. They walked with practiced grace along the paths twisting throughout the city. Often, Ha Jun would catch them staring at him with awe. As the governor had said, many stories circulated about his feats on the island, and he knew parents had already begun approaching his father so they could introduce their daughters to him as potential brides.

As he went about business in the city, he would notice girls staring at him. They would quickly look away, their cheeks reddening, and Ha Jun could not deny that something new stirred in him, too.

At times like this, Ha Jun often thought back to his father's speech delivered at the beginning of his first quest to Nagane-upseong Fortress.

"Other fathers on this island, do you know what they want for their children?" Kang Jeong Seok had said. "An ordinary life. To fight in some war where the Emperor gets all the glory. To come back home to take over the family business. To be married off to some girl. To sire children to take care of them when they are old. That is what other fathers want for their sons."

His father had insisted Ha Jun must become a hero before he married. As the year passed, with two quests successfully completed by Ha Jun, his father seemed to become more worried about the attention the opposite sex gave his son. During the few times they were together in the northern city, his father would rush him through the streets. He scowled at the girls who weren't fast enough to avert their gaze as he and his son took care of business so they could return to the grove as quickly as possible.

Ha Jun would have liked to tell him that he needn't concern himself. Though he found many of the South Hanguk girls quite pretty, his own gaze lingering on their hips and chests accentuated by their hanboks, he felt they all paled in comparison to Windshine. Her exotic beauty made his heart leap with excitement. If only his father knew it was the very quests he pushed Ha Jun upon that gave him the opportunity to be in the Dark Elf's presence.

Even though he only saw her during quests, Windshine's presence was a balm to his troubled spirit. Nights when he couldn't sleep, thoughts of her would be the only respite from the faces of the dead. His growing depression, always attempting to imprison him in darkness, was held off by the knowledge that somewhere on the island, the Dark Elf lived, alone, in a home he'd never seen.

Windshine was the most perfectly beautiful female he had ever known. He would conjure the image of her violet skin and luminescent hair cascading like a wild mane past her shoulders to her hips. her pointy ears, the strange blue corneas with brown pupils that shifted like desert sands.

Windshine's uniqueness left him stunned every time he saw her on quests. Since this was his third, he had seen her more than almost all other Jeju people, many of whom had never glimpsed the foreigner at all. Even Ha Jun hadn't met Windshine's counterpart, the second Dark Elf on the island who taught magic to a handful of elite scholars.

Being in Windshine's presence once again lifted his spirit. As with his previous two quests, Ha Jun was sure tragedy awaited him; yet with the Dark Elf at his side, he knew he would have the strength to walk through valleys of death and climb mountains of pain.

"The ceremony has come to an end." The governor's announcement cut through Ha Jun's thoughts. "May your journey be full of adventure and danger so your triumphs and victories will be repeated by the mouths of young and old in homes across Jeju and beyond!"

The governor rose, and everyone in attendance bowed low as he descended the stairs to the official *gama*. Four porters in white pants and black vests waited until he entered the palanquin. Then they squatted down, took the poles in hand, and gently lifted the litter. Slowly, they started down the lane, the *gama* gently swaying between them until they had gone through the governor's office gate in the direction of the governor's home.

The three Jang brothers and Ha Jun rose, and one of the officials led them back down the steps to the gate.

"You four will depart on the night ferry and sail west alongside the Hanguk Strait until you reach the southern coast of

Incheon," he told them. "Jang Jae Jin, as you are the eldest, you will be in charge of the finances."

The official took a pouch of coins from the pocket of his hanbok and handed it to Jae Jin, who accepted it with both hands. "You should arrive at your destination in two days. There will be many stops along the way as other passengers disembark. We have obtained a map from the mainland."

He handed Jae Jin a rolled scroll. "You should be able to find Majeon with this. It is a small village, and not easily identified by those who are not familiar with the region."

"There is only one giant that we must defeat?" Jae Jin asked. "It sounds too simple a task. I wonder why it was necessary for governors to send out the summons for an official quest to vanquish it."

"Because of our ongoing war with North Hanguk, small villages are the most vulnerable," the official replied. "They are often left with only a handful of defenders, and those defenders are often old, or no longer regularly trained for combat. In matters such as this, it is easy for a small threat to become a big problem if not dealt with immediately. Remember, however, slaying the giant is not your only hurdle. You must also beat the other provinces to the glory of the kill. On a quest like this, that is your true objective."

The four companions bowed as the official took his leave. The sun had long since set, dusk sweeping through Busan. The drone of crickets reverberated against the walls. Overhead, birds circled about chasing insects before descending into the trees to roost for the night.

The companions exited the governor's office grounds so the caretakers could lock the gates for the evening.

"We're scheduled to leave immediately," Jae Jin said. "Have you brought provisions to last for several days?"

Ha Jun held up his bag and nodded.

"Then let us depart."

The three brothers turned toward the ports and started away, but Ha Jun hesitated.

"Elder brothers," he said, and they turned back to him. "On our last journey, we had no time for proper introductions."

The Jang brothers arched their eyebrows. This, of course, wasn't true, as the eight companions who had gone from Jeju to the village of children had announced each other's names and ages before setting off.

"With your permission," Ha Jun continued, "I would appreciate it if we all introduced ourselves to the Chronicler, and she introduced herself to us."

Understanding dawned on the Jang brothers' faces, and they exchanged glances. Ha Jun had suggested this same request at the beginning of their last quest. At the time, the eldest of their group, the solider In-Su, had refused, pointing out that the foreigner was only there to observe, not to interact with them.

Jae Jin stepped toward Ha Jun and inclined his head in agreement. A brief smile touched Ha Jun's lips, and he turned around to look for Windshine. As usual, she waited at the periphery of the companions, so he went to the pool of shadows in which she stood under a tree. He fought to slow his breathing as his heartbeat picked up.

"Windshine," he said quietly in Elvish, "would you be so kind as to join us before we set off on the quest? We are about to make introductions."

On their return journey from the last quest, she had taught him basic vocabulary and grammar from her language that Ha Jun had repeated to himself many times since. She had written down notes in scrolls she gave him as a parting gift, and he had practiced them during the long intervals they weren't together to make sure he could speak to her in Elvish when next they met.

The Dark Elf regarded him with surprise in her blue-brown eyes, making Ha Jun flush, his skin warming. He yearned to reach out and touch her angular face, to caress her cheek, to come closer to her and inhale the stinging-sweet aroma of her sweat clinging to her bright red dress embroidered with gold Elvish lettering. A breeze jostled the beads hanging from the red cap covering her pale hair. For several moments, the beads' hollow clinking was the only sound that existed between them.

Finally, Windshine nodded. Ha Jun exhaled the breath he hadn't realized he'd been holding in, his nerves so tight he felt like he'd just been in a battle. He led her back to the three brothers, who stared awkwardly at her. Despite traveling with the Dark Elf on the last quest, they had never actually spoken to her before.

"Elder brothers," Ha Jun said with a bow, "I am honored to journey once again on a quest with you. I am Kang Ha Jun, and I am eighteen years old."

"We are pleased to have you join us once again, Kang Ha Jun. I am Jang Jae Jin, a champion of the spirit, and I am twenty-five years old."

Ki Ha stepped forward. "I am happy to see you well and strong again after the last quest, Kang Ha Jun. I am Jang Ki Ha, and I am twenty-three years old."

Jae Ho bowed to his older brothers, then to Ha Jun, then to the Dark Elf. "I have great hope that all of us who leave today will soon return to Jeju Island, whole and in health. I am Jang Jae Ho, and I am twenty-one years old."

Now the three brothers paused, their eyes politely averted from the Dark Elf until she spoke.

Windshine inhaled, then said, "I am the recorder of your

adventures, and I wish you grand success. My name is Windshine, and I am over a thousand years old."

The three brothers gasped sharply, their eyes opening wide at this revelation.

"Can that be possible?" Ki Ha asked in awe.

Windshine smiled gently. "As I am standing here before you, it must be, for I am real, and I speak truly. I have indeed lived ten of your centuries, though time exists differently for humans than for my race. When I am alone, months pass so swiftly I hardly notice. It is when I interact with humans I most feel the passage of time, your presence slowing the *now* of my perception."

Confusion swept the companions' faces, and Windshine smiled again. "I suggest you contemplate it another time," she advised them. "The ferry awaits, and though I cannot interfere in your quest, I do wonder if you want to miss it here in conversation about relativity."

Jae Jin laughed, and his two brothers joined him.

"Though you cannot interfere, we respect and will take your suggestion." He looked to Ha Jun. "The introductions have been made, and it is time we set off."

The Jang brothers turned back toward the ports. Ha Jun looked at Windshine, and—in Elvish—said, "Thank you for your patience and kindness."

Windshine reached over and touched his arm.

The brush of her flesh against his made the world temporarily cease to exist around Ha Jun. Sounds and sights faded away into nothingness, and all he saw was this foreign woman, this Dark Elf, a creation more wonderful than he felt he could bear without bursting.

30. PRISON

N am-Gi had thought he would die the first night.

He had been wrong. Instead, his body gave birth to new torments, each moment bringing fresh suffering.

Days had passed since he was tossed into the wagon, spat upon by the yangban, and imprisoned in Busan Prison, the long, dark red building at the edge of the city. He lived in a narrow cell of four damp brick walls and slept on a thin mat that created no buffer between himself and the packed floor. Jagged nails of pain afflicted his twisted back, leaving Nam-Gi sobbing throughout the day. The intense humidity of the cell absorbed his tears and sweat, making the air even heavier, the temperature hotter.

The jailers allowed Gu In-Hye to visit once. She swept into the cell and hugged him, though he was filthy and knew he smelled from lack of regular bathing. His little sisters hadn't come with her, nor his father, whom Nam-Gi was terrified to see.

"Do they feed you every day?" she asked, staring into his eyes with such motherly love Nam-Gi's heart felt as if it'd been stabbed.

"Yes," he said, which wasn't exactly a lie. They gave him seaweed soup and rice, and occasionally a piece of dried fish. His constant hunger had become a part of his punishment.

"They wouldn't allow me to bring you anything except this." She reached into her hanbok and retrieved a two-week supply of his medicine in a tiny vial. Nam-Gi wanted to snatch it from her hands, so desperate was he to take some of it now to ease his suffering. Yet he would not worry his mother more, so struggled against the urge and simply stared at it.

"It's all I could afford," his mother continued, her voice breaking.

Nam-Gi tore his eyes away from the vial to look at his mother again. "The restaurant? There are fewer guests now?"

His mother avoided his gaze and held out the vial to him. "Take it," she said, but Nam-Gi did not reach for the medicine.

"The restaurant, eo-ma," he insisted. "Are there guests still?"

When she attempted to force the medicine into his grasp, and again Nam-Gi refused, she met his eyes briefly, before averting hers again.

"It's been shuttered," Gu In-Hye finally admitted in a strained whisper. "The yangban came back the day after they took you away. We have nothing left."

"What will you all do now?" he asked her, but she had no answer, lowering her head so that her hair fell over her thin face.

The jailer came to tell his mother she must leave. For a final time, she thrust the medicine into his hands, limp now as he absorbed the news of his family's misfortune. "I will bring you a substitute," she promised him.

"How will you all survive?" he asked as she stepped out of the cell at the prodding of the jailer. She could not answer, and finally, when the jailer's impatience manifested as a prod from his halberd, she left her son and followed the scowling man down the dim hall.

The guards would give him no promise as to when his mother would be given permission to return. As tears ran down Nam-Gi's face, he despaired they might never allow her to visit him again for the remainder of his prison sentence, an added punishment for his crimes.

Nam-Gi tried to take less than his usual dose so he could stretch the medicine as long as possible. The terrible effects of his jailed existence quickly forced him to swallow a regular amount, however, then double to soothe the never-ending affliction. When he saw how quickly the medicine was running out, he tried again to sip it only sparingly, hoping to just take the edge off his pain for as long as he could.

A government advocate came one day and told him his trial was scheduled to be held in several weeks. The yangban were busy tracking down and interviewing patrons who had visited the restaurant. These people would testify against him—their accounts sure to seal his fate. The yangban were extremely interested in talking to the regulars, those whom Nam-Gi had been manipulating for years and who had trusted him most.

As he was informed of this news, Nam-Gi thought of his father, who would be ruined. Their family's name would be associated with deception, and all of the city would learn they had been cheating their customers. Though only Nam-Gi was responsible, the people of Busan would assume the lies had been going on longer. They might even believe his grandfather, who had been famous for the quality of his food around the ports in his day, had used the same trickery.

These thoughts created a new type of torment. As he sat in the cell in his bubble of misery, he often thought his life would end there, in the terrible heat and suffocating humidity, his body plagued by pain, his mind wracked by guilt.

Yet his life didn't end, and he continued to exist despite it all. Nam-Gi had fought all his life for everything he'd ever gained. Even now, the desire to be more, to overcome his challenges, wouldn't allow him to die. His jeong-shin burned within him even as he wished it would grow cold. Each new day he opened his eyes to a fresh morning, disappointed he had not slipped into the eternal darkness of death while he slept.

One night, as Nam-Gi leaned his throbbing back against the brick walls, the persistent needles knifing through his twisted bones, the shadows near the door began to swirl. Even when awake, he had been drifting in and out of consciousness so he only stared dully at the phenomenon, sure his mind was playing tricks on him. Often these days, his dreams seemed as substantial as reality.

The shadows rotated slowly in concentric circles, giving Nam-Gi a sense of vertigo. He blinked to steady himself, and their speed increased, startling him. Awareness dawned over him that something fantastic was happening. The fact he had no control over the occurrence frightened him. He wanted to move as far away from it as he could, but in his cell, where would he go? He was trapped with whatever was happening before his eyes, at the mercy of yet another affliction about to be thrust upon him.

The twirling shadows suddenly fell in upon themselves, giving Nam-Gi the sense he would tip over and fall into the manifesting vortex. A constellation of multi-colored lights popped into existence within the darkness

This was too much for Nam-Gi. He pushed back against the wall with a low gasp of terror. The needles in his spine seared him at the unexpected pressure he was forcing upon himself. The shadows rent themselves apart, and from their interior, Daesh Seon-saeng-nim stepped forward.

Nam-Gi, crushing himself against the wall now, breath coming out in sharp gasps, realized this must all be a fevered dream. His teacher couldn't truly be in this cell, standing opposite him and regarding him with those blue-brown eyes, a bemused expression on his face.

"What I admire most about you, Nam-Gi," Daesh said, breaking the deep silence between them, "what has always drawn me to you, was your ability to endure the fate life has dealt you no matter how terrible it was."

Daesh stepped forward and crouched down next to Nam-Gi, who could only stare as he tried to collect his scattered thoughts.

Finally, Nam-Gi managed a simple question. "Seon-saeng-nim—are you really here?"

Daesh smiled. "This is not an illusion," he said. "I am really here."

Daesh reached inside his robe and revealed a vial of golden liquid. "Take this and drink. It will restore some of your strength and ease your pain."

Without hesitation, Nam-Gi took it, uncorked it, and placed the vial to his lips. He tilted his head back and swallowed the liquid. Fire rushed down his throat and spread out from his chest to his arms and legs. Wherever the heat touched, the pain melted away. Nam-Gi had eaten very little since he was put in the cell, but the weakness from his constant hunger dissipated, and he was filled with strength. His thoughts, dulled by the overbearing and ever-present heat, sharpened. Spells that had been impossible to recall to his addled mind sprang into his head once more.

"It is incredible!" Nam-Gi breathed out. "How is this possible?"

Daesh's smile dwindled. "It's a vitality potion, but it is made with Elvish physiology in mind. Giving it to humans carries grave consequences." He gazed into Nam-Gi's eyes. "Everything has a cost, and the price you pay for drinking this is immense. Months will be lost from your life each time you consume the potion. It'll eat away at your internal organs even as it gives you incredible mental prowess. The small amount I just gave you has already caused irreparable damage that will manifest itself physically years from now."

Daesh reached into his robes and took out a small jade box. He opened the lid and revealed a dozen more vials of the same golden liquid. "These I brought for you, though it must be you who decides to take them. It is only through consuming these you will be able to make your dreams come true. Tomorrow, four young men will be issued a quest, and I will accompany them. You can follow us, but only if you escape this prison. Like a shadow, you can trail after us. When they reach the destination of the quest and engage the opponent that must be vanquished, you can make your appearance then and surprise the others with feats that will be sung about for generations."

Daesh held the box out to Nam-Gi. "But you can only do these things I speak of if you drink these potions, for the jeong-shin you currently possess simply isn't developed enough to work the magic you will be called upon to utilize." Daesh paused. "So, what will you do, Nam-Gi?"

Again, Nam-Gi didn't hesitate, taking the box from his teacher with both hands. "Thank you, Daesh Seon-saeng-nim."

The smile returned to Daesh's lips. "Now, let us begin."

Daesh offered his arm to Nam-Gi, whose breath caught at the prospect of touching his teacher. Seldom had any part of him rested upon any part of the Dark Elf. Now he had to lean upon Daesh to support himself. The slender body beneath his teacher's robes felt strong, and healthy, probably much unlike his own crooked and sickly form.

Daesh directed his attention to the shadows by the door.

"You must learn to push aside the veil of this reality and step into the neighboring one."

Nam-Gi watched in fascination as the darkness began to swirl once more. This time, he closely observed the cyclone of shadows and flickering lights. The more he studied the display, the clearer a pattern started to take shape. He concentrated harder upon it to bring greater clarity to the phenomenon. This, however, had an opposite effect from the one he desired, for the more he focused, the more complicated the pattern became, causing him to lose the thread.

Nam-Gi calmed his mind, easing back his focused attention. He watched the pattern out of the corner of his mind's eye, and it became clear enough he could make sense of it.

"Delve into your jeong-shin," his teacher said. "Reach out to the event, but do not cling, for if you do, you won't be able to grasp the puzzle of the veil. What you are attempting to deal with is beyond human comprehension. Even for Dark Elves with long lives, this discipline pushes the limits of understanding. The invigorating potion has amplified your abilities, but it is not brute force you need now, but a gentle touch. You must brush against the veil, with awe and humility."

Daesh spoke of the separation of realities as if it was alive. Nam-Gi tried to heed his advice and do as his teacher instructed. Steadying himself, he reached out with both hands and bowed. The swirling shadows and light remained in the periphery of his vision. The pattern resolved itself more the less he directly studied it. Straightening, he leaned forward and touched the myriad lights and shadows with the tips of his fingers. The colors danced up into his palms and brought wisps of darkness along with them. The veil felt almost insubstantial, but when Nam-Gi tried to ease it apart, it was like pushing against the side of a mountain.

"The veil cannot be torn asunder," Daesh said, his voice quiet and full of amusement. "Existence requires order, which the separation ensures. You can only shift the veil a little, opening up tiny cracks for brief moments of time so you can pass through it. Always remember, Nam-Gi, that in comparison to what you are dealing with, you are only a grain of sand in the wide desert, and just as insignificant.

"However," Daesh added, "even a single particle, when wielded properly, holds fathomless power."

Nam-Gi did not fully understand, but relaxed his body as instructed. In his mind, and in full humility of the awesomeness he was attempting to connect with, he sent a plea, a wish to be allowed to pass into whatever awaited him on the other side. Teasing apart his hands, he glimpsed, out of the corner of his eyes, the veil parting to reveal a reality adjacent to the prison cell.

"Excellent," his teacher said, pleased. "Now, step through."

With his teacher supporting him, Nam-Gi left the reality he'd known all of his life and entered another existing right alongside that he'd never been aware of. Terror of the unknown washed over him, but even that was dwarfed by a truth revealed to him. Nam-Gi stepped away from Daesh and straightened his back. In this reality, he stood tall. The pain that had plagued him since birth became nothing but a dream that belonged to a Nam-Gi in another time, in a different place.

In this reality, he was completely healed.

"It is true." His teacher stood beside Nam-Gi and gazed at him with blue-brown eyes. Daesh's appearance had changed, too. He appeared more regal, and more alien. The velvet color of his flesh seemed to flow about him, alive and rippling. His hair pulsed, a continuous wave washing up from his scalp and cascading down his back.

"Pay careful attention to the details of this reality," Daesh warned him. "You must remain ever vigilant, for like every other pocket of existence, there is danger here. Strange beings with unknown motivations prowl this realm, and if the desire takes them, they will devour you in an instant."

31. WINDSHINE

The Jeju governing officials reserved the same ferry company every time to take questing groups to the mainland. Windshine, walking behind the three Jang brothers and next to Ha Jun, kept her gaze unfocused as they ascended the gangway to the ship. She knew the crew would be looking down at her, their gazes darkened with hatred. She knew the captain, who had tried to assassinate her, would be on deck, his wide-brimmed hat flopping in the sea breeze. She'd seen him wearing a silk glove over his damaged hand. Ha Jun had crushed the thin bones of the captain's fingers when the young warrior had stopped the captain's attack on her. This had left the man permanently crippled and had certainly deepened his hatred of the Dark Elf.

Windshine didn't know if word of the murder plot had ever made it past the ferry, but she suspected it had. She hadn't told Ha Jun that Woo Jin had also tried to kill her. She had had a brief vision of the young archer in the afterlife before Ji Su had pulled her soul back to her body. Windshine had garnered many enemies in Jeju during her centuries living on the island, the animosity directed at her stretching back generations. Each time she went on one of these quests, she exposed herself to fresh threats of violence. The only real danger, however, was if she were to actually harm a human, an action she had refrained from doing even at risk to her own life.

The four companions and Windshine went down the ladder into the familiar cargo hold. They settled on crates stacked along the hull and against the walls. The Jang brothers set their instruments at their feet, and Ha Jun leaned his fire lance and glyph sword against the wooden boxes. He sat down beside Windshine. This time, she didn't force away the small smile that curved her lips.

"Have you already eaten?" he asked her politely.

Windshine nodded, knowing from human culture that the question was meant to start a conversation. "I haven't been to Incheon in several years," she said.

"I have never been that far north, actually," Ha Jun admitted. "Do you think this quest will be an easy one?"

His question brought to mind the dozens of young men Windshine had journeyed with over the centuries. So many of them had died. The truth was that there were no easy quests where fragile male bodies were concerned.

"I think you are strong," she said to Ha Jun, "and that you will survive."

"But will I win?"

The question was like a blow to her stomach. Windshine inhaled deeply as memories of her younger sister, Blythe, flooded her.

"I'm sorry." Ha Jun laid a hand on her arm. "I didn't mean to hurt you."

Windshine met Ha Jun's gaze. A flush crept up his face, but he didn't look away, and he didn't remove his hand. The powerful sphere of energy made up of violence and rage burned brightly inside of him still. When she saw it the very first time not so long ago, she had been reminded of the Dark Elves of her homeland. This is what had initially drawn her to him, and continued to do so each time she was in his presence. Her attraction to the human male was stronger now than it had been when she'd run the tips of her fingers over his bicep as he dashed by her to his first quest ceremony.

Confusing emotions stirred within Windshine. She knew she should look away, but Ha Jun gave her a sense of completeness she missed while living in South Hanguk, on Jeju, in isolation. The only other Dark Elf on the island she rarely saw, for the Emperor did not like the foreigners communicating with each other. This left only Ha Jun, this mortal human, this foreigner, who created nostalgia for her own war-torn country.

Though that vibrating ball of rage reminded Windshine of the people of her country, it was the capacity for gentleness Ha Jun still possessed, the ability to reach out past his race and culture in an attempt to form a connection with her—a rarity in South Hanguk—that reminded Windshine of her father, Denevius.

Denevius had wanted to cast aside the cycle of revenge the Dark Elves had been engaged in during their forever war. His responsibility to their clan was too important, however, and he could not simply abandon his responsibilities to his people, leaving them weakened and vulnerable to slaughter and enslavement by the other clans. Denevius had, instead, sent away his two daughters, Windshine and Blythe, in the company of twenty-three other Dark Elves seeking peace. Across the seas they sailed until they finally landed in the country of South Hanguk. After centuries alone and lonely in the world of humans, Windshine finally met Ha Jun.

Staring at him now, sitting so close to her, his hand still touching her arm, Windshine reminded herself he was only eighteen, while she was over a thousand years old. Worse still, he would only live another fifty or so years, whereas Windshine could see several thousand more. It was their long lives that made peace in her home country impossible, for the tens of centuries elves walked the earth ensured they did not forget past injustices, and so they did not forgive.

Windshine shrugged off Ha Jun's apology. He had killed her sister, Blythe, who had been trying to destroy the people of South Hanguk. His actions had been justified, though the pain of Blythe's death was like a missing limb to her, a piece of herself forever lost.

"Blythe is gone now," she told, bottling her immense grief so it did not spill out onto her face. "There is no bringing her back. Her actions were evil, and someone had to stop it."

She laid her hand over his, her black fingers touching his pale skin. "You humans set out on these quests in the hopes of gaining what we Elves already have. A longer life, but not in your physical form, which is impossible. You want to make names for yourselves, you want future generations to remember your legacy. In this way, you will still live, and have influence in a world in which you no longer exist.

"I have been recording the adventures of quest males in South Hanguk for 400 years. Those who prevail through multiple journeys are truly the best your race have to offer. But, Ha Jun, never question whether or not you were victorious in your earlier quests, for it is not only strength and power that is gained at each end. It is also something here," she touched his chest, "something that can only grow after enduring great hardships. Pain is its soil, sorrow its sun, wisdom its rain. When I look at you, I see it in your face, as I saw it in others I have traveled with and recorded. You are close to becoming a hero."

The slapping of the waves against the hull, and the creaking of crates swaying in the ropes tying them down, reminded Windshine that others sat in the hull with them. The

Jang brothers, who were politely trying to give the two of them their space, spoke quietly among themselves.

Ha Jun had that effect on her. There were moments like this with him when the rest of the world ceased to exist, and all of her thoughts flowed around him, the center of the maelstrom that was her conflicting emotions.

"I do not know if this quest will be easy or not," she said, finally answering his other question. She moved away from him, and immediately missed the warmth of his body and the musky smell of his hanbok. "But in my experience, life is full of surprises, and death is a frequent guest to humans."

32. TOWERS

The pleasure of a healed body was short-lived as Nam-Gi became aware of the landscape around him. An opaque sky of shifting shades of gray occupied the wide horizon. The flat ground had sudden drops that fell into a hazy distance. Tall angular shapes towered like trees; flashing lights emitted from their smooth surfaces.

These sights overwhelmed Nam-Gi, but what distressed him most were the objects that moved. Of different sizes and with a variety of sharp angles, they glided noiselessly on all sides high above him.

Daesh Seon-saeng-nim, standing by his side, said, "You must maintain a connection with your reality, or you will become lost in here."

Nam-Gi looked to his right and left. He saw nothing of South Hanguk.

"On the periphery of your vision, you will be able to see your homeland. Relax your mind. Do not focus too hard, and you will glimpse your world again."

If he had not drunk the potion, Nam-Gi wondered if he would have been able to maintain control in this realm.

Calming his thoughts, he expanded his awareness to the edges of his perception and made out the faint details of the cell in Busan Prison. He still stood inside of it, he realized with a start.

"Start walking forward if you want to leave this room," Daesh instructed him.

Using the same technique he had employed in order to lift the veil, Nam-Gi looked without seeing, and hesitantly stepped toward the door. He reached out to push the thick frame open, and his hand passed through the wooden surface.

Was what was physical in one world immaterial in the other?

Nam-Gi walked through the door and continued down the hall. He listened closely, sure he would soon hear the footsteps of jailers rushing in to stop him from escaping. Moments passed, and when he heard nothing in either reality, he asked Daesh, "Does sound exist here?"

Daesh smiled. "You speak now," he said, "and so sound exists. But always know that what your senses interpret in this reality, and what actually *exists* in this reality, are not the same. You do not belong here, Nam-Gi, and your mind will not be able to bring into focus the true existence of this place. With more practice, perhaps you will truly see what is here, but there will always be limits to what you will be able to learn. Your life-span as a human is simply too short. Seventy years is but a blink of time. Seven hundred years, crossing continually over into this realm, and you might begin to perceive where you really stand when you step into this world."

They passed out of Busan prison, and Daesh took the lead. Nam-Gi walked beside him, keeping his vision focused between both realities so he would not miss a thing. A feeling of being watched slowly crept over him. Nam-Gi glanced around. The gliding shapes continued to pass overhead, the patterns along their surfaces blinking in a myriad of hues he could not make sense of.

The sensation of being observed grew stronger, and Nam-Gi asked in a furtive whisper, "Those things moving through the sky. Are they alive?"

Daesh laughed. "As life is known in this reality, yes."

"Do they know I am here?"

"The ones that have noticed you, yes."

Nam-Gi felt reluctant to ask the next question, but if he were to visit this place again, he knew it would be better to know now. "Can they hurt me?"

"Think of it this way," Daesh replied, "in the land of South Hanguk, there are many creatures. If you chance upon a dragon, you probably know your life would soon be over. Dragons see humans as prey, so when they see a human, they are likely to roast them alive with their fire before consuming the cooked meat from their bones. But if you were walking through the countryside and came upon a herd of cattle, you would feel safe. They may look at you curiously, but they mean you no harm, for they do not eat meat. In fact, you are more a threat to a cow than a cow is a threat to you. It is the same here, Nam-Gi. Some of what exists in this reality, if they pay attention to you, will simply be curious as to what you are. Others, however, will see you as prey. If the desire takes them, they may very well swallow you whole."

Nam-Gi considered this for several moments. "So, they can hurt me," he said, watching the moving shapes gliding along, "but can I also defend myself?"

Daesh turned to Nam-Gi. "Of course," he replied. "If you have the courage to stand in the face of the unknown and maintain your composure, you may be able to elude that which would harm you."

Nam-Gi recognized the path they took now. They were nearing the office of the governor of Busan.

Daesh stopped walking. "We have arrived back at the school. We must leave this reality and enter South Hanguk again. Part the veil," he commanded Nam-Gi.

"How?"

"The same way you did before."

Daesh stepped back. The school Nam-Gi had been studying at for years stood before him, the alleys stretching away behind him. Without gazing directly at any one aspect of his home reality, Nam-Gi sought a rift similar to that he had seen before, in Busan prison. He noticed a ripple in space and approached it. Whereas the veil into this dimension had looked like shadows and flickering lights, the veil leading back to South Hanguk had a completely different appearance. It carried an odor of the life he'd always known. Someone, somewhere, was frying meats with spicy *gochu* paste. The sharp fishy smell of the nearby sea drifted on a breeze blowing in from the ports.

The veil back to his reality also contained sounds: wagons rumbling over paths leading back and forth from the docked boats; the piercing cries of birds greeting the rising sun; human voices resonating through the city as people started a new day.

When Nam-Gi reached out and touched the rift, he felt as if he was sticking his hand into thick honey that coated his fingers and slid up his wrist to his arm. For a brief moment, he wondered if that which existed in this reality could also part the veil and enter South Hanguk? How would they perceive these everyday human sights, sounds, and sensations?

He didn't have time to ponder, however. Slowly, Nam-Gi parted the veil, and his teacher stepped forward. Side by side, they left the strange reality and entered the familiar one. Immediately, he felt his twisted spine again. The potion Daesh had given him still coursed through his veins, but the torment from being in Busan prison, and the usual pain his crippled body delivered unto him, hovered on the borders of his senses. Any moment, he knew, they would close in upon him, gripping tightly and making him suffer.

"The young men who have been chosen for the quest will arrive at the Busan Governor's Office later today," Daesh said as he opened the wooden door to his school. "I will write the ingredients to the potion in a scroll and teach you how to properly mix it over the next several days as we journey."

Daesh motioned for him to step inside, but Nam-Gi leaned against the wall instead. If he tried to move now without his cane, he would probably fall. His legs were too unsteady without the familiar support of his walking stick.

Understanding dawned on his teacher's face. Once more, Daesh offered Nam-Gi his arm. "We will have to find a substitute device for you. There is much you have to do and very little time to do it."

Nam-Gi didn't understand what his teacher meant by that as they entered the school, but before he could ask, Daesh continued.

"When you have learned how to make the potion for yourself, you must remember that every time you take it, you shorten your lifespan. You will not notice the damage being done to your health initially, but the potion will be attacking your internal organs. Each time you consume it, a toxin is building inside of you. Your body will gradually start to fail you. Your kidneys, your liver, your stomach, your heart. There is no cure for the poison you will ingest, Nam-Gi, so it is a decision you will have to make with each dose you consume."

They stopped before a shelf of scrolls. Daesh took one down and unfurled it. He paused and looked at Nam-Gi with his blue-brown eyes.

"You will not be able to enter the other dimension unless

you take the potion," Daesh said. "But when you do, you will be free to move in a way you cannot with your current physical limitations. Greatness, you will achieve, but the price will be illness, and a death that will come sooner. You will not live to see old age."

The words, spoken so bluntly, struck Nam-Gi with feeble blows. If he could get what he wanted—if he could make his dreams come true and become a hero—he would trade his far future for a better present.

Daesh wrote the ingredients in Elvish. "We will not have much time, but when I can be alone, I will come to you and give you further instructions on combining the ingredients properly to create the potion. You will have to follow us as we travel from Busan."

The question that had been bothering Nam-Gi now came to his lips. "Where are we going?"

Daesh paused and turned to Nam-Gi. "To Incheon. You must follow the chosen four, slipping in and out of this reality to the other reality using the potions I have already given you."

Nam-Gi could not stop the smile that spread across his face. After wishing for so long, he was finally going to be able to do it. He was going on a quest. He was going to become a hero.

33. EMERALD AND JADE

Until Daesh landed on the shores of South Hanguk, he had never met a crippled person. Dark Elves were all born healthy. Their magic and advanced medical skills ensured that pregnancies and births were easy. Even illness was foreign to their race.

Here in the world of humans, however, sickness plagued their bodies, creating a host of negative effects that robbed men and women of their vitality and strength. Sometimes, like Nam-Gi, disease left them misshapen and weak throughout their brief lifespans.

Though Dark Elves did have to contend with injuries received during battle, even these were usually not permanent. Their healing magics could regrow limbs and close gaping wounds. Each clan had members that specialized in the healing arts. Anything their powers could not mend meant the person had died during the conflict in question. If one of his kind made it off the battlefield, then they could be made whole again. This too, however, only fueled the forever war amongst themselves.

Daesh had seen only a few corpses in his homeland. He was

still relatively young for a Dark Elf when he finally sailed away. Outright slaughter had not been the preferred method of warfare. Instead, the clans of Dark Elves preferred to enslave each other, using their captives to generate greater magics against their enemies. This led to the tides of power continuously ebbing and flowing, with dominance shifting from one clan to another for thousands of years. It was also why the separate clans of the Dark Elves finally realized that, if they were ever going to escape the endless cycle of war, they would have to engage in genocide. One clan would have to kill off all the other clans until only they remained. Differences could not be allowed to exist in the country of Dark Elves.

As this solution took root and the number of dead started to rise exponentially, several families in a loose federation of clans formed to protect themselves decided to send twenty-five of their children across the sea to foreign lands. They chose those who were believed to have the potential to be the best and brightest of their race, for the clan members who were currently the most powerful could not afford to be sent, as they were needed to protect all those who remained.

And so, centuries ago, Daesh and twenty-four others had boarded a boat and set sail to find a new home. Eventually, they landed in the country of South Hanguk.

None of them had ever seen humans before, though they had studied them, and had learned some of their ways and cultures. Before they sailed from home, their elders had warned them that Dark Elves were significantly more powerful than humans, so when the refugees first stood before the Emperor of South Hanguk, they used their simplest spells and offered their services to the kingdom if they would be allowed to settle there. It was only afterwards they realized that even their simplest spells overwhelmed humans, but by then, it was too late.

That long dead Emperor and his advisers had decided the

Dark Elves were too powerful to send to a neighboring country's land, and too dangerous to remain as a single group in South Hanguk. The court officials divided the twenty-five Dark Elves, separated them so that only two were allowed to exist in each province. Even then, the Dark Elves were forced to promise they would not communicate with their counterparts. Men were placed with men, and women with women so they could not sire children. As a result, the Dark Elves lived a lonesome and lonely existence in South Hanguk.

This is why Daesh felt as he did for Nam-Gi. Daesh had taught many humans over the hundreds of years he'd lived in Busan. Only a handful had he ever formed a genuine connection with, and it never lasted long, for human lives were absurdly short. Even the lucky few who lived to an age considered old for humans only saw seventy or eighty years. Most died before then, either from conflict, misfortune, or illness.

As Daesh had taught Nam-Gi over the past seven years, he found himself increasingly attracted to the youth. The boy, crippled and walking with great difficulty, didn't seem to understand the concept of giving up. Life had dealt him a terrible disease, one of the worse Daesh had ever seen in mortals, but still, Nam-Gi strove to show the world what he was capable of. He wanted to prove his worth, he wanted to go on a quest even though his disabilities prevented him from traveling far easily. Nam-Gi wanted to be known as a hero, and gain life beyond his physical form in the minds of future generations.

Daesh thought about all of these things as he wrote down the ingredients to the deadly vitality spell. He wished there was another way to help the disabled human, but he knew there wasn't. The potions would eventually kill Nam-Gi, and Daesh suspected the death would be most painful, as tumors blossomed to consume the human mage's body. Yet even now, despite the warning Daesh had given him twice, Nam-Gi still wanted to take the potions. He would not be denied what nature had tried to take away from him; the ability to travel far and wide on two good legs with a straight back that did not continuously torture him.

When Daesh finished writing the potion recipe, he showed the Elvish script to Nam-Gi. "I'll go over the words with you later to confirm you understand what's needed, and in what exact proportions. You already know all of the Elvish phrases, but it's essential you do not add or subtract even the smallest item from the list. The mixture must be perfect if it is to have the desired effect." He held the scroll out to his pupil, who took it with both hands. The action made Nam-Gi lose balance, and Daesh watched him catch himself against the wall of shelves.

"You need a new walking stick."

Daesh went into a side room, his private chamber. He had no cane available, never having had the need for one himself. During the long periods of solitude, however, he had been practicing to create magical items, a skill that still eluded him. One of the twenty-five Dark Elves who had arrived with him in South Hanguk had shown great potential in crafting magical items, but Daesh had never risked trying to contact her to ask for advice.

On his own, he had tried to add glyphs to clothing, rings, necklaces, and weapons. All of the items disintegrated under the force of the magic when he tried activating them. Looking around the room now, he reached for a staff leaning against the wall he had been planning to practice on but had not yet attempted to enchant. It was as tall as he was and made of black volcanic rock and jade. At its top, an emerald bird of prey was poised to leap into the sky, its wings spread, its sharp beak pointed toward the heavens.

Daesh went back to Nam-Gi, whose mouth dropped open in astonishment upon seeing the staff.

"Daesh Seon-saeng-nim," he gasped. "It is incredible!"

Daesh held it out to Nam-Gi, who seemed afraid to touch it. Finally, the boy took it in his right hand, and leaned upon it for support, his eyes roving up and down the jade and emerald.

"As with everything else, there is a price to pay," Daesh said. "When you are around others, you must cast an illusion upon the staff. It is worth a fortune here in South Hanguk, and men will kill you for it. Make no mistake about this."

He paused and studied Nam-Gi's reaction. "Do you still want it despite the risk?"

"Yes," Nam-Gi said without hesitation.

Daesh nodded, a fierce pride welling up inside of him toward this fearless human. "The morning grows late, and soon I will have to go to the quest ceremony. We should eat now."

Food was delivered to Daesh several times a week. He went to the back of the school and saw a crate had been left for him against the wall outside. He brought it in and unpacked dried fish, salted strips of pork, kimchi, rice, and eggs. The vegetables and fruit would have been recently picked and delivered to him fresh, as Daesh couldn't go out to the market for produce. Humans didn't trust the Dark Elves, yet Daesh still lived a lifestyle far above many of the poor and hungry of the country. Money, truly, was not a concern of his.

He brought the food inside and lit a small fire in the hearth of the kitchen to prepare the rice and tea. He always ate alone, but the governor of Busan made sure he would never be hungry, and there was more than enough to share with Nam-Gi—especially as he was about to depart on a quest. Daesh waved off any attempt by the boy to help prepare the meal and set out dishes and cups himself. Soon they sat across from each other on mats on the floor, the food set upon a squat wooden table between them. They did not speak while they ate, Daesh being unused to company, and

Nam-Gi seeming too awed by the events of the day to make conversation.

When they finished, Daesh cleared the table and told Nam-Gi, "Take out the scroll and let me instruct you on the exact mixture of its contents."

Only after he was sure Nam-Gi understood the proper way to mix the components for making the potion did he end the brief lesson, satisfied.

"Your Elvish is coming along nicely," Daesh told Nam-Gi, who beamed at the compliment. "I have one last gift to give you." Daesh went back into his private room and returned with a gold and silver cape with a hood. "The material is light and made by my hands. You will still feel the heat and humidity of this time of year, but the fabric will not add to it."

Daesh draped the cape around Nam-Gi's shoulders and tied the dangling cord around his neck. Pulling the hood over the youth's head, he stepped back and looked over the outfit with a critical eye. "You are a fugitive from Busan Prison now, Nam-Gi," he said. "One day—after you have shown your worth in quests—you may be able to reveal your identity to the people of South Hanguk. The path you take now is exceedingly difficult. You will have to follow questing groups, from the periphery, coming forward to show your power as a stranger to all. In time, the people will hear rumors of your existence and your incredible abilities. That will hopefully persuade the governor of Busan to show leniency when you finally allow your identity to be known."

Daesh gazed at his student. "When the time is appropriate, I will use my influence with the governor to ask for your pardon. This cannot be done now, but do not despair, Nam-Gi. Though the hurdle is high, if you remain steadfast, if you do not give up, you *will* become a hero. No matter what happens, never lose faith in yourself, and you will eventually triumph over everything that stands in your way."

Daesh knew that, when the time came, he would lend all the support he could so that these would be more than just encouraging words he shared with his student today. He would make a difference in the lifespan of this crippled human. Nam-Gi would rise up, and he would be great.

One day, Kim Nam-Gi would be remembered by the people of South Hanguk. He would gain the title of *Hero*.

34. THE CLAY BOWL

When the crescent moon shone bright among the endless stars dominating the night sky above the mountains of Majeon, the Orsieg stirred. It rarely slept, hardly needing it. Often, though, it curled up so the meat would not be able to see it. In that way, it maintained an advantage over them when they tried to move unnoticed through the trees.

Unfurling itself from a fetal position, it straightened its muscular form until it stood taller than the tallest trees of the forests. Its stomach rumbled, breaking the silence like thunder and signaling the beginning of the night's hunt.

The Orsieg gazed out from the mountainside and saw the sea in the far distance. The place where it had first been brought ashore on the fishermen's boat was to its south. The Orsieg turned its gaze north, however, deciding it would search the meat herds there tonight. Returning to the same source made the hunt more difficult, for the meat had set up sentries.

Sometimes, the prey displayed actions that almost made them seem intelligent, but the Orsieg knew their evasions were no different than a school of fish evading the shark. The sea life the Orsieg had sometimes fed upon in the waters surrounding the crag had also tried to avoid its grasp. Prey sought to escape the predator, from the lowly ant to the biggest animals roaming the land on two and four legs. In the end, all that lived had to feed to survive, and the Orsieg was no different.

It reached its long arm into the cave behind it and brought out a wide bowl fashioned from the clay of the earth. The strong odor of rotting blood congealing inside the bowl wafted up to its nose. The Orsieg waved away buzzing flies that hovered on the surface of the thick red liquid.

The bowl fitting comfortably in both its hands, the Orsieg raised the clay vessel to its lips and took long, noisy slurps, the limbs of meat mixed in the blood stew sliding down its wide throat. When it had drunk the last swallow, it wiped its mouth with the back of its hand and returned the bowl to the cave.

Now the Orsieg had a little more strength for the night's hunt, the grumbling of its stomach dwindling to a low but persistent rumble. It had realized from the beginning most of the herd along the coast was too thin. Their meat was scrawny, their skin wrapped tight around their bones. Those that had fought back in the beginning had been plump, but it made a meal out of almost all of them when they followed it into the forest in the first days of its arrival. They had taken to staying close to the brick shells the meat lived in now, rarely straying far from their herd.

The Orsieg climbed to the top of the mountain and looked out upon the rest of this land spread out as far as the eye could see. When it had eaten everything living along the coast, it would have to travel to find new sources of meat. The Orsieg didn't know if it would be easier or more difficult, but it realized that it should be as big and strong as possible before it went forward into the unknown in search of sustenance.

It picked up the net made from rope it had salvaged one night on the coast. Throwing it over its shoulder, it started down the mountainside. It moved silently, but its presence still disturbed the roosting birds that took flight as the branches shook from its passage. Small animals scurried under foot. The Orsieg continued north until it picked up the musky smell of meat on the breeze. It paused, dropping to all fours so its head could no longer be seen above the treetops. The meat had surprised it once, the Orsieg coming under a fierce onslaught from sharp projectiles that had lodged in its tough skin. Though it had chased them down, it had only managed to snatch up a couple before the rest had retreated back to their brick shells.

The Orsieg worried about its eyes, the only spot on its body it felt the meat could do it real damage. So, it crept through the forest now, going in a wide arc from its current position until it approached the humans downwind and to their right. It spied three waiting in the branches. They peered out into the darkness with wide eyes. It inhaled the spicy scent of their fear. Saliva filled its mouth in anticipation of the sharp taste of their blood filling its clay bowl. Slowly, it crawled towards them, stopping when they stirred and waiting until they settled down again.

Finally, they were within arm's reach. Quick as lightning, its hand darted out and caught all three squirming pieces of meat in its palm. Before they could make a noise, it closed its hand and slammed them into the ground. When it opened its fist, the meat's ragged breathing and deep moans floated up to its ears. Again it closed its hand and slammed them into the ground, stunning them but making sure to leave the meat alive. Now their arms and legs were twisted at odd angles, but they made no other noise. After checking to see that their chests still rose and fell, it stuck them into the net and slung them over its shoulder.

Ducking back down under the cover of trees, the Orsieg

continued along, crawling through the trees looking for more sentries. It moved cautiously again and saw nothing until it finally reached the outskirts of the brick shells. It had been easier when the Orsieg had first started feeding upon this herd of meat. That's when they still slept in the shells close to the forest so that all it had to do was creep forward, smash through a wall, and grab the squirming food.

The meat had shown animal cunning once more and stayed in a large group near the coast during the night. This forced the Orsieg to have to hunt from the air. Tensing its body, it flung itself into the night sky and spread its long black wings. It cast a deep shadow over the brick shells. The meat started to scream as it flew over them. A projectile sped from the ground in its direction, which the Orsieg easily dodged. Now, it knew exactly where they were cowering. It swooped down and saw them pointing and screaming at it. The Orsieg landed, rumbling the ground, and snatched up four as the others scattered. As it had done before, it slammed them into the ground, twice, stunning them, then stuffed them into its net.

The meat were running, but a small one had fallen and lay in the mud crying. The Orsieg picked it up and popped it into its mouth. Chewing, it thought once again how much bone and little meat the smallest ones had, and hoped the herds living in the interior of the unexplored land had more fat to their bodies.

Flapping its wings, it took off from the ground, its hunt finished for the night. It would have enough to make blood stew to last several days before it would have to go out and search for more meat.

Swallowing the tiny morsel it had consumed, it returned back to the cave and its clay bowl.

35. BUSAN GOVERNOR'S OFFICE

Walking beside his teacher through the lanes of Busan, Nam-Gi was, for once, glad of his twisted back and hunched-over gait. The hood of the cape fell over his head and easily covered the features of his face. He used his jeong-shin to create a continuous mirage around the staff so it appeared old and knobbed. In this manner, he didn't have to reach directly into the minds of everyone he passed.

"You'll have to get used to the expenditure of energy," his teacher told him as they walked toward the governor's office. "The mirage will force you to expend a low level of concentration to maintain it, but over time, this continuous exertion will strengthen your jeong-shin. For now, it will leave you feeling a little more fatigued than usual, but there is nothing to be done about it if you wish to keep the staff."

For Nam-Gi, it felt like he had assumed a physical position, one that wouldn't normally be particularly difficult if only done for a few moments. But as time stretched on, the pose began to wear on him.

The streets of Busan were crowded with people going about their daily business. Store owners called to passersby, while merchants with wagons—pulled by hand or by horse—rode throughout the city with their wares. Children darted by Nam-Gi. Only the occasional small child could see his face under the deep hood. When one glanced up and caught his eye, Nam-Gi's heart lurched, pounding in his chest for fear of being recognized. How long, he wondered, before word traveled around the city that a fugitive was on the loose?

The guards standing throughout the city to keep the peace —their hats with bright-colored plumes sticking out among the crowds; their tall halberds with sharp-bladed points grasped in their hands—made Nam-Gi grip his staff tighter each time he spied them. Often he thought of fleeing into a dark alley, especially since the Dark Elf drew curious stares from the people, many of whom had never seen him since he only walked from his school to the governor's office for a quest ceremony.

"You must turn off here," Daesh told Nam-Gi when they were still a little way from the office. "Go to the east side of the gates. There you will see a cluster of trees. From that position, you will be able to observe the ceremony and hear the governor's speech. You will not be alone, as these ceremonies attract viewers not allowed on the official grounds without appointments. Do nothing to draw attention to yourself, and you should be safe."

Daesh touched Nam-Gi on the shoulder before departing. Without his teacher at his side, the attention flowed away from him to trail after the Dark Elf, which made Nam-Gi breathe a little easier. Now he did step into the alleys and went in the general direction of the governor's office. A few times he got turned around as narrow paths became dead ends. Finally, he emerged back into sunlight and saw the metal fence and gates surrounding the wide hall without walls symbolizing the transparency of Busan's government.

The four young men who would go on the journey waited

at the bottom of the stairs for the summons to come up to the governor's platform. They stood upright, their physical health a shining example to all watching the ceremony. Nam-Gi gazed at them in envy from the shadows of his hood. He recognized one of his classmates, Dae-Hwan, among the chosen few. The unfairness of it all! Nam-Gi's jeong-shin burned so much brighter than that of either of his classmates, yet here he stood, outside the gate, hidden away from the eyes of others for fear of being taken back to Busan Prison. And there Dae-Hwan stood, with three other tall young men carrying swords in sheaths tucked into their hanboks.

Nam-Gi hissed curses to himself in frustration, but when a person standing nearby inclined their head in his direction, he fell silent again.

An official beckoned to the young men. They climbed the stairs and sat down seiza-style before the governor seated in his ornate wooden chair. The governor beamed down at them. Opening his arms wide, he said, "Welcome, young warriors of Busan! On this bright day full of hope, we send you forth on a grand journey to bravely face the incredible dangers of the world. We send you forth so that you may prove your worth— to your families, to your neighbors, to your peers. You are the best Busan has to offer and, on your journey, you will perform acts that one day will be recorded to be repeated long after you are gone. For it is your destiny to become legend. It is your fate to walk among the stars, high over the ordinary deeds of ordinary people doomed to be forgotten by the ravishes of time."

The governor held out his hand, and an official brought him a scroll. Unfurling it, the governor read its contents, a broad smile curving his lips under his black mustache.

"The quest is indeed a grand one and will test the might of you four gathered here. Only the strongest can prevail over this foe, for a giant has come to the villagers along the coast of

Incheon and harasses the fishermen, their wives and children there. They have begged the neighboring provinces for help, and the cries of their woe have reached the ears of the Emperor.

"So that we can maintain military might and remain vigilant of the ever-present threat of North Hanguk's attack, the Emperor has called upon the governors to send young men to take care of this terrible curse afflicting the people of South Hanguk that he so loves. And you four are among the chosen!"

With a flourish, the governor handed the scroll back to the official, who took it with both hands and bowed low.

"Now rise, warriors of Busan, and go forth with all the vigor and vitality of youth. Journey to Incheon with courage and brave hearts, and do great deeds to be written down and recorded by our ageless chronicler of human deeds."

The governor motioned to the Dark Elf, who stepped forward and nodded to the four companions.

"Come back to us victorious," the governor said in a booming voice. "Come back to us glorious! Come back to us one step closer to being called a hero!"

The four young men rose and bowed deeply before being led back down the steps by the official carrying the scroll. The ceremonial words the governor had spoken went round and round in Nam-Gi's mind so that he felt lightheaded. *Fate. Victory. Courage. Hero.* How he wished he could have been there, kneeling before the governor having those words spoken to him.

Nam-Gi walked down the length of the fence, coming as near its opening as he dared as the young men joined their waiting families and introduced themselves. He imagined what it would have been like if he had been among them, introducing his three companions to his father, who had never believed his son would be selected to go on a quest. How proud his father would have been, standing there among the other parents as the companions told their family names.

But no. Instead, Nam-Gi had shamed his family by getting caught cheating patrons with magic. Now the restaurant his great-grandfather had built was ruined, and he didn't know what had become of his grandmother, mother, and young sisters. What were they doing as he stood there in the heat and humidity of Busan watching young men do what had been denied to him?

Nam-Gi noticed Daesh standing at a distance from the group of companions in the shadows of the trees near the governor's front gate. He remembered what his teacher had told him so long ago when he'd gone to complain about his father not allowing him to put his name forward to go on a quest. Nam-Gi burned away his gnawing disappointment with anger. Then he stoked his anger into rage.

He would come back to his parents one day and make right what he had done wrong. He would restore the name of his family, and he would rebuild the restaurant he had destroyed through his deceit and manipulations. Nam-Gi vowed to become a great man in South Hanguk.

Nothing would stop him, no matter how high the mountain he must climb with this twisted back and crippled legs.

He would become a hero.

36. INCHEON

Ha Jun and his companions landed at the port of Incheon. Morning was just dawning, the sun rising from the horizon into a cloudy sky. From the deck, they saw the piers teeming with people already busy preparing for the coming day. Birds swooped overhead, their cries echoing across the wooden boards of the docks. Waves slapped against the hulls of boats, the heavy fragrance of rain coming in from the sea and filling the morning breeze.

Only when Ha Jun was walking down the gangplank, coming at the rear of the Jang brothers and Windshine, his hand on the hilt of his sword, did he finally relax his grip. He didn't like the sailors or the first mate. He especially disliked the captain with the wide-brimmed hat. The way in which the crew stared at them with dead expressions told Ha Jun that they hated him, too. The whole trip, he had feared they would attack Windshine, and had remained vigilant, sleeping little, his sword within easy reach. He hadn't been able to share his concerns with the Jang brothers, who had commented upon the perceived hostility of the crew with deep confusion. But Ha Jun could say nothing in response because then the brothers might start asking questions. The details of the first quest he journeyed on could not be revealed. Much of that experience remained secret between himself, Windshine and the soldier, Seong Min. The public knowledge of that quest, the tales the Jang brothers would be familiar with, was quite different from the reality.

So while the Jang brothers had rested, Ha Jun watched the ladders leading down into the cargo hold. He had stiffened whenever the sound of footsteps approached them across the wooden planks of the deck. Windshine didn't seem concerned, her face stoic as they sailed across the Hanguk Strait north to Incheon. She was in no real physical danger, Ha Jun knew, for Windshine's true powers were awesome to behold.

The knowledge of the depths of her magical abilities only increased his worry. It was Windshine's incredible powers that made the situation on the ferry even more precarious. If the sailors attacked, Windshine would not try to defend herself for fear she, a foreigner, might end up hurting, or accidentally killing, one of the people of South Hanguk. This possibility of an accidental casualty was where the real risk lay for her.

While she would show restraint, Ha Jun knew the tethered ball inside of *him*—that sphere of dark emotions created during his years of training at his father's hand and secured in that inner universe where he'd stuffed it—would leak out into his consciousness. If that happened, the repressed suffering and rage he harbored would flood Ha Jun, and he would show no mercy to Windshine's attackers. To protect her, he would kill one, then another and another, until all who might harm her would be torn apart and hurled into the sea.

So he had sat on the crates during the sea voyage, tense and watchful, and could only relax now that they were in Incheon on solid ground again. The three brothers and Ha Jun gathered around a food stall selling breakfast. They bought bowls of rice porridge topped by fresh shrimp, and a pot of lentil soup they shared between themselves. When Ha Jun asked Windshine to join them, the Jang brothers made room for her so they could all sit together.

"We'll need horses," Jae Jin said. "We should start out immediately. A storm's coming, and we need to get as far as possible before the rain slows us down." He looked at Ha Jun. "We'll trust you on this again, as last time."

After they finished, Ha Jun asked the food vendor for the nearest carriage house. The first one they passed, the man refused to rent out to anyone going on a quest. "Too many of my horses don't come back," he told them with an apologetic bow, while wishing them success on their journey. "I have the highest respect for you," he said, "but I just can't afford to keep losing my strongest horses, and quest companions never want to settle for anything less."

They had to travel further to the outskirts of the city to find the next carriage house, which had wider grounds and a larger number of grazing horses. The stable master looked at their weapons, then at the Dark Elf.

"You'll have to buy them," he said, a strong breeze blowing in from the sea and tugging at the loose sleeves and pants of his hanbok. The morning was still bright, but dark clouds gathered far out over the waters and were speeding their way towards land.

"I'll buy them back if you return—at a reduced price, of course. The better the condition they're in, the more I'll give you back when next we meet."

"Have you heard anything of the terror of Majeon?" Jae Jin asked. "Have any of the villagers along the coast made it to Incheon?"

"No people, no. But there've been rumors aplenty." The man stroked his beard and gazed out at the coast the companions planned to follow north. "The forest between here and the fishing villagers is thick and wild. Even in the best of times, you have to be on continuous guard for threats. Many have entered those trees never to return. And of course, we must always be wary of tigers that steal our forms and cause havoc among humans. They've ripped apart whole families, and up until now, have been considered the worst danger in the forest."

The stable master shook his head. "But whatever it is that's preying upon the villagers along the coast has proven even more lethal than the tigers. This monster isn't letting *anyone* get in and out. It is believed to stalk the forest, snatching up anyone that tries to pass through."

The companions exchanged glances. Perhaps this quest wouldn't be as simple as they'd thought back the governor's office when they'd heard it was just a giant they had to behead.

"We'll take the horses," Jae Jin said finally. He paid the stable master the full sum asked for five horses, which nearly depleted their allotted funds.

Jae Jin thought it best to have a locally drawn map to Majeon in addition to the one given them by the governor. They were drawn a simple sketch that would take them directly to the village on well-known paths. Then they used what few coins they had left to buy dried food to bolster the supplies they already carried.

"Remember what happened in the village of Goseong," Jae Jin said. "We almost ran out of supplies and had to rely on the villagers, who had depleted all of their stores during their long siege. We should try and avoid a similar scenario at Majeon if we can."

The stable master had pointed them to the stone wall surrounding Incheon, and they exited the gate against a stream of people entering the city for the day. The trees rose up high on both sides of the wide road. The humidity increased even as a steady wind swept over them. The long column of dark clouds coming in from the sea finally made landfall, and what began as a persistent rain soon become a downpour. The ground became mud, and the horses trudged slowly forward. Bright flashes of lightning illuminated the land, and loud booms of thunder made the mares skittish.

"Should we take shelter?" Jae Ho asked Jae Jin, who shook his head.

"Don't forget, we're not the only ones going to behead the giant. If our competitors don't rest, we shouldn't, either. And if they do stop because of the weather, then we will get to the glory of the kill before they arrive."

Despite the storm raging around them, the three Jang brothers, Ha Jun, and Windshine rode forward toward the village of Majeon.

37. JOURNEY TO MAJEON

Nam-Gi watched the four Busan companions mount horses one of their fathers had prepared for them. Though no one spoke to Daesh Seon-saeng-nim, there was also one for him. His teacher stared off into the distance as the young men said their final farewells to family and friends. Nam-Gi knew it was time for him to leave also. He scanned the people still milling about after the ceremony to make sure he received no scrutiny before hobbling off to a nearby alley. He went a little ways and found a narrow aperture between two buildings set closely together. He squeezed himself between them to make sure no one would see what he did next.

Taking the jade box from an inner pocket of his hanbok, he removed a vial and uncorked it. His hand shook at the idea of working the magic by himself and, for a few moments, doubt made him stand there alone, his shoulders scraping against the brick walls. The truth of his situation was undeniable. If he was to go on this quest, then he must work this magic. After everything he'd done to get to this point, would he allow his fear of the unknown to win out over him now?

With a violent shake of his head, Nam-Gi uncorked the

vial, placed it to his lips, and swallowed. His jeong-shin flared inside of him, flowing through his body with an incredible level of energy. He turned to the shadows and focused on perceiving the veil separating the realities. When the blinking multicolored lights started to dance in the darkness, he knew he had found what he was looking for.

Extending his hand, he plunged his fingers into the veil and, without applying too much force, shifted it until a crack formed. Again, he suffered a moment of hesitation, a moment of fear, before taking a deep breath and stepping into the strange other world, this time without his master. The immediate pleasure of a healed body was short-lived as he gazed upon the tall towers; the sudden drops into further unknowns in the opaque ground; and the silently gliding shapes covered with the dancing lights. He didn't have time to stand there and let his anxiety slow him further, however. By keeping track of his own world, still visible in the periphery of his vision, Nam-Gi stepped out of the alley and walked back to the governor's office. He propped the staff on his shoulder, as here he would not need it.

The world of humans seemed to slide by on the edges of his perception, as if it was on wheels, or he was in a wagon. He reached the four questing companions just as they were riding off and followed them to the city gates. In the alternate dimension, he kept a wary eye on the passing shapes, and noticed that occasionally, as some neared him, they seemed to slow down, the lights facing him blinking faster. Daesh had warned him that what he saw was only how his mind perceived the reality he visited now. The thought of what those things hovering around him really looked like made Nam-Gi shudder. Again he found himself fighting down his panic and an overwhelming desire to exit this world back into his own.

The companions traveled all day, and Nam-Gi followed

alongside them. They rode through valleys with tall mountains on either side, the path winding through the countryside past farms. The four men talked often, preparing for the eventual encounter with the giant. They couldn't guess how big the monster would be. His classmate, Dae-Hwan, devised a plan to confuse the giant with illusions as the other three crept up on it from behind.

"If it's strong, a frontal assault would work against us," Dae-Hwan said. "But I can make it see warriors riding down upon it while you all cut it down from behind."

If there was truly only one giant, the four companions figured perhaps the quest would be easy. The biggest challenge would be reaching Majeon before other questing groups.

The sun rose high over the land, their hanboks clinging to their bodies with sweat. Nam-Gi couldn't feel the heat in the strange reality he walked. In fact, there seemed to be no temperature at all. Though he inhaled and exhaled out of habit, he was not sure it was air his body was breathing, or if he needed to breathe at all in this altered state.

The sun eventually fell behind the trees so that the moon could claim her throne in the sky. The companions decided to rest for the night and start out again early the next morning. They took out the provisions they'd brought. Sitting in a circle, they shared the food among themselves.

Nam-Gi went back down the road to a farmhouse they'd recently passed. He walked through a field of bean sprouts and stopped in front of a brick home with a thatch roof. He walked through the wall as if it wasn't there and stood in the main room. Several people sleeping close together on mats remained undisturbed by his ghostly presence.

Nam-Gi went to a smaller room and inspected their larder. Dried fish neatly wrapped, kimchi in a squat pot, and brown eggs in a bowl were sitting in a small wooden box in the corner.

Nam-Gi couldn't pick up any of it without reentering his reality. Focusing on the human world, he detected the sounds of humans snoring, the smell of stale sweat from sleeping bodies, and a slight breeze blowing through the open window. Using this as a guide, he pushed aside the veil and stepped into the reality of the farmhouse.

Gingerly, he picked up the fish, kimchi, and eggs. As quietly as he could, he hobbled around the family sleeping side by side so he could reach the door. He tried not to tap the staff too hard on the floor as he used it to support himself once again. He unclasped the heavy latch and stepped out into the night. In the dark of the rural countryside, Nam-Gi didn't want to travel far by himself. The four companions and Daesh were nearby, but he couldn't risk being seen. He also didn't want to put himself in danger of wild animals wandering the darkened landscape. Plus, now he had stepped back out into the human reality, the aches of his body assaulted him anew. His head throbbed with a steady pounding, as if a hammer was beating against metal. He ground his teeth as sharp pains stabbed into his back, making each step he took a familiar torture.

Nam-Gi decided to sit down outside the farmhouse. Leaning the staff against the rough brick wall, he gingerly lowered himself to the damp ground. He ate the dried fish, chewing the leathery skin repeatedly so that he could build up enough saliva to swallow since he had no soup to wash it down. In between strips of flesh, he added kimchi to give the meal flavor. When finished, Nam-Gi cracked the brown eggs and swallowed the yoke raw. The pangs of hunger in his stomach had subsided by the time he finished his stolen meal, but every other ache remained. He stared up into the dark night and blinked away tears of frustration.

Now that he was no longer moving, the difficulties of his current life rose up to engulf him. Only yesterday, he had been a prisoner in Busan prison. Today he was a fugitive and, though he had gotten what he wanted—a quest—it had come at a high cost. He wanted to be excited at this opportunity to show others what a cripple like him could do, but all of the problems of his new lifestyle shaded his future in darkness. Was becoming a hero worth it when he was being forced to sacrifice so much?

Nam-Gi closed his eyes and didn't reopen them again until rough hands shook him awake. His stiff body wouldn't allow him to start with surprise. He could only crack his eyes to see the horizon had paled, though the sky above him was still dark. Morning wasn't far off. Standing over him was the farmer who he had seen sleeping not so long ago. Nam-Gi heard movement inside the brick home and knew the rest of the man's family had already risen and were preparing to get ready for the day's work.

"Who are you?" the farmer asked in a surprisingly calm voice.

Nam-Gi cleared his throat and coughed. "I am just a traveler, Elder Brother. I had no food," he admitted, knowing the remnants of his stolen meal were at his side. "I am deeply ashamed to have stolen from you, and I am sorry."

The farmer stared down at him, his face gaunt. Nam-Gi noted the simple cream pants and shirt he wore, and the many times it had been mended. The man had a strong, sinewy frame, his hands calloused from years of hard work. Behind him, Nam-Gi saw several younger boys staring at him in curiosity. They wore similar-colored hanboks to their father's. Life was difficult for the farmers of South Hanguk. They worked from early morning until late afternoon taking care of their land just so that they could survive from season to season. A bad crop would be their ruin, as the farms were all they had.

"If you were hungry, we don't mind you having some of

our food," the farmer said, "though you would have had to come in while we slept." The man shook his head. "But you did us no harm, and that's something to consider."

"I will be going now, Elder Brother." Nam-Gi made to stand. The pain that swept through him made him gasp, fresh tears filling his eyes. He hauled himself to his feet, his back assuming its familiar bent-over posture, and put his weight upon the staff once more.

The farmer's eyes never left him, and he stared closely at Nam-Gi. "You can rest inside before you start your journey again. We won't come back home until sunset."

The pale sky drew Nam-Gi's attention again. He said, "May you point me to the privy, Elder Brother?"

The farmer nodded and led Nam-Gi to a narrow trench behind the house. Nam-Gi nodded his thanks, and when the man left to allow him privacy, Nam-Gi uncorked another vial, swallowed it, and stepped back into the alternate dimension. He had to make it back to the companions' camp before the quest group left. Even in this world where he moved easily, finding them again if he actually lost their position in the human world would probably be difficult, if not impossible.

Propping the staff on his shoulder, Nam-Gi quickly walked away from the farmer and his family, who were still milling around outside of their home. He went back across the field and made his way to where the companions had made camp last night.

The towers still stood around him in this strange reality, and the shapes still glided silently through the air. Near the camp, however, Nam-Gi noticed something unusual. It was hard to tell at first, as he knew so little about this reality, and had little idea what was a normal occurrence, and what was unusual. But he saw a shape with twenty-four sides hovering near the camp. Like everything else in this world, multicolored lights blinked along its geometric angles. But with this object, the lights had all gathered near a single point at the top and seemed to be projecting a shaft of light forward.

Nam-Gi slowed his approach, unsure what this manifestation meant. He noticed movement to his right and turned to see a figure. At first he couldn't make out if the person existed in this world or the human world. The figure's bright hair burned with the intensity of the sun, and his eyes were like blue orbs glowing in his face. He walked towards the camp, and Nam-Gi made out a curved bow in his hand and a sword on his waist.

"What's going on?" Nam-Gi wondered to himself, and could only stand and watch in awe to see what would happen next.

38. WARNING

The wind, blowing in an array of storm clouds across the horizon, swept back Tsierus's golden hair. He stood atop a hill and gazed down at the Dark Elf and four men rising for the morning. The poison infecting him from his last battle had been purged from the physical body he manifested in this plane. He had become strong again, and anxious at the thought of the evil twisting the minds of humans while he recuperated.

He had finally reached his third target. He wanted to kill the menace quickly, but he had no wish to put the men in harm's way in the ensuing battle between himself and the Dark Elf.

"Guardian," he called, and the disembodied Eye popped into existence above him.

"How do you think I can separate the humans from the Dark Elf?"

"I can create a distraction for you," the Eye replied. "But this will be a dangerous elimination, Tsierus. Before, you had the element of surprise, and the extermination did not take long. Here, the humans are in close proximity to the Dark Elf.

He may use them against you even as I try and draw them away to a different location."

Tsierus thought back to the crying child on the farm, and the angry father who had tried to attack him. He couldn't stand the idea of upsetting the people of this world again, yet he had to take out the pervasive influence of the Dark Elves. He would simply have to be careful, quick, and efficient. In this way, he could achieve all his objectives.

The Eye added, "I will try and take care of the humans as quickly as possible so I can come back to help you. Be careful, Tsierus. These Dark Elves have existed in this world longer than you have and understand this reality better than you do. You do not know what surprises lay in store for you."

"Thank you for your concern, Guardian," Tsierus said. "I've gotten a little more used to this world and its strange conditions. I believe I'll be fine."

"Be that as it may," the guardian replied, "remember that while you linger here, the cords connecting your body and your spirit are put under duress. At any moment they may snap, and you will die."

Tsierus nodded. "The chance to cleanse this land of the evil that taints it is worth the risk of death," he said. "When the innocent face a threat they cannot handle, it is the duty of the strong to save them. The humans are not powerful enough to withstand the influence of the Dark Elves. It is only my kind that can remove their perverted influence from these lands. We are the only ones powerful enough."

Tsierus fitted an arrow to his bow. "The humans and the Dark Elf have mounted their horses. Shall we begin?"

The Eye blinked away. Tsierus felt its presence become distant from him, and the pressure of this world settled upon his physical form. His movements became awkward, his arms weighed down as if by stones, his legs unsteady, his footsteps heavy. His ability to concentrate lessened, and he found it difficult to focus.

Tsierus inhaled, pushing against the alien forces limiting his potential. He had been in this world for several days now and had been building his mental fortitude for just such a moment. A gradual easing occurred, his muscles becoming lighter as vitality returned. Without the Eye nearby, however, he would only be able to maintain his power for a limited time. He had to resolve this situation quickly so his strength would return to him as fast as possible.

Tsierus ran down the hill, his gait lacking its normal grace. His guardian blinked back into existence far from him, hovering behind the party of men as they rode their horses down the path. The Eye glowed and, in the tall grass along the road, smoke rose in thin trails. Soon, sparks popped along the shrubbery. A wall of fire erupted alongside the traveling companions. The horses reared, and one of the men, caught off guard, was thrown violently from its back. The Dark Elf, riding further apart from the men, gazed at the fire, curiosity budding on his features.

Tsierus pulled the bowstring back so that the fletchings touched his cheek. He aimed at the Dark Elf's chest though his blurry vision. He stumbled, briefly losing his target. Again he lifted the bow, aimed, and calmed his mind so he could take out the target in one shot. The other three humans had dismounted to help their comrade, who moaned from an injury he had suffered in his fall.

Now, Tsierus thought.

Right before he released the arrow, a fifth human appeared to the Dark Elf's right. This one was hunched over, a golden hood covering his head, a tall staff clutched in his hand.

"Daesh Seon-saeng-nim," the hunchback called out, "someone is trying to kill you!"

Daesh, Tsierus thought in disgust. Even the name had a vile ring to it.

He released the arrow. It sped from the bow at incredible speed straight toward the Dark Elf's heart. Right before it impaled his target through the chest, the arrow's shaft dissolved and rained to the ground as grains of dust.

Tsierus nocked another arrow, but now he had the attention of Daesh. The element of surprise was lost, and Daesh gazed directly at him with those demonic blue and brown eyes.

Tsierus aimed the bow towards the sky and released the string. The arrow shot into the storm clouds, then exploded in a flash of blinding light. Daesh and the newcomer both cried out and covered their eyes as the brilliant glow bathed them. Tsierus immediately nocked a third arrow, but before he had time to release it, the humans and the Dark Elf shivered, then multiplied so that twelve stood before him. Those twelve shivered and multiplied again, and again, until ninety-six individuals crowded his field of vision. The humans on foot were trying to control their horses, with Daesh's sixteen figures mounted—the sixteen hooded strangers beside him.

It had to be an illusion, yet Tsierus couldn't tell who was real and who wasn't. He would need the Eye for that, and called out, "Guardian! I need you!"

The Eye reappeared over the Cloud Elf. Immediately, renewed strength flowed through Tsierus again.

"I am here," the Eye said.

"Thank you." Tsierus, refreshed, gazed down at Daesh. "Let's go down and kill him."

39. DAESH VS THE CLOUD ELF

Daesh's bloodline had played in the space between realities. Unlike other Dark Elves, his lineage had never forgotten the existence of Cloud Elves.

Dark Elves had been banished to the lands Daesh grew up in long before he was born. Their race lived to ancient ages, yet few remembered the beginnings of this punishment that stretched back beyond the time of almost all Dark Elves still alive today. Only occasionally would Cloud Elves visit their country to ensure the Dark Elves had not tried to sail for other shores. Rarely were these wardens seen. The Cloud Elves would blaze through the skies in fiery chariots. They only briefly took form, their hair blond like the sun, their eyes the deep blue of the sky.

Those in Daesh's clan were the exceptions. They made note of the Cloud Elves' comings and goings. They told no other member outside of their group, not daring to interfere with the Cloud Elves' observations of the Dark Elves for fear their advantage over the blond-haired elves would be lost.

When Daesh came to South Hanguk, he would occasionally see the chariots blazing through space. He would glimpse the forms of the Cloud Elves, who appeared as wisps of brightly glowing smoke encased in orbs of brilliant light. From his studies, he had learned what they appeared like in physical form.

Gazing at the figure with the bow and arrow seeking to kill him now, Daesh knew he was dealing with an executioner. The Dark Elves were not supposed to be in South Hanguk; they were not supposed to have left the land they had been placed in. Daesh and his twenty-four companions who had arrived in South Hanguk centuries ago could be hunted down for disobeying the decree of a greater individual, the Lord Daesh had learned about but could not, even now, envision.

He did not know how long the Cloud Elf had been in South Hanguk, but he had to warn the others. As the illusion of men and horses he'd conjured charged the golden-haired figure, Daesh turned to Nam-Gi.

"You must continue on to Majeon," he instructed his young pupil. "Another Dark Elf may be there with a questing group. You have to warn them our people are being targeted for extermination." Daesh pointed to the Cloud Elf. "Describe him to them and tell them he will be powerful. He will show us no mercy. They must treat him the same way if they wish to survive an encounter."

Nam-Gi stared at the Cloud Elf standing still as the illusion of the oncoming horses and warriors dashed upon him.

"I do not understand what I am to say," Nam-Gi said. "Please, come with me, Seon-saeng-nim. Your words will be more convincing than anything I could utter."

Daesh looked at the Eye hovering above the Cloud Elf and shook his head. "I can't risk confronting that entity in any reality but this one. Here, I may have a chance. In an alternate dimension, I would be at too great a disadvantage."

Daesh turned back to Nam-Gi. "I aided you over the years

because I believe in you and wish to see you succeed. Now I need your help, Nam-Gi. My people need your help. If they're not warned, they may all be killed. By him." He motioned to the Cloud Elf again. "I cannot allow that to happen."

Daesh pulled the reins of his horse, and it reared up with a wild neigh. "I go to challenge him now, but you must flee. Go to Majeon and warn my people."

Daesh spurred his horse forward without looking back. He had to have faith Nam-Gi would obey his request. He had no more time to convince his student further. Daesh only had a limited chance to defeat the Cloud Elf.

Unlike other people of his race, his magic did not help much in feats of overwhelming strength. Daesh's clan worked with deception, manipulating the reality their enemies perceived in order to win the battle. They worked better as a group, however, and Daesh was alone. Never before had this proven to be a problem in South Hanguk. Never before, until today, with this golden-haired visitor from somewhere far distant to their current reality.

Focusing on the illusions charging towards the Cloud Elf, Daesh multiplied the number of images further. Ninety-six became one hundred ninety-two, which became three hundred eighty-four. The companions on horses unsheathed long swords with one hand and held curved daggers in the other. The Cloud Elf looked at them rushing upon him with wide blue eyes and fitted an arrow in his bow. The first shot went through an illusion of Daesh. The following ones did the same, and Daesh realized that the Cloud Elf was purposely avoiding the humans.

So he only wants to kill me, Daesh thought, and does not wish to take the chance of harming one of the people of South Hanguk.

Daesh changed his form, while allowing the other images

of himself to stay the same. Now he appeared as his student Dae-Hwan and directed the illusions to attack. They swung their swords at the Cloud Elf, riding in two and three at a time. They flung their daggers at him to confuse the Cloud Elf further so he would not know where the true attack originated from.

Daesh watched The Cloud Elf avoid the phantom blows and dodge the daggers as they whirled past him. Excellent, he thought. Whether or not the Cloud Elf knew the warriors didn't really exist, the more the warriors made him react, the more real they would become in his head. With Daesh's magic empowering them, if the Cloud Elf eventually believed the weapons to be dangerous—if he came to think they would actually cause him harm if they hit him—then his mind would register pain if his body was struck.

Enough mental pain could be the very death of someone.

Daesh would not rely only upon that technique, however. He pulled his own dagger from the folds of his robes, and gradually rode closer to the Cloud Elf, keeping himself hidden in the tumult. He didn't rush forward, not wanting to give himself away. Yet always he neared the whirling figure, who had dropped his bow and was now using two scimitars to block the sword blows of the illusions when they swiped out at him.

Closer Daesh came, until he could hear the Cloud Elf's heavy breathing and see the sweat glistening on his body. The Cloud Elf moved with incredible grace, a dance of death that would have killed dozens of humans if they actually existed. Yet the Cloud Elf continued to play defense, and the illusions reacted accordingly, falling when he struck them in non-vital areas so that the facade of reality would not be broken.

It mattered not, for now Daesh was close enough. With a leap forward, he would be able to plunge the knife into the Cloud Elf's neck and carve out his throat.

He tensed to leap.

The Eye suddenly appeared before Daesh. He stumbled, and before he could react, the Cloud Elf leapt through the illusions, ignoring them as if he had never truly believed they were actually there. Too late, Daesh realized the Cloud Elf had been drawing him in. The Cloud Elf must have known all along the warriors on the horses were not real.

Daesh yanked on the reins of his steed, but he wasn't fast enough. The Cloud Elf plunged the two blades into his chest, and twisted his arms in a fluid crescent motion, cutting through Daesh's ribs, lungs, and slicing through his heart. Blood filled Daesh's mouth. With a pained cry, he fell to the ground. The Cloud Elf was immediately on top of him. Daesh was no longer able to focus, and the illusions of the warriors crowded around him shivered, then dissipated into the air.

The Cloud Elf brought his head close to Daesh, his hair a golden waterfall flowing around Daesh's temples. "Your evil ends today," the Cloud Elf hissed at him. "Your ability to corrupt humans will be vanquished with your death."

Daesh gazed up into the bright blue eyes of the Cloud Elf. Through the pain, he managed to laugh. It erupted in his chest, blood spurting up from his mouth to spill down the sides of his chin. He thought of the crippled boy, Nam-Gi, on his way to Majeon through the other reality that allowed him to walk and move through space without being limited by his physical deformities. Nam-Gi's dream to become a hero despite the limitations he was born with was one step closer to becoming a reality.

As the light faded around him, Daesh whispered to the Cloud Elf, "I gave everything I could to help one of the human race. If that makes me evil, so be it. But I wouldn't change a thing."

The Cloud Elf yanked the two blades out of Daesh, who

moaned in agony at the searing fire ripping through his chest. With bright blue eyes so clear they seemed soulless, the Cloud Elf said, "No, you wouldn't repent your transgressions. For your kind, there is no hope, for you are beyond redemption. And this, I do with pleasure."

The Cloud Elf swung both swords and removed Daesh's head from his shoulders.

40. RACE TO WINDSHINE

In the reality of South Hanguk, Nam-Gi could do nothing as he watched Daesh ride off to face the bright-haired foreigner. Worse yet, he could not be helped in carrying out his teacher's last command: find another foreigner and warn them.

Who was this mysterious stranger from a different world? Why did he want to kill the Dark Elves who'd been living peacefully in South Hanguk since time immemorial?

Uncertain of his next move, Nam-Gi stood rooted to the spot. A nearby commotion jerked him back to his precarious situation. While the illusions of Daesh and the four young men mounted on horses charged ahead, the real companions of the quest group remained close by. One of them had been thrown from his horse during the initial attack but had since recovered. Now they were trying to make sense out of what had happened. Who had attacked them, and why had the foreigner ridden away amid a host of their exact replicas?

"It's not real," his classmate, Dae-Hwan, explained to the companions.

"But they smell like us," one replied, wonder in his voice. "How can that be possible?"

"It is the power of the foreigner," Dae-Hwan said. "It is awesome to behold."

Nam-Gi wanted to reveal himself. He wanted to ask the people of his hometown for help, yet how would they react upon seeing him? Would they welcome his sudden appearance? Did they already know he was a criminal recently escaped from Busan prison?

Weighing the risk of being seen against the benefit of being aided, Nam-Gi decided not to reveal himself. With his heart pounding, he ducked away and sought out a veil of shadows and dancing lights in the crevice of reality. When it manifested itself to him, he eased the veil aside and stepped into the alternate reality.

Immediately, he sought out the shape with twenty-four sides. It stood near the bright-haired figure. When he had first seen the stranger, he hadn't known what to make of him. Unlike everything else he perceived in this reality of geometric angles, the stranger appeared as a brilliant fog swirling continuously into the form of a bipedal figure. There appeared to be strings extending from him and stretching up into the hazy sky. Where those strings terminated, Nam-Gi could not guess.

The twenty-four-sided shape and the strange smoky figure spoke. To Nam-Gi's surprise, he understood snatches of the conversation, and realized it was the Elvish tongue. Normally, Nam-Gi struggled to translate Elvish writing and language into Hangugeo, but the potion he had drunk must have enhanced his capabilities. He discerned their plot to kill Daesh. Though he did not know why they wanted to do so, he knew he had to warn his teacher of the added danger of the mysterious shape.

Out of the periphery of his vision, he watched his teacher riding forward at the edge of the illusion of warriors. The golden-haired foreigner evaded attacks from the illusions, yet Nam-Gi noticed the concentration of multicolored lights from the twenty-four-sided shape blazed a bright cone of light on the field, bathing everything it touched in a yellow glow.

His teacher, Daesh, neared the golden-haired foreigner. When it seemed like he was about to strike, the golden-haired foreigner suddenly leapt forward, and Daesh was thrown from his horse.

Nam-Gi had to help him! But his teacher had given him an order, and he would not disobey it. He had to find the other Dark Elf, and looking at the map Daesh had given him, he started in the direction of Majeon. The human world passed swiftly around him. He got the impression in South Hanguk, it had started to rain, though he did not know how strong the storm was that whipped the earth around him.

Nam-Gi entered a thick forest. If he had been traveling through the human world, the difficulty of the terrain would have proven impossible in his crippled condition. In this realm, however, he walked through the trees effortlessly, his healthy legs carrying him towards his goal at a rapid pace. He was approaching his destination faster than he could have imagined. He wondered if the other questing group had already arrived. If not, how long would he have to wait before he could find another Dark Elf of South Hanguk? And how would he get the foreigner to believe him?

Daesh was the only Dark Elf Nam-Gi had ever seen. Legends said there were about two dozen living in South Hanguk altogether, though Nam-Gi suspected only the Emperor and his inner circle knew exactly how many and where each of them dwelt. Nam-Gi wasn't even sure if Daesh was privy to that information.

This brought a fresh round of worry to Nam-Gi. The golden-haired foreigner had unhorsed his teacher. Daesh was powerful, more so than any human. Nam-Gi hoped Daesh would be able to hold off against the attack until help arrived.

Nam-Gi came to an abrupt stop as he rushed down the path, his mouth dropping open in awe. At first, he wasn't sure if the thing he saw walking before him existed in this strange realm or the human realm. Yet, when he tried to stare directly at it, it disappeared. Nam-Gi realized two things simultaneously: first, whatever the thing was existed in the human world; secondly, it had to be the giant terrorizing the coastal villages the questing groups had come to kill, because the creature was enormous!

The monster stood at least three times as tall as the tallest tree. It wore no clothes, and with each step it took, its body rippled with muscle. Tied its waist was a net similar to that of fishermen, except much wider, with thick, corded rope. Nam-Gi saw the giant also had wings growing from its shoulders and draping down to its feet. It moved carefully, the trees barely swaying at its passage. Nam-Gi didn't have to ponder what it was doing and where it was headed. Blood stained the cords of the net.

He followed after it, getting as close as he dared so he could inspect the monster in greater detail.

Nam-Gi had seen so many strange sights in the past few days the giant walking through the trees didn't startle him as much as it would have weeks ago. Studying it, he thought a strong sword blow would be enough to take it down, unless the giant had abilities not apparent from merely looking at it.

The giant's gait slowed. Nam-Gi gazed ahead of him and realized they had reached the coastline.

The giant spread its wings and crouched, the muscles in its legs tensing. Then it pounced up into the sky, flapped its massive wings and flew right beneath the clouds filling the sky over the village of Majeon.

41. MAJEON UNDER SIEGE

Han-Jae swirled rice wine in a wooden bowl before taking a sip of the bitter liquor. He let it swish around his mouth to wet his tongue. He swallowed, the sound of it going down his throat echoing in his ears.

No one was left, and the swift boats and fishing boats had all been destroyed. Only one fisherman had managed to escape by water before the rocks tossed by the giant had smashed the others who had attempted to flee.

Isolation pushed in upon him with a force that pulsed with a life of its own. Gazing at the stone walls of the coastal fort, he repeated the names of his men one at a time, his voice going dimmer as he recited all twenty-four once, then again. Each of those who had called him leader, who had looked to him for guidance, had been consumed by the giant.

Han-Jae lapsed into silence. He was last of the sea guards in the village of Majeon.

His grip tightened on the wooden bowl. Raising it to his lips once more, he drank deeply, the coarse liquor streaming down his throat and dribbling down his chin. Grief, which had taken residence in his mind, bobbed up and down, adrift on the wave of alcohol he'd been imbibing since he'd jerked awake at sunset. Outside, a bright flash of lightning illuminated the sky, followed by a boom of thunder that shook the fort. A storm had roared ashore earlier and lashed the village, setting the Hanguk Strait to crash against the coast with relentless fury.

Somewhere nearby, he imagined the people of Majeon, hopeless and miserable in their stone homes. Over the days of loneliness he'd endured since the last of his men perished, Han-Jae had been left to dark imaginings. He found himself wondering what past lives must have cursed the villagers to the fate they presently suffered. In their current incarnations, the people of Majeon had never struck him as devious. Simple fishing folk who could barely survive against the larger city of Incheon, they were basically harmless and more deserving of pity than retribution from the gods.

What had these wretched souls done to warrant the punishment they received at the hands of the giant? Even this night, above the roar of the storm, he thought he could hear the wails of children who had lost their parents, grandparents, and siblings to the monster, for that was almost all that remained: the very young, who had been defended till this bitter end.

Their time would come soon.

Han-Jae reached out and stroked the shaft of a spear, the only one left in the fort. He'd been saving it. Once the swift boats were destroyed, the sea guards had fought to the last man. Han-Jae wouldn't lie and say they had all confronted the threat bravely in their final moments. Most had died weeping, on their knees. Terrified. In the end, it made no difference. The giant showed no mercy, and all, except for himself, had ended up in the belly of the monster, which seemed to have an endless appetite.

As the weeks passed, villagers had tried to flee on foot through the forest. The desperate and foolish had attempted to escape through the trees during the day, leaving their children behind in hopes they could get through and return with help. Eventually, a few even tried at night. It mattered not. The giant kept careful watch, and before long, screams drifted through the trees back to Majeon. They didn't know when, or if, the monster slept, for it always seemed to be watching them. The forest between here and Incheon was simply too vast. No one made it to the road. Those left in the village knew this, for the giant would often deposit the remnants of humans it had not eaten in places easy to find. The terror of the villagers had grown with each new discovery until now they waited like sheep for the slaughter, no one left brave enough to try and escape.

If the fisherman who had escaped the hail of rocks that sunk the boats made it to a distant village, perhaps help was on the way. Would heroes get to Majeon in time, and if they did, would they stand a chance against the giant?

Han-Jae finished off the liquor and refilled the wooden bowl. They had had several casks of the wine brought in right before the giant arrived, but he had drunk almost all of it. When he finally finished his store, Han-Jae would be left to deal with his thoughts completely sober. That left a foul taste in his mouth, and he knew he would not be able to bear it for long.

When the wine was gone, he would challenge the giant, and then he himself would be gone. The liquor was the only worthwhile thing in his life now. Nothing else held value for him. He had seen too much grief and misery.

Another flash of lightning, and then a boom of thunder, shook the fort. The thin sounds of high-pitched wails became the deeper cries of familiar screams. Han-Jae's hand trembled, the rice wine rippling in the bowl. Once, he would have rushed outside with his men at his side. Alone, though, he had no heart, and waited, along with the rest, for his time to come.

He sat there on his mat with his wine and ignored the distant sobs, pretending they didn't exist. He pushed himself into a corner of the fort, and let the giant's hunt continue unimpeded. In his mind's eye, he saw the slaughter, the villagers being taken one by one as they begged for a mercy that would not come.

Han-Jae slammed the wooden bowl to the floor, the wine jumping up over the edge. He pushed himself to his feet. His mind cleared, sobered by the fear and adrenaline racing through him. If his time was to come, it would be of his own choosing. The choice would be his to make, and he decided it would be this night as the wind howled around him and the rain pummeled the earth. He would challenge the giant, and he would die.

Han-Jae picked up the spear, inhaled, and bellowed a war cry that sent a thrilling shiver though his body. Then he plunged out into the storm.

For a few moments, he saw nothing but darkness, the moon and stars invisible behind the wall of clouds blocking the sky. A lightning strike brightened the coast like day, and Han-Jae plunged forward down the slippery shell path towards the village. He had walked this way many times over the years, and his footsteps were sure despite his pants clinging to his legs and the rain stinging his eyes. To his left, the Hanguk Strait lashed against the shore, the waves whipped up into a fury by the gale blowing in from the water.

Han-Jae heard a fresh round of screams but could see nothing more until the lightning struck again. The brick homes stood out clearly, the trees of the cursed forest waving wildly back and forth. Some had toppled under the ferocity of the storm. Darkness blanketed the coast again, but Han-Jae still reached the nearest fisherman's home and followed the sound of weaker screams. Whoever had been taken, hope had left them. Han-Jae knew that, at this moment, they would just be waiting for their lives to be over.

Another flash of lightning, and Han-Jae saw the giant. He stopped cold. The monster stood much taller than any tree, its body corded with muscle. It ripped the brick walls of a home apart with massive hands. Han-Jae saw the net hanging at its side. Several scrawny villagers had already been thrust inside. The giant bent down and grabbed someone squirming—a child by the look of it. Then darkness stole the scene away again.

Han-Jae crept forward, tense. He realized warm tears were streaming down his face slicked with cool rainwater. Ragged breathing tore from his throat, his hands shivering, his heart beating so hard in his chest the left side of his body went numb.

He saw nothing and heard little of the victims except a low groan that somehow penetrated the overwhelming roar of the storm. Was it his imagination? He didn't know how close or how far he was from the giant and took one quaking step forward after another. Lightning flashed again; looming right in front of him was the giant. Han-Jae froze, and—as he gazed up into the wide eyes of the monster staring down at him—compartments of his mind unlocked, and memories flooded him.

Visions of his parents in the village he grew up in, his mother clearest of all. He would grumble when she called him in from playing with his brothers and sisters, but would watch her graceful movements with delight as she prepared food for their family of seven. Her soft words of comfort, which could turn stern when he disobeyed her, were heard with startling clarity in his mind as the storm roared overhead. It almost felt as if she was there with him now, her protective arms wrapped around him.

Then he heard the voice of his father. Always stern, always

complaining to his wife she would make Han-Jae weak the way she mothered him. His father had always looked tired to Han-Jae, the long hours of work from dawn to evening wearing down on him throughout the years. Like the villagers, his family had often been hungry. Somehow, they had survived, and one day, Han-Jae had joined the Emperor's navy, which took him far from Gwangju.

He had spent years chasing North Hanguk pirates. Many skirmishes he had engaged in with his comrades-in-arms on the rolling waves between the two warring countries. Han-Jae had never distinguished himself, but he was reliable, and had a good rapport with the crew he served alongside. His superiors had noticed, and when his obligation to the Emperor was over, they had asked him to join the sea guards and continue policing the ocean to keep the northerners from mischief in South Hanguk's territorial waters.

Han-Jae had first returned to his village and married the woman his parents had arranged for him. After he left her with a child, he took up the position here at Majeon as captain of the sea guards. Once every four months, he would travel home to see his first son, then his second and third, with full confidence his mother was helping his wife raise their children.

Han-Jae had never cared about being assigned to Incheon. That was his wife, who had probably been influenced by his father. Yes, there would be more prestige and increased earnings, and he admitted he had grown tired of the people of Majeon. Their poverty was depressing. Their reproachful looks made the sea guards, all better paid and better fed, feel guilty when they went about their duties on the coast of the village.

Han-Jae disliked the way the villagers blamed them for the Incheon fishermen, who had bigger boats and bigger crews, and were territorial of the most abundant fishing spots. The villagers seemed to believe Han-Jae and his men could solve all the problems of the world and make their lives better. When he thought about it, he could almost understand why the foolish brothers had brought ashore a corpse that was much more alive than dead, no matter how it first appeared. In their own way, they were looking for a way to get ahead and make the lives of their wives and children better. They had—of course—failed, and brought doom to themselves and their fellow villagers. That small, shriveled-up creature with black wings laid on Han-Jae's breakfast table had grown into this giant looming over him now. Han-Jae, gazing up at it, feebly raised his spear.

Lightning zipped across the sky, and the world brightened in a series of brilliant flashes. The giant reached toward Han-Jae with its long arm. Han-Jae had seen it do this so many times, and even as darkness fell, he knew what was coming next. He poked out halfheartedly with the spear, but knew it would do no good. Soon the monster would grab him in its wide grip, lift him up, and then slam him onto the ground to stun him. If he resisted any further, the monster would slam him again, though not enough to kill him. The giant seldom killed anyone outright, though it would sometimes consume little children as if they were snacks. No, the giant liked to take them away while they were still breathing. Somewhere on the mountainside, Han-Jae knew he would meet his final fate. There, he would be devoured like so much meat.

Even in the darkness, he saw the outline of the fingers closing in upon him, and he smelled the stench of rot and death on the flesh of the giant. He could do nothing else. Dropping the spear, Han-Jae waited for the inevitable.

Suddenly, it was the giant that cried out, and in the next flash of lightning, Han-Jae saw the monster swiftly raise up, clutching a hand from which a dagger protruded. Han-Jae heard a booming voice louder than the thunder, and he looked across the village to see four figures standing on the outskirts of the ruined homes. The stranger that had called out stood at the forefront, and before the light died away, Han-Jae noted his size, saw how he stood there challenging the giant, a two-handed sword in his hands.

Manic laughter escaped Han-Jae's lips, and he collapsed to his knees in the mud. They had finally made it. The heroes had come to kill the giant of Majeon.

42. THE ORSIEG

The Orsieg knocked the stinger from its hand and whirled to the meat that had thrown it. It had come to finish off what was left in the brick shells, taking everything back to its roost with it before moving on to the next batch along the coast, then the next. The meat dwelling in these parts no longer satisfied it. Too scrawny, too dry and lacking a good flow of blood, the subsistence here would not do. The Orsieg wanted to finally find other hunting grounds with better meat to feast upon.

It stared down now at the four figures standing before it at the edge of the trees, its stomach rumbling. These seemed much healthier, with broader bodies and thicker limbs. It wanted to catch them and smash them against the earth, but it had to be careful. The figure standing at the head of the pack was one of the biggest humans it had ever seen. He held a pincer that glowed with a dangerous light. The Orsieg was not afraid, but it also did not want to take a risk.

Crouching down, it sprang up into the air and spread its wings. With a mighty flap, it soared high above the brick shells. In an ensuing lightning strike, it memorized the position of the humans watching it take to the sky. Darkness fell, and it lost sight of them as it climbed higher. Powerful winds buffeted its body, but it was strong, and it fought against the wild currents so it could maneuver over the four humans. It could do nothing just yet—it had to wait until lightning flashed again across the sky.

The coast lit up brightly. The Orsieg saw its target, and with a mighty flap of its wings, propelled itself down to slam into the ground, rumbling the earth. It cocked its arm back so it could stun the human with a blow strong enough to knock it out, but not strong enough to kill it outright.

Its fist sped downwards, but the meat was faster. Swinging his glowing sword, the human shouted a strange word, and a gust of wind slammed into the Orsieg, lifting it off of its feet and hurling it across the village. The Orsieg spun through the air, surprised at the invisible attack, and slammed into the water off the coast. It sank up to its hips, the storm waves crashing over its lower body.

Once again, the Orsieg couldn't see the human as darkness descended, but it quickly came to a realization. This meat could not be taken to its cave and ripped apart to make a fresh bowl of blood stew. This meat had to be killed here and now. The Orsieg had to eat it despite the loss of blood it would be unable to catch.

The Orsieg scooped up a handful of mud from the bottom of the Strait. At the next lightning strike, it twisted its body back and spun forward, hurling the sediment with incredible force. The mud slammed into the human and knocked him from his feet. The Orsieg scooped up another handful, and— without wasting a moment—crouched and leapt forward before the meat could recover. It tossed the sludge downward with an explosion of force, burying the human. Landing in the spot it hoped the human was buried, it raised both hands, clasped them together, and prepared to bring them down in a fatal blow.

An echoing boom rolled across the land, but there was no lightning strike preceding it. The Orsieg paused, hands raised high over its head. A second boom followed that shook the giant to its core. Trying to find the source of the sound, it discovered the other three humans hadn't been caught in the mud, and now each held strange objects in their tiny hands.

A third boom vibrated the Orsieg's very bones. From the mud, the big human pounced, his pincer grasped in his hands. The sharp end slashed across the Orsieg's chest, biting deep through its tough flesh to open a gaping wound. An odd sensation pierced the Orsieg, a terrible, awful burning that penetrated its body and seared its very heart. The Orsieg peered down and saw a river of blood leaking from a deep gash in its torso.

The meat had caused it pain, the first time the Orsieg had experienced the sensation at this intensity. It opened its mouth wide, and a great cry escaped its lips. *Meat had hurt it!* The absurdity of this truth increased the ferocity filling its roar.

These small little creatures it had been feeding upon since it crawled out of the fissure in the earth. *They* had caused it to bleed!

The big human spun around, but the Orsieg was faster. It kicked the ground, and clumps of soaked earth and rock slammed into the human. It grabbed the tops of trees and ripped them out by the roots. Spinning to the other three humans, it hurled the uprooted trees, and watched its prey try to leap. The thick trunks slammed into them, burying them beneath leaves and branches. The Orsieg rushed forward before they could recover. Ripping another tree from the earth to use as a club, it raised it high over its head to bludgeon the three men.

Yet another man suddenly appeared, darting under its legs. The Orsieg dimly recognized the meat from the first day it had arrived. It had feasted upon his companions, and now this lone, ragged animal was all that was left of that herd.

Ignoring the lesser threat, the Orsieg focused its attention on the three fallen meat, but the ragged man screamed at him.

"Monster! For my comrades, for this village, for the Kwan family, I strike at you!"

The man carried one of the sharp projectiles and hurled it with such force the giant froze in surprise. The wooden projectile flew strong and true, slamming into the Orsieg's right eye and immediately ending its vision there.

The Orsieg reared back its head in an anguished cry. It lumbered backwards as it tried to maintain its footing. Stabs of painful bright light filled its head, and among its thoughts of rage, bewilderment flourished. How were they doing this? How *could* they be doing this? The humans were food: meat and blood to fill its clay bowl. The Orsieg was the hunter, towering over them, stronger than them. On its crag, it had ruled without contest, the wooden shells floating by no match when it hovered in the sky over them.

Yet here—now—these humans were fighting back with a determination that bordered on intelligence. *They were just meat!* They were only meant for consumption and nothing more. Yet they fought, and simply would not give up and let it feed its appetite with their flesh and bone.

The Orsieg lunged at the small man, who was whooping and hollering, pointing with mad glee at the damage he had wrought upon the giant. Before the Orsieg could wrap its massive hands around the man, a fresh slash of pain tore across its back. It craned its head to see the big human soaring over its shoulder from behind it, an arc of blood trailing him. The

Orsieg spun to this renewed threat to try and grab the man as soon as he landed.

One of the other three men, knocked down by the trees, had recovered, and a boom of thunder shook the world once more. The sound seemed to make the big human faster and stronger, for he spun to the Orsieg, swinging his sword and crying out another word that carried above the storm. Another gale of wind slammed into the giant and sent it tumbling down to slam into the brick shells.

The Orsieg tried to stand, but before it could regain its feet, the big human leapt up again on his powerful legs. With a merciless swipe, the man cut through the Orsieg's throat. The Orsieg saw a fountain of blood sprout up to mist its vision red. It felt its heart pumping out the life-sustaining liquid, and it grasped its neck in a tight grip.

Lightning flashed. The world was brightly lit again as it watched the big human leap up into the air one final time. The glowing pincer descended upon it with a terrific speed, and when it fell, it cut clear through the left side of the Orsieg's neck.

The flames of thought that animated the Orsieg slowly blew out one by one as its blood poured from its throat until only a single light remained in the darkness. With its last thought, the Orsieg wondered, "How?"

The candle blinked out, and never sparked with life again.

43. THE GOLDEN CLOAK

Ha Jun brought his glyph sword down several more times, hacking away at the flesh, then thick muscle and rock-hard bone before he was able to completely cut off the head. His hanbok was covered with blood from the deluge spraying up from the giant. With the storm finally abating and the clouds breaking up above them so the stars and moon became visible, Ha Jun peered down at the Hanguk Strait. He was eager to dive in and clean himself off.

Despite the evil of the monster he had just killed, Ha Jun still marveled at the inhuman body beneath him. The giant was massive. He'd never seen anything like it before—or even dreamed such a thing was possible. He stepped carefully down the length of the torso and came to a sharp stop. He hadn't seen it when he fought the giant, but there was a net tied around its waist. Tangled in the thick cords were humans. As Ha Jun approached, he saw the twisted limbs of the crushed bodies, and knew that none caught within remained living. Had they died before he attacked the giant, or had they died during?

Ha Jun bowed his head, grief washing over him. Once more, he had reached the end of a quest, but instead of feeling triumphant, he felt only despair. Is this what it was like to attain greatness? He thought of the governors, who had all gone on multiple quests to become heroes. He only saw them at the ceremonies, but now he wondered what type of men they truly were. Did all of them feel as he did as he came closer to standing in front of the Emperor and being declared a hero?

Ha Jun wiped the blood from his blade and sheathed it. He went in search of survivors in the village and came upon a few huddled amid the rubble of their homes.

"The giant is dead," he told them, his voice heavy. "The people he took—" Ha Jun paused. "I am sorry, but they perished during the battle."

No expression touched the villagers' tired faces. No tears dampened their eyes. In silence, they stared at Ha Jun as if he had not just told them of the demise of their friends and family. Gazing back at them, he understood they had been through too much. Despair had affected them so thoroughly it could affect their weary souls no further.

He turned from those blank faces and went back to the giant. Cutting the netting apart so the bodies spilled out, he watched the corpses roll onto the wet ground. The Jang brothers came over to him as he stared dumbly down at the broken bodies of women and children, all that was left of Majeon.

"We have put to rest a great evil," Jae Jin said, his voice heavy. Tears streaked down the Jang brothers' faces. Their red hanboks were ripped in places, and scratches—some deeper than others—from the trees falling upon them, marked them. For the most part, however, their injuries were minor. They would soon recover from their physical injuries, but the grief Ha Jun saw in their faces reflected his own. How long would that take before it scabbed over, and what type of scar would it leave on them all?

The spear-thrower accompanied them. Ha Jun had been surprised by the man's sudden appearance when the giant had reached down to snatch up the Jang brothers. The expression the man wore now was different from the other villagers. His eyes wild, he suffered involuntary twitches, his body revealing a lack of control as emotions raged deep inside of him.

"Thank you for helping us," Jae Jin said, and bowed deeply to him. His two brothers, and Ha Jun, followed suit.

"Tell us who you are," Jae Jin said, "so your name will be recorded by our chronicler, and your deed will live on to be known for generations to come."

The man jerked his head up and gazed dumbly at Jae Jin.

"Who am I?" He paused, his body shivering. "I was captain of two dozen men, now all dead. I was supposed to be a protector of this village, but because of foolish selfishness, I doomed them all." His eyes roved around the desolation. "I stripped everything from these people, and have had everything important to me here taken from me as well; and now you ask me, who am I?" He sighed, deeply, his body relaxing as some great inner turmoil became still. "My name is Kwan Han-Jae, and I am the last of the sea guards of Majeon. When the full story is known, will I be jailed for my crimes?"

Ha Jun could not begin to understand what the man was going on about. The brothers were equally confused and exchanged pitying glances among themselves.

"You have done no wrong," Jae Jin finally said, breaking the awkward silence. If they expected relief from the man, they were wrong, for he laughed and sobbed at the same time.

"We will return to Incheon," Jae Jin said to his brothers and Ha Jun. "Our horses are not far off. We'll have to secure a wagon to bring the giant's head back to Jeju. Before we return, we'll visit the governor's office here at Incheon and ask him to send aid to help the people leave this area so they can settle elsewhere."

"There is nothing left for any of them here," Han-Jae agreed through ragged gasps. "One day someone may resettle Majeon. One day a fresh deployment of sea guards will be sent here to protect those villagers." Han-Jae looked down at the corpses spilled forth from the bloody net. "I will not see that day. For my sins, I will be condemned."

Again, the companions exchanged glances, unsure what to say to the disturbed captain. Jae Jin motioned to the three others. They stepped away from Han-Jae and went back towards where Windshine waited at the edge of the village.

"Elder Brother, is there nothing more we can do for them?" Ha Jun asked.

Jae Jin shook his head. "The recovery of these villagers is the duty of the province. We have succeeded in our quest, and there are people waiting for us back home. We should leave as quickly as we can."

Ha Jun wished it could be different, but he knew it was true. When he turned to speak to Windshine, two things happened. First, a young, hunched-over youth blinked into existence beside the Dark Elf.

"They are trying to kill you!" He shouted at Windshine, and did a complicated series of motions with his hands. Suddenly, where Windshine had stood, there were now three more of her.

Before anything more could be said, an arrow slammed into the ground at the feet of one of the images of the Dark Elf, and the earth exploded upwards, throwing all of them off their feet. Ha Jun fell hard, the air knocked from his body. His first thought was of Windshine, and quickly he regained his feet. He saw Windshine had been knocked backwards, all four of her, and he did not know which one was the real Dark Elf. It didn't matter, he quickly decided. He would have to protect them all.

Ha Jun ripped the glyph sword from its sheath, but he didn't know from which direction the attack had come. He ran towards Windshine, figuring she would be the target once again. To his right, he saw the Jang brothers regaining their feet also, and Jae Jin called out, "What's going on?"

Ha Jun shook his head, having no answer to give him. Another arrow struck the earth near one of the Windshines. A second explosion erupted, knocking Ha Jun from his feet once more. This time, he had an idea which way the attack had originated. When he regained his feet, he ran straight towards it.

That's how he got his first glimpse of the attacker.

Ha Jun gasped. The figure standing in front of him was an elf, though he looked nothing like Windshine. Where her skin was black as the night sky, this elf's skin tone was white, like clouds on a breezy day. His hair, instead of pale like the moon, blazed with an orange fire imitating the sun. He held a bow in his hands, an arrow nocked on its string.

Ha Jun didn't know who this stranger was, or why he was attempting to kill Windshine. At this moment, he didn't care. The rage tethered inside of him erupted, and he charged towards the strange elf with a roar.

The elf aimed the arrow at him but didn't release it. He tried to readjust it to get a better shot behind the warrior, but Ha Jun quickly changed his course to keep his body between the golden-haired elf and Windshine. The elf shouted something Ha Jun didn't understand, but once more, he didn't care. Raising his sword up high, Ha Jun slammed it into the ground and cried out in Elvish, "Earth!"

An earthquake rocked the ground and opened a wide chasm that stretched ahead of Ha Jun to the elf. With a cry, the stranger lost his footing and fell into the crack that opened at his feet. Ha Jun skirted around the chasm and dashed forward with the plan to hop into the hole and cut the elf in half. A shaft of light enveloped the elf, and he stopped in mid-fall and was whipped up out of the hole to hover in the air. Ha Jun followed the path of the light, and emitted yet another sharp gasp.

Floating over the shoulder of the elf was a disembodied eye.

Ha Jun ran towards it. The eye emitted a glow, and a force slammed into him. Stumbling, he fell back for a moment, but immediately started forward again. Again, the force hit him, but it wasn't enough to injure him. Ha Jun swung his sword and shouted the Elvish word for lightning. A current shot from the blade. The eye immediately vanished, and the elf fell lightly to his feet.

Ha Jun had used both of the wind spells against the giant, and now one of the earth spells and one of the lightning spells against the elf and the eye. He only had one each of earth and lightning spells left, and both of the fire and water spells. Until he figured out what the eye was and how he could kill it, he didn't know if any further attack would have any effect. Once the spells were depleted, he would only have his strength to fight the elf. If the golden-haired stranger was anything like Windshine, physical prowess might not be enough to defeat him.

Ha Jun was just about to race forward again when the hooded, hunchbacked teen appeared beside him.

"You can't destroy it out here," the teen said, blood leaking from his nose. He held a thin vial clenched between his fingers. Swallowing the liquid, he tossed the vial aside and held out his hand to Ha Jun.

"I think I can take you with me the way Daesh Seon-saeng-nim took me with him," the teen said.

"I don't know what you're talking about," Ha Jun replied, and focused on the second lightning spell inscribed on his blade.

"If you don't follow me, they'll kill the Dark Elf. Trust me, and we can save her." The hunchback pointed to the disembodied eye that had reappeared. "You'll never be able to harm that thing. It doesn't even exist in this world."

Ha Jun, however, would not be dissuaded. Turning from the stranger, he faced the golden-haired elf once more and raised the glyph sword up high. Crying out, "Earth," he used the second glyph spell and rocked the world again, causing the earth to quake and tossing the attacker into another deep crevice.

44. WINDSHINE VS THE
CLOUD ELF

Windshine regained her footing from the second quake that had sent her to her knees. Ha Jun, she knew immediately, had used both earth glyphs against this new threat. After battling the giant, he would only have a few glyphs left to continue fighting.

Who was this new stranger intent upon killing her? She thought back to the young archer, Woo Jin, who had attempted the same thing. She had never told Ha Jun, as the two young men had become friends as they journeyed to the village of children. Windshine had never discovered why Woo Jin had been sent to assassinate her, or who had ordered it. She knew, however, she had many enemies in the land of South Hanguk, going back generations. From the very beginning, the Dark Elves had been distrusted in this foreign land they had immigrated to.

Now, someone else wanted to take her life. The thought exhausted Windshine. This time, though, she wanted to keep the person alive so she could interrogate them. If she could find a direct source of the conspiracy, perhaps she could better identify its manifestations later so she would not be taken by surprise again.

"Speed," she said, activating one of the spells inscribed on her boots. She darted across the land towards the attacker hoping to reach him before he had a chance to recover. The attacker thwarted that hope, however, levitating out of the crack in the ground into which he'd fallen. For the first time, Windshine glimpsed him. Shocked at what she beheld, she stumbled, her concentration disrupted by the impossible. What was this person hovering before her with hair that shone bright as the sun and startlingly blue eyes that burned with hatred as they gazed down upon her? Was this truly another elf? And if so, was he as powerful as she?

Her hesitation was all he needed. The stranger fitted an arrow, nocked it, and released the bow string.

"Shield!"

An inscription woven into her vest created an invisible barrier, and the arrow disintegrated upon contact. The stranger didn't seem concerned. He nocked another arrow and released it, to also be blocked by the shield. Recovered from her surprise, Windshine dashed towards him again, but a roar from her left distracted her. Out of the corner of her eye, she saw Ha Jun charging something, his powerful legs propelling him forward. She directed her gaze in the direction he headed and gasped. Behind the strange elf, a large, disembodied eye hovered.

Now what?

A beam from the disembodied eye inundated Windshine. To her disbelief, the shield shattered. The strange elf smiled in satisfaction and immediately nocked another arrow. Just as he was about to release it, Ha Jun leapt up high into the air and shouted, "Water."

A wave swept down from the blade of the sword and

washed over the elf, smashing him to the ground with its deluge and sending him tumbling down the hill. Not wasting a moment, Windshine said, "Bind." Her robes shimmered, and a dozen threads shot forward, snaking above the water towards her target. She didn't know exactly where he would surface, but she had to be ready the moment he emerged from the waves so she could immobilize him.

There! The elf swam to the top, gasping for breath. The threads from her robes sped towards him, reared up to wrap around him, but were suddenly covered with a light that set them on fire. Above the water, the hovering eye was emitting that glow again from its pupil. The flames raced back along the threads of cloth towards Windshine. Quickly, she disconnected them and leapt just in time as a wave of fire rose up and smashed where she had stood seconds ago.

Windshine didn't know which of the two was the greater threat, but she decided to go after the floating eye to see how the elf would react.

"Fly."

A glyph in her boot took her up into the air.

"Cover."

From a spell woven into her pants, inky darkness flowed out, whirling around her in a cloud and masking her exact location from any gazing upon her.

"Lightning."

A charge built up on her clothing. Sparks flickered to life along her limbs and gathered into a prism in front of her.

"Cage."

The prism darted forward toward the disembodied eye. She planned to imprison it only, determined not to destroy this unknown entity that had made her its enemy. Before the cage reached it, however, the eye blinked from existence, then reappeared within the inky darkness where Windshine hid. She spun to it, uttering, "Barrier," just in time to block a blow of radiant energy that emitted from the eye, slamming into her. Tremendous heat washed over her, and Windshine fell from the sky, the smell of burning hair filling her nose as she crashed down onto the wet earth.

"Tunnel," she gasped as another beam slammed into the ground, creating a powerful explosion. Her glyph spell whirled her deep into the earth, then changed direction, sending her perpendicular to the surface until it propelled her upwards. She paused before breaking the ground above her head, her breathing ragged.

"Sight."

The earth above her became transparent. She saw the elf standing strong, poised, a fresh arrow nocked. The disembodied eye hovered over his shoulder, and suddenly swung in her direction. An invisible force gripped her, tore her out of the ground, and clamped down hard upon her, squeezing her tight.

Words of powerful spells, the kind her race had used in her own land, which possessed destructive capabilities the like of which had never been unleashed in South Hanguk, came to her mind. She could kill them both with those glyphs woven into her clothing. Windshine gazed at the elf, who pulled the bow string taut.

The spark to fight extinguished inside of Windshine. Anger led to hatred, hatred led to violence. The cycle was unending.

She didn't know what good the elf thought he would accomplish by killing her, but Windshine would not annihilate him before he did so to her. She would not utter the spells woven into her clothes that could wipe enemies from existence. Instead, she waited, almost impatiently, for death to liberate her from this life of sorrow and unending woe.

45. THE OTHER WORLD

Nam-Gi gaped in stunned silence for only a moment as the bull-headed warrior, Ha Jun, prepared to attack the eye and elf again. He had tried two spells using Elvish words to unleash powerful magics from his sword, but both had failed. Why didn't the stubborn warrior understand he couldn't defeat these foes that way?

Nam-Gi quickly slipped into the alien dimension, dashed to Ha Jun, and parted the curtain slightly so he could extend only part of his body through. "I don't have time to explain this to you!"

He grabbed a distracted Ha Jun by the wrist and yanked him through the portal into the other world. Ha Jun immediately spun toward him, sword raised high.

"What did you do?" he roared at Nam-Gi. "Where am I?"

Nam-Gi stumbled back, his hand raised over his eyes at the sight of the warrior in this reality. He had seen Daesh's appearance in this realm and had glimpsed the golden-elf's appearance here, but this was the first time he had beheld another human inside this strange world.

Ha Jun still held the shape of a bipedal creature, yet

concentric rings blazed crimson around him with an explosion of power that created bright light in the opaque gloom. The geometric shapes nearest them backed away from the warrior, their own multicolored lights blinking furiously.

"Where is Windshine?"

His voice manifested as a physical force that swept over Nam-Gi like a gale and shook the very foundations of this reality. Ha Jun's sword gleamed with a cold sheen that extended up from its sharp point to pierce the void above them.

Nam-Gi, finding his own voice, pointed. "She's there."

Ha Jun spun around. "I can barely see anything here." The concentric rings encircling him flared to even brighter life. "That's her there! What's wrong with her, why isn't she moving?"

"That thing is attacking her." Nam-Gi pointed to the twenty-four-sided shape. "You have to destroy it if you hope to save her. I haven't fought with it yet, I don't even know what it is."

Ha Jun, however, didn't seem to care about the mystery of his new target. He charged the twenty-four-sided shape, the ground beneath him fragmenting each time his foot pounded its surface. The twenty-four-sided shape's flickering lights, which had all been focused upon Windshine, divided. Some slid across its body to view the warrior.

"Human."

The voice sounded as if it came from some hollow place far away, yet Nam-Gi was sure he detected a note of shock in its tone.

"You do not belong in this space."

Ha Jun leapt high up into the air, sword raised over his head, and dropped down upon the twenty-four-sided shape. The flickering lights pulsed, then emitted a beam that slammed into the sword, shattering its top half. Pieces of the ruined blade rained from the sky to litter the colorless ground with its glittering shards.

"I do not want to hurt you, human," the shape intoned. "Leave here and let me return my attention back to my master."

Nam-Gi peered again into the land of South Hanguk and saw the golden-haired elf was now bent over as if under some great invisible weight. The cords tethering the elf to whatever existed in the sky above them were growing thinner. They appeared on the verge of snapping at any moment.

Ha Jun landed, tossed the hilt of the broken sword aside, and charged the twenty-four-sided shape again. The concentric circles around him became blood red and burned bright hot. Another beam from the flickering lights slammed into Ha Jun, lifting him up and throwing him back with its force.

"I give you one final warning, human." Now, all of the flickering lights had slid along the body to view Ha Jun. The warrior was rising to his feet once more, his skin blistered, his clothes smoking. The determination on his face had not faltered, however. With awe, Nam-Gi beheld the rage twisting Ha Jun's expression, the overwhelming desire for vengeance burning brightly in the other's gaze.

"Return to your realm, and let me help my master save your race of Man."

Ha Jun's lips parted, and a bellow erupted from his mouth as he charged forward a third time. The beam of light struck him, but the crimson rings swirling around him deflected the attack, so the destructive shaft of energy struck the land of this world. Nam-Gi dodged the pieces of alien ground blown up into the air and crashing on the landscape around him.

Ha Jun reached the twenty-four-sided shape, drew back his arm, and slammed his fist into its side. A wide fissure opened up in the shape, spreading up and along it. A white gas erupted from the crack. The sound of voices screaming in a language Nam-Gi did not understand issued forth from the interior.

Ha Jun brought his arm back and again smashed his fist into the twenty-four-sided shape. The fissures widened to overtake the entire structure. It pulsed, as if struggling to remain whole. Then it broke apart, big pieces breaking into smaller bits, all of which crumbled up into the opaque sky with a howl of strange alien screams and trails of smoke.

The swiftly spinning rings surrounding Ha Jun slowed as silence fell over the alien world.

46. THE DECISION

Windshine quenched the destructive spells rising in her mind, her lips pressed tightly together in defiance against those glyphs woven throughout her clothing. The golden-haired elf above her grinned in triumph, then suddenly stumbled. The arrow sprang from the bow and whipped past Windshine, grazing her cheek in its passage. Trickles of blood slid down her cheek, its metal kiss a biting sting.

The golden-haired elf cast his gaze behind him to the disembodied eye. To Windshine's astonishment, the eye seemed to be phasing in and out of existence, flickering like a candle in the path of a strong wind.

"Guardian!" The elf cried out. "What's happening to you?"

The disembodied eye splintered. A milky white light flowed into its pupil.

"Master—"

Its voice was filled with deep grief and unending love. "We have failed."

The disembodied eye shattered into sparkling pieces, then faded away. The force that had captured Windshine dissipated, and she dropped to the ground. The golden-haired elf tried to stand as she approached him, tried to raise his bow, but his entire body trembled as if some great pressure exerted itself upon him.

She knew nothing about this stranger who had tried to kill her. He was an elf, but not like her. He had tried to eliminate her without speaking to her, without a hint to his motivations. Even now, he gazed with revulsion upon her, a burning hate embedded deep in his eyes.

At the same time, he looked as if he was dying, when before he had appeared so strong. Pity touched Windshine's heart. If she had held no intention of killing him before, she certainly wouldn't now that he seemed so broken. She reached out to help him stand. Before she could touch him, Ha Jun popped into reality beside her. Grasping the hilt of his broken glyph sword, he raised the jagged blade high over his head and stabbed it down at the golden elf.

Windshine quickly stepped between him and his target. "Wait!"

Ha Jun jerked to a stop as another figure stepped out of nothing behind him. Windshine looked from Ha Jun to a crippled teen, then back to Ha Jun.

"Where have you been?" she asked him.

"I do not know," he replied, shaking his head. "I cannot explain to you anything that just happened to me. I only know he tried to kill you." He looked past her to the golden-haired elf. "If you step out of the way, I will kill him."

Windshine laid a hand on Ha Jun's chest. His eyes widened, and he placed his bigger hand over hers.

"Let me talk to him first," she said. "Be patient, Ha Jun, and wait just a moment."

She turned from him to the golden-haired elf gazing up at her in fury.

"You have corrupted them," he spat at her with an Elvish

accent she had never heard before. Despite the harsh accusation, the beauty of its melody pierced her.

Before she could reply, the teen who had appeared after Ha Jun limped forward and threw back his hood.

"Where is Daesh Seon-saeng-nim?" he demanded of the stranger.

Windshine recognized her old companion's name even in the crude manner of the boy's question. She had not seen Daesh for many centuries, but she realized he must have been the chronicler for the boy's province. Even more interesting, he had taught the boy some Elvish, for that was the language he spoke to the elf.

"He is dead," the elf snarled in his beautiful voice. "I have freed you to take your life back from the perversity he has wrought upon your soul. I have freed you from one of *their kind.*"

Dead?

The revelation reverberated through Windshine. Tears sprang to her eyes. Daesh had possessed the most powerful intellect of the twenty-five that had left their homeland centuries ago. He had understood aspects of reality many of their race could hardly grasp. His gift of understanding the intricacies of existence was a result of a special sphere of knowledge his clan excelled at. Windshine hadn't spoken to Daesh since they were separated by the Emperor hundreds of years ago, and now she never would again.

"Did you kill him?" she asked the golden-haired elf.

"Of course."

The teen gasped in horror. Clutching Ha Jun's arm, he shouted in Hangugeo, "Kill him! He murdered my Seon-saeng-nim, and he will do the same to yours, too. He wants to destroy all of the Dark Elves of South Hanguk. I heard him say it from the alternate reality. Strike him down and save the foreigner!"

Ha Jun stepped forward, raised the jagged bladed again, and stabbed at the elf's exposed throat. Windshine darted out her hand to shield the elf from the fatal blow. Ha Jun jerked the weapon away just before he pierced her skin.

He turned to her, confusion sweeping his features. "Why?"

"Will you kill him without first hearing his story? As well as his." She nodded to the crippled teen. "We don't even know his name."

"My name is Kim Nam-Gi, and I come from the village of Busan." The boy's voice quivered with anger and grief, his eyes never leaving the elf kneeling weakly before them. "My master was Daesh, a Dark Elf. He taught me from when I was a child. When no one else believed in me because of my illness, Daesh gave me the confidence and the power to overcome my deformity." Tears sprang to the boy's eyes, and he brushed them away with a furious swipe of his hand. "Now I am left with nothing because of him." He jabbed a finger at the golden-haired elf. "He has taken everything from me!"

Windshine gazed at the hunchbacked boy with wonder. The devotion in his voice for one of her kind bordered on love. Perhaps that's exactly what it was. The boy reminded her of Ha Jun. Both were so angry, so full of rage. From those raw emotions, they were both able to achieve amazing feats.

She turned to the elf again. "This human, Nam-Gi, wants to kill you," she said. "This human, Ha Jun, will carry out his wish if I do not stop them. Before the act is done, I would like to know who you are, and why you want me dead."

The elf shot her a venomous look. "You know who I am and why I must kill you. The Lord sent your kind into the dark lands and forbade you ever to leave them. You Dark Elves are cursed to violence and evil. You will corrupt all that you come in contact with." His voice quivered with righteous fury. "Yet here you stand in this land of humans, having broken the order of the Lord. I am duty bound to kill you, and all of your kind that have trespassed here."

"You say you have already killed this boy's teacher?"

"As well as two others," the elf said.

The reality of his words sank deep into Windshine. The Dark Elves all wielded incredible magics, yet he had killed three? She saw no injuries to indicate the lengthy battle she would have imagined they had. Did killing Dark Elves prove no challenge to him and that disembodied eye that seemed to have disappeared?

"You would do the same to me if you have the chance?" Windshine asked him.

The elf smiled. "I gladly would, for you have broken the vow to the Lord. For that, I would shoot you through the heart with this," he touched the bow that had slipped from his fingers to the ground, "or take your head with these two blades on my back. Just as I took the head of the boy's master."

"Do it now!" Nam-Gi urged Ha Jun. "You're strong, I saw you slay the giant. With one strike, he will be dead."

Ha Jun raised his blade again, and again Windshine stopped him. She stared at the golden-haired elf for a long time, unsure of what she should do. If she allowed Ha Jun to kill him, she would never know the riddle of his being in South Hanguk. She would never know where he came from, how he arrived here, and where he planned on going after he finished eliminating her kind from South Hanguk.

Yet if she let him live, he would pose a constant danger to her. She didn't know the extent of his power. If he was as old as she was, then it might end up taking a long time to unlock his secrets. If he was actually older than her thousand years, it might prove impossible. His mental powers could dwarf hers, especially if she allowed him to regain his full strength.

But as she stared at him, weak and barely able to rise, she

knew she could not allow him to be killed in his current condition. She was no judge, and she would not use Ha Jun as her executioner. She had not come to this land to take life, but to live in whatever peace she was able to find.

"He will live," she announced.

"No!" Nam-Gi looked at her, stricken. "He must die."

Windshine shook her head. "You and Ha Jun are similar. Both of you are capable of greatness in the short span of your human lives. But how that greatness will manifest depends on if you learn to tame the anger inside of you. Will you be its master, or will it be *your* master?"

Windshine felt the blue eyes of the elf boring into her, and she turned back to him. "Are you surprised I have decided to spare you?"

The elf shook his head. "I am familiar with your kind. This is a trick, nothing more than some sort of manipulation. I do not know what your ultimate goal is, but I will figure it out. And when I do, I will destroy you."

Windshine suppressed a grim laugh. Whoever this stranger was, he truly believed the worst of Dark Elves. Perhaps he had good reason to. The Dark Elves had been warring against each other for so long, their homeland ripped apart by great magics only they could wield. If this elf had met her sister, Blythe, instead of her, he would have been right. Blythe had planned to kill off the people of South Hanguk so the Dark Elves could repopulate the country. She had abandoned her father's ideals of peace in favor of conflict and conquest.

Windshine, however, hadn't agreed with her perspective. She had no desire to hurt anyone.

She looked at Nam-Gi, who gazed at the golden-haired elf with contempt. "You have lost your Seon-saeng-nim. When you return home, who will continue to instruct you on the ways of our magic?"

Nam-Gi's face fell, a forlorn look overcoming him. "My story is long," he said quietly. "I cannot go back home. I have nowhere to go. I have no one to teach me."

Windshine sighed. Yet another problem she had to deal with.

The Jang brothers stood in the distance. They would not have overheard anything that had just transpired, which gave her an opportunity.

"You are skilled in illusion, are you not?"

Nam-Gi nodded. "I am."

"Then I have a request of you," she said. "Create an illusion of Ha Jun killing our visitor. Make it big so there is chaos around us. I will secure the elf in the folds of my clothing and take care of him until we return back to Jeju."

"Windshine." Ha Jun held up his sword. "It was broken in the strange battle I fought in a place I cannot name."

Windshine, inspecting the broken blade, shook her head. "Look closely, Ha Jun. You have not been paying attention to it since you reappeared. Do you not notice anything about the blade?"

Ha Jun gazed at the glyph sword, and he and the crippled teen both gasped. The blade, indeed, had grown longer, and was swiftly returning to its full length again.

"How?" Ha Jun asked.

Windshine wondered if she should tell him the truth. The sword had become bonded to rage and thirst for violence over the time he had used it. As long as there was hatred and vengeance in his heart, it would reform, ready to strike down a new target.

"It will always be remade," she told him. "I created it to be used in this world, and in this world, it will always have a use."

"And what of me?" Nam-Gi asked her. "What am I to do now?"

Windshine sighed. "After you create the illusion of Ha Jun killing the elf, you will come with me. I will be your new teacher. You helped me capture this elf, and I wish to repay you as I can." She reached out and touched the staff he held. "This was made by the hands of one of my kind. Was it your teacher?"

Nam-Gi nodded. "He gave it to me before we left Busan. I cannot walk without it."

"When we return to Jeju, I will imbue it with glyphs. Powerful spells will be locked inside of the jade that should help you on your journey. For I can see it in your eyes, even as I see it in Ha Jun's. Your life leads towards a greatness few of your race ever achieve. One day, you may very well be called a hero."

47. BURIAL

Han-Jae's thoughts drifted like the splintered wood of a shipwreck. He walked among the ruins of Majeon village. He was supposed to be searching for survivors, yet images of Myong-Sook and his children floated in his vision. Overshadowing them was his father, who gazed down upon Han-Jae as if waiting for some type of grand announcement to be made.

He paused, a barely audible sound reaching his ears. He went towards a home that had crumbled during last night's battle. Pressing his ear against the stones, he listened carefully. Behind him, he heard footsteps.

"Is there someone beneath the rubble?"

Han-Jae turned to the massive warrior, Ha Jun, and shrank back. Ha Jun didn't seem to notice as he reached down, took one of the bigger stones in his hands, and lifted it away.

"Is there someone there?" he called into the darkness.

A moment passed, then a soft voice said, "Help me, Elder brother."

Han-Jae yearned to help Ha Jun, but the gaping hole of blackness stared at him, and he could not bear to meet its gaze.

Ha Jun only glanced back at him before starting to carefully lift more stones away, widening the hole. When the warrior reached into the darkness, Han-Jae gritted his teeth. Was that laughter he heard coming from the other side? He blinked away the tears that sprang to his eyes as he remembered the monk at the burial mounds of his family.

Ha Jun moved back from the hole with a small girl in his arms. She was caked in mud, her hair wild around her head. She clutched tightly to Ha Jun as he asked her, "Is there anyone else in there?"

"My brother," the girl whispered, "but he hasn't moved in a long time."

Ha Jun turned to Han-Jae. "Elder brother, will you take the child so I can try and pull out the boy?"

Han-Jae's body shook, but the way Ha Jun and the girl waited for him to respond shamed him. He jerked forward and took the child from the warrior's grasp. She immediately wrapped her arms and legs around him while Ha Jun ducked back into the hole. She weighed almost nothing, her skin tight around her fragile bones. Again, Han-Jae's mind drifted to the faces of Dora, Kyung Wan, and the other sea guards bobbing on the surface of his thoughts.

The warrior, Ha Jun, climbed out of the darkness of the rubble a moment later, a body cradled in his arms. Han-Jae immediately knew the girl's brother was dead.

"We will have to bury the dead," Ha Jun said to Han-Jae. "Are the burial mounds far?"

Han-Jae opened his mouth to speak, but no words came out. Tears blurred his vision, and he looked away. Eventually, the warrior tapped his shoulder, and together they went back to the Jang brothers.

"Shall we bury the remains of those who are left?" Ha Jun asked them.

Jae Jin stared at the broken body in Ha Jun's arms. "If we leave them here, the carrion eaters will get to them before those from the city can arrive. We will bury them." He looked to Han-Jae, but Han-Jae still could not manage to speak. His voice had deserted him, so one of the other villagers directed the companions to the burial mounds outside the boundary of the village. The four companions searched the rubble, and when they were assured all of the dead had been collected, they carried the corpses to the tombs. They took spades with them. Digging into the earth, they laid the bodies in the proper mounds as instructed by the survivors.

They worked throughout the day until night fell. Han-Jae held the girl, who refused to let go. He stood at the periphery of the companions as they buried the dead. When finished, Jae Jin said, "We are all exhausted, but I do not think anyone wants to spend any more time in this cursed village. Let us start toward Incheon and make camp on the road there. Leaving this sad place will do all of our souls good."

The three Jang brothers took the lead, their torn, mud-splattered red hanboks like bright flames in the thick trees between Majeon and the road leading to Incheon. Ha Jun, pulling a wagon he had recovered from the debris of the village, came at the rear.

In the wagon was the head of the giant, covered in a sail he had ripped down from the rigging of one of the sea guard's destroyed boats.

Though the remaining villagers all knew the giant was defeated, they still peered fearfully through the trees. Han-Jae was no different, his body tense as he glanced to his right and left at the least sound of rustling leaves or the flapping of wings from birds flitting through the branches over their heads. Children began to cry. The Jang brothers, looking back upon them all with pity, readied their instruments. Soon, a light drumming raised their spirits, while the comforting melodies of the flute and *haegum*—a string bamboo fiddle—wove around the weary travelers to quicken their step.

They walked steadily until they finally broke through the trees onto the wide path leading to Incheon, the moon a bright disk surrounded by a multitude of stars.

"We will rest now," Jae Jin told the group.

While the villagers settled down, the four companions divided what food they'd been able to salvage among them. There was no fish, but they started a small fire and boiled rice. There was seaweed that they added to it. Rolling the two into small compact balls, they handed them out to the children, who took and ate them without a word.

The little girl had finally left Han-Jae's arms to sleep among the other children. Han-Jae sat at the edge of the group and gazed into the fire. Darkness deepened around him, and he regretted he had no weapon left. Ha Jun had left the wagon with the giant's head further away from the group, but still Han-Jae did not trust it. When he had first glimpsed the monster, he had assumed it was dead. How could he be sure now it was truly defeated?

The four companions sat down near him.

"Kwan Han-Jae," Jae Jin said. "What will you do after we leave the villagers with the government of Incheon?"

Han-Jae regarded the people of Majeon silently. "I must speak with the officials of Incheon and give my formal report. After that, I will go wherever they instruct me to."

Jae Jin nodded. "You fought bravely," he said, "and saved our lives when the giant attacked."

Han-Jae slowly turned his gaze to Jae Jin, a hollow feeling opening in his chest.

"We have decided we would like to speak on your behalf to the officials of Incheon and tell them of your deeds. Though

Ha Jun is the one who finally slew the giant, we would like to tell them the role you played in aiding us."

From the darkness at the edge of his vision—the shadows gathered thickly beneath the forest trees at the edge of the road leading to Incheon—the sound of children laughing floated to Han-Jae. He started and looked from one face to another of the four companions seated before him, gratitude bright in their eyes.

"The village of Majeon is no more," Jae Jin continued, "but we believe we will be able to get you promoted to a high position with the sea guards of Incheon. The four of us will also write up reports before we depart back to Jeju. We are confident our efforts will secure you high recognition among the officials of Incheon."

Han-Jae looked from brother to brother until his gaze fell upon Ha Jun. The young warrior stared at him with an expression of—what? There was a deep sadness in Ha Jun's eyes, along with a shared understanding. All of this destruction had been the price of Han-Jae's promotion.

In the end, what would the young warrior have to pay to finally reach his goal, and become a hero?

The End

ABOUT THE AUTHOR

Todd Sullivan attended his first serious writing class in 1995 at Stanford University. Between 1997 and 2002, he participated in the National Book Foundation's 10 day summer writing retreats. In 2006, he graduated with a Bachelors in English with Concentrations in Creative Writing from Georgia State University. He moved to New York that same year, and received a Masters of Fine Arts from Queens College in Flushing, New York in 2009. Todd moved to Jeju, South Korea, where he taught English in the public school system for five years. He currently lives in Seoul, and is studying the Korean language at Yonsei University. He is also working on a speculative fiction/urban horror novel that takes place in Korea.